F

D0261461

EYE CONTACT

About the Author

Fergus McNeill has been creating computer games since the early eighties, writing his first interactive fiction titles while still at school. Over the years he has designed, directed and illustrated games for all sorts of systems, including the BBC Micro, the Apple iPad, and almost everything in between.

Now running an app development studio, Fergus lives in Hampshire with his wife and teenage son. *Eye Contact* is his first novel.

EYE CONTACT

FERGUS McNEILL

HODDER &
STOUGHTON

First published in Great Britain in 2012 by
Hodder & Stoughton
An Hachette UK company

I

Copyright © Fergus McNeill 2012

The right of Fergus McNeill to be identified as
the Author of the Work has been asserted
by him in accordance with the Copyright,
Designs and Patents Act 1988.

A CIP catalogue record for this title is available from the British Library

Hardback ISBN 978 1 444 73961 9
Trade paperback ISBN 978 1 444 73962 6
EBook ISBN 978 1 444 73963 3

Typeset in Plantin Light by Palimpsest Book Production Ltd,
Falkirk, Stirlingshire

Printed and bound by Clays Ltd, St Ives plc

Hodder & Stoughton policy is to use papers that are natural, renewable and
recyclable products and made from wood grown in sustainable forests.
The logging and manufacturing processes are expected to conform
to the environmental regulations of the country of origin.

Hodder & Stoughton Ltd
338 Euston Road
London NW1 3BH

www.hodder.co.uk

For Anna & Cameron
Always & Completely

He realised very early on that he'd have to set rules. Otherwise, there would be no structure, no real challenge . . . and what would be the point if there was no challenge? He wondered how many others might have walked this road before him, moving unseen through society, their actions sending out little ripples over the surface of the news, while they remained quietly anonymous, hidden in plain sight.

Little ripples.

He smiled at the thought. It was certainly harder to do now, so much more challenging than it would have been even twenty years ago – tougher surveillance, tougher forensics – but in many ways that was the appeal of it.

Little ripples.

He watched them spreading away into the twilight, glittering with reflected street lamps from across the otherwise calm water. He watched them fading as they expanded outwards, silent rings around the face-down figure, now so still after moments of such struggle. And then, like the last of the ripples, he was gone.

part 1
SEVERN BEACH

I

Wednesday, 2 May

Robert Naysmith peered thoughtfully at the typewritten menu in the window, then pushed open the door with his forearm, the sleeve of his jacket preventing any direct contact with the glass.

Old habits.

A little bell clinked above the doorway as he stepped inside, his polished shoes tapping quietly across the scrubbed wooden floor. Eight tables, neatly squeezed in, with linen tablecloths and flowers in slender vases, artistic photographs on the walls. But only one customer – an owlish old man lost in his newspaper, a half-empty mug at his elbow.

Naysmith walked over to the counter, his eyes on the woman with her back to him, studying the shape of her – those narrow shoulders, the straight brown hair – then calmly switched his gaze to the menu board as she started to turn round.

'Can I help you?'

She had a soft voice, warm, with a slight West Country lilt. He allowed his eyes to drift back from the menu, as though he hadn't been watching her before, his smile mirroring hers.

'Are you still serving breakfast?' he asked.

She glanced up at the wall clock, then looked back to him with a slight shake of her head.

'We're only supposed to do that till ten thirty . . .'

'I understand,' Naysmith sympathised. 'I wouldn't want you to get into trouble . . .'

He held her gaze, a hint of mischief in his unblinking eyes, until she smiled again and looked away.

'Well,' she admitted, pushing an errant strand of hair away from her face, 'it's not as though we're busy. What was it you wanted?'

Naysmith turned to the menu board.

'Eggs Benedict?'

'I think we can do that for you.' She called the order through to the kitchen.

'Anything to drink?'

'Black coffee, thanks.'

She turned and picked up an empty mug, while Naysmith reached for his wallet. She was wearing a blue sweater – plain, but just tight enough to show that she had a pleasing figure. Very little make-up, but that sort of sleepy beauty he'd always found rather appealing.

'So is this your place?' he asked. 'Or are you a rebel employee who serves breakfast whenever the mood takes you?'

The woman laughed as she placed the mug under the coffee machine.

'A bit of both,' she replied. 'I run it with my sister, so I suppose I can do whatever I like.'

'Must be nice to be your own boss.'

She placed his coffee on the counter and took the money he offered.

'Sometimes,' she nodded as she turned to the till. 'You get to meet some nice people.'

Naysmith smiled at her as she handed him his change.

'Thanks.' He remained at the counter, inhaling the steam rising from his coffee.

'And you?' the woman asked him after a moment. She had a wonderfully shy expression.

'I'm just one of those nice people,' he lied.

Naysmith had always liked Clifton. It was quite beautiful in parts, especially up near the suspension bridge. Leafy streets with grand old houses, narrow lanes that fell away down steep inclines, boutiques and cafés and the well-dressed people who frequented them. So different from the rest of Bristol – a little island of calm, looking out across the hazy urban sea below.

He stopped by a second-hand bookshop, smiling as he studied the sign taped to the door: *Back in 10 mins.* The ink was faded and some of the tape looked older – the shopkeeper was obviously out a lot – but somehow that made the place even more charming. Yellowing paperbacks were stacked high in the window, larger volumes propped up against them in a precariously balanced display. He thought about coming back to browse and checked his watch – quarter to twelve. The Merentha Group meeting wasn't until three. Plenty of time if he did decide to return this way.

The smell of warm bread came to him from a bakery across the road but he continued up the hill, enjoying the sunshine and shop windows, happy to see where his feet would take him.

At first, it was just a flicker of an idea, a nagging feeling that he couldn't quite recognise, but it grew stronger in his mind as he walked.

It had been months since his work had taken him to Bristol, and even longer since he'd been up here. There was something about this part of the city that drew him, and some good memories from a couple of summers back when he'd chanced to meet a particularly interesting woman in a tiny private gallery. They'd discovered a shared dislike for modernist sculpture – she'd joked that even bad art could bring people together. Absently, he wondered if she still lived in that same flat, the bedroom windows overlooking the Downs, but then quickly dismissed the idea.

That wasn't the sort of encounter he was thinking about.

It had certainly been a while. And coming here today on business might be the perfect opportunity to find a new challenge. To find someone new.

He stopped outside an antiques shop, his gaze wandering across the tarnished medals, dusty uniforms and other militaria that would normally fascinate him. But not today. Instead he found himself staring at the reflection of the street behind him. The people walking by, unaware of his presence in their midst, or his scrutiny. It could be any one of them . . .

His own reflection smiled back at him – late thirties, tall and slim, well groomed, with short dark hair that showed no sign of thinning. Searching dark eyes surveyed his jacket and shirt, stylishly casual as befitted a successful sales director, but smart.

He realised now that he had been trying to distract himself all morning, but the restless excitement was growing, the sense of inevitability.

Wandering on in the direction of Clifton Down, he savoured that curious mix of anticipation and regret that always seemed to stir in him at this moment. A familiar feeling now.

He checked his watch again. Five to twelve. There was really no sense putting it off any longer. He'd already made the decision – had made it years ago – and he felt the cold thrill stirring in his stomach as he prepared himself to begin.

Okay.

The park lay in front of him. He would walk across it; all the way across. The first person to make eye contact after twelve o'clock would be the one.

He bowed his head for a moment, took a breath to calm himself and clear his thoughts, then set off.

It was a bright day, and the high, open parkland of Clifton Down stretched out around him, a swathe of green beneath a vast blue sky. Newly cut grass filled the air with a wonderful, fresh smell. The edges of the straight tarmac path were dotted with benches, all occupied, and the warm weather had even tempted people to sit out beneath the trees, though it was still quite early for lunch. He smiled again. What a glorious day for it.

A dour little man on one of the benches glanced up at him as he passed, a mean-spirited face scowling behind a tightly held sandwich, clearly unhappy at the thought of sharing anything, especially his seat. Naysmith checked his watch – 11.58. A pity, but it encouraged him to think that he might find someone suitable, someone *deserving*. He walked on.

This was always such an exciting part of the game. So much of it was down to skill and strategy, but here, at the outset, he would give up the control and surrender himself to fate. It could be anyone, and therein lay the real challenge.

Anyone.

This was the random factor that made the game real, that made the skill and the strategy meaningful. There were rules, of course – the twenty-four-hour head start, only pursuing one target at a time, and so on – all carefully considered to make the whole thing more interesting. But without a genuine element of chance what would be the point in playing?

Somewhere in the distance, a church bell was chiming.

Noon.

Though it might be tempting to loop back round and find the man with the sandwich, he knew that would be cheating. He had to do it properly – continue walking *all* the way across the park before he could turn back.

There were people on the path ahead of him. A young man came first, Chinese by the look of him, a little under six foot tall, spiked hair, slight build, listening to his iPod. Clean, white trainers. His clothes seemed too good for a student but he couldn't have been older than early twenties. They drew closer, until Naysmith could hear the tinny beat from his earphones . . . but he passed by without ever looking up.

A moment later, a heavy-set woman in her fifties – somebody's aunt. Greying hair, floral-print top, expensive bag. She had an aura of disapproval about her, steering herself towards the edge of the path as they came near each other and carefully avoiding his eye – her type often did. On another day, he might have felt a slight twinge of offence at this deliberate evasion, so determinedly keeping herself to herself – after all, there was nothing about him or his manner that anyone should find threatening. And yet, today, she was quite right.

Next were two younger women sitting on a bench – late twenties or early thirties, one fair-haired, the other a redhead. Both were smartly dressed, midday fugitives from an office perhaps. They were talking as he approached, catching up on gossip before they had to return to work. The redhead had her back to him as he approached, but her friend looked up as he passed, her eyes flickering to his for just a second before she continued her conversation.

She would be the one.

And now his pace faltered just a little as he bent his whole attention to her, taking in each detail, remembering, fixing her in his mind.

She looked to be of average height – hard to say while she was seated – with a relatively slim, athletic figure. Her grey trouser suit was presentable, if not flattering, and there was no ring on the hand that held her Starbucks cup.

He took another step . . .

Shoulder-length hair, straight, with cheap plastic clips to keep it out of her face, mousy with fading blonde highlights.

. . . another step . . .

Pale skin, delicate chin, high cheekbones, small nose, not too much make-up, pierced ears with small lobes. He burned her mouth shape into his mind, the slightly too pronounced pout of her lips, then gave the last seconds over to her eyes – pale grey-green with nice lashes.

And then he was past her. A fleeting moment, but that was all it took.

He *never* forgot a face.

One more glance at the watch – it was 12.07. She had twenty-four hours' grace, and he had a meeting at three. Grinning cheerfully, he turned off the path and headed back towards the city centre.

★   ★   ★

Naysmith slept late next morning, and the hotel reception was busy with guests checking out when he came downstairs to catch the end of the breakfast sitting. He chose a table near the window and a nod summoned the attentive young waiter, who was immediately sent for coffee. The breakfast menu held no surprises, and Naysmith was already checking emails on his phone when the coffee pot was placed before him.

He ordered without looking up and finished tapping out a short reply to one of his subordinates. The dining room was almost empty now, just him and a few other late-risers – an overweight businessman tackling bacon and eggs, and an older couple looking around the room as they quietly ate their toast.

He poured himself some coffee and raised the cup to his nose, savouring the aroma before taking a sip. Heaven.

The place looked different this morning, sunlight from the windows infusing everything with a golden glow. He'd done his entertaining on the other side of the room last night.

The Merentha Group meeting had gone even better than expected. Jakob Nilsson, their dealmaker, was a large, friendly Norwegian with a vigorous handshake and a booming laugh – heftier and a little older than he'd sounded on the phone. He'd been refreshingly sensible about the numbers and they'd managed to agree terms there and then in his office. He wore a very good suit and Naysmith had taken to him almost at once.

Jakob's colleague, Michaela, had turned out to be both intelligent and attractive in an understated way, with shoulder-length auburn hair, a guarded smile and dark, lingering eyes. She dressed with a classical elegance – black jacket, nicely tailored, with a simple cream blouse, and the confidence to wear a skirt. There was a quiet calm about the way she discussed their delivery requirements that he found oddly appealing, and he'd invited them both out for a drink. They'd started at a nearby bar on the waterfront.

'So tell me,' Jakob gestured towards him with his glass, 'how did you come to be with Winterhill?'

Naysmith leaned back in his chair.

'I like a challenge,' he replied, allowing his eyes to engage Michaela's for a moment, then returning to Jakob. 'Winterhill gave me the opportunity to build my own department from the ground up, to run things the way I want.'

'They are good to work for?'

'Very.' Naysmith smiled. 'I usually do one day a week in the Woking office, but the rest of my time is flexible. I work the hours I need to and, so long as I keep delivering the numbers, the directors are happy.'

'I read that you recently expanded into Germany?' Michaela had the faintest hint of a Welsh accent when she spoke. 'Business must be good.'

'You've done your homework,' he nodded. 'Germany's our second-largest market and one of our resellers was based in Hamburg. It made sense to acquire them, bring their expertise in-house. It also eases the workload for my UK team, who were getting quite stretched. I just wish more of our clients were like you – it usually takes a lot more than one meeting to get a deal memo.'

'Ah, but we know what we want.' Jakob laughed.

Naysmith smiled at Michaela.

'So do I.'

By 7 p.m. it was clear that nobody was in a hurry to go home, so Naysmith suggested they all eat at a nearby hotel. He remembered the restaurant there as being rather good, and there was a comfortable lounge as well. He could get a room – that would save him the misery of the slow evening train home, and it would afford him a legitimate excuse to spend the night and be in Bristol the next day.

Dinner was surprisingly enjoyable. Naysmith had known some very dreary Scandinavians, but Jakob was well travelled and Michaela added some welcome chemistry to their talk. At first, he had wondered if Jakob was fucking her – there did seem to be a faint spark between them – but as the meal progressed he had revised his opinion. The big Norwegian was keen on her, and she enjoyed the attention, but that was as far as they had gone, or seemed able to go.

Conversation drifted easily from business to pleasure as they ate.

'Oh, I wish I'd known.' Michaela brightened as they discussed music. 'There's a place on King Street that has great live jazz most evenings.'

Naysmith shrugged. 'Next time I have an evening in Bristol . . .'

'Absolutely.' She smiled.

It was perfect. He'd never have risked a deal like this over a woman – if she and Jakob had been an item, he'd have kept his distance. As it was, though, he had a pleasing evening, asking her lots of open questions, carefully empathising, and verbally fencing with Jakob over her, letting everyone enjoy the agreeable tingle of flirtation in their talk.

It was almost ten when Jakob went to retrieve his jacket from the cloakroom. Sitting with Michaela, Naysmith casually reached into his pocket and stole a glance at her business card. There were three telephone numbers on it. He leaned forward, closing the distance between them.

'This is your mobile number?' he asked her, indicating the card.

'Yes.' She answered quietly, without looking at it, allowing him to hold her gaze far too long.

It was so tempting, to put his hand over hers, to ask her back for a drink in his room, but he reluctantly decided against it. She had something special about her, something that he didn't want to rush. He could imagine slow summer afternoons with her, seeing her shy smile when she woke next to him, someone he might actually enjoy listening to.

'I'll hold you to that promise . . .' he pointedly placed her card in his pocket, then smiled, '. . . next time I have an evening here.'

And then Jakob had returned and the moment passed, with just a hint of regret in her eyes to assure him that he was right.

She was something to look forward to when he had more time . . .

He savoured that thought as his breakfast arrived.

2

Naysmith called the office later on that morning and caught up on some emails before checking out of the hotel just before eleven. It wouldn't do to be early, but he was eager to be back up at Clifton Down by noon.

He told the taxi to drop him at Sion Hill, a little over a mile away from the park – intentionally distant. It was better to be careful even at this early stage, and he had plenty of time. He took a few minutes to walk out onto the Clifton suspension bridge, stopping at the halfway point, alone, far above the Avon Gorge with its ribbon of silvery water and its tiny cars hurrying along below. He looked south across the city, out to the pale horizon beyond, then closed his eyes and enjoyed the breeze, the tremendous sensation of height, like standing in the sky.

There was nothing he couldn't do.

A narrow footpath wound its way up to an open expanse of grass, scattered with benches where people could sit and take in the view of the bridge. An enthusiastic young Labrador came bounding towards him as he crested the hilltop and he stooped to make a fuss over it as its owner, a large woman in her forties, hurried forward, vainly calling, 'Sammy. *Sammy!*'

'I don't think he heard you.' Naysmith grinned, rubbing the dog behind its ears.

The woman shook her head, catching her breath. 'I'm so sorry.'

'Don't be, it's fine,' he laughed. 'Are you all right, though? Looks like he's been giving you quite a workout.'

'I never thought having a dog could be so exhausting.' She smiled ruefully. 'It's worse than going to the gym.'

'Better company though.' He gave the dog a friendly pat and stood up. 'You wouldn't have the right time, would you?'

The woman quickly frowned at her watch. 'Twenty to twelve.'

'I'd better get along.' Naysmith smiled. 'There's someone I have to catch up with.'

The footpath led down through a stand of overhanging trees, then out to the main road. He crossed over and walked up a long hill, admiring the tall houses that looked out over the park.

Somewhere, a bell chimed noon. Seven minutes to go and her twenty-four hours would be up. He gave them all this grace period, a head start, so they had the chance to disappear before he came looking. She could be anywhere now, but that just made the challenge more interesting. And of course, she didn't know he was coming.

At the top of the hill, the road bent round to the right and he followed it, measuring his pace, resisting the temptation to hurry.

A buzzing in his pocket slowed him and he cursed under his breath. Taking his phone from his jacket, he looked at the name on the screen, sighed, and diverted the call. *Not now.*

Switching off his phone, he cleared his mind of everything but her, summoning her face from his memory, recalling her eyes, the small nose and straight, shoulder-length hair. A sense of calm spread through him as he focused on her image.

He was just a couple of hundred yards from the corner of
Stoke Road. It was 12.06, but he waited, willing the second
hand on his watch to crawl right round to the top before he
looked up.

12.07 – and the game was on!

Quickly, his eyes swept the park, studying the various
distant figures for anyone that might possibly be her. He
crossed the road but ignored the path, cutting straight across
the grass in the direction of the bench where she'd been
twenty-four hours before.

Picture her now, slim figure, about five foot six, mousy blonde . . .

He moved purposefully towards the middle of the park,
his gaze flickering left and right – it was vital that he saw her
before she saw him – but there was no sign of her as he drew
near the bench and found it deserted. He paused for a
moment, then sat down where she had sat, placing his palms
flat on the rough grey wood of the seat and leaning back.

It would have been her lunch hour. He turned his head,
looking out over the park stretching away into the distance,
then considered the buildings to his left, the shops and offices
he'd passed on his walk yesterday.

Thoughtfully, he stood up and started back along the
tarmac path, retracing his route from the day before. Still
alert, he scrutinised every approaching figure, but the sky
was overcast now and it was colder – the park was quiet
today.

He reached the road and waited at the busy junction until
he could cross over, his eyes drawn to the crescent of four-
storey buildings that curved down to Whiteladies Road ahead
of him. A bridal store, sports shop, Indian restaurant . . .

Picture her now. Smart grey trouser suit.

His eyes drifted up to the second- and third-storey
windows. Some had net curtains – obviously flats – but as

he walked down the hill he began to see more with vertical blinds, sterile fluorescent lights and stencilled business names.

She worked in an office.

He drifted slowly down the road, relaxed but watchful, stopping now and then to peer through the windows of cafés and sandwich shops – anywhere that workers might visit on an overcast lunchtime. His gaze flitted around the people on the street, resting longer on anyone slim, anyone about five foot six, anyone with mousy hair . . .

By 1 p.m., he began to sense that he'd missed his chance. Her lunch hour would be over and she'd be back at work. He looked up and down the road, lined on both sides with offices. There was no way of knowing which one she was in, or even if this was the right place to search. It was a daunting challenge, but he found the prospect pleasing.

Tired of walking up and down past the same shops, he turned his back on the park and followed the road as it sloped down in the general direction of the city centre. He decided to look in on the second-hand bookshop he'd passed the day before and see if it was open. Crossing the street, he continued to watch the people around him, just in case . . .

Two young women were walking up the hill towards him, deep in conversation. Both were casually dressed – one with short blonde hair, faded jeans and a tight green sweater, the other looked Asian with a tan suede jacket and dark trousers. He knew immediately that neither of them was his target, but the Asian girl was rather attractive and held his attention as she came closer, long dark hair swaying as she walked. As they drew level, she placed her hand on her friend's arm and whispered something, almost spilling her companion's coffee as they both giggled. She had a nice smile, but as they passed Naysmith stopped short.

Sitting on that bench in the park, average height, slim athletic figure . . .

He frowned, concentrating on the image in his mind.

. . . grey trouser suit, no ring . . .

The two women passed by, oblivious.

. . . and what was she holding?

'Excuse me?' Naysmith called after the two women, who turned and regarded him with puzzlement.

'Sorry to bother you.' He offered a wry grin, then pointed at the coffee cup in the blonde's hand. 'Just wondering if you could tell me where Starbucks is?'

The Asian girl pointed back down the hill. 'Just keep going down there and you'll see it on the right.'

'Next to the station,' her friend added.

The entrance to Clifton Down station was only a couple of minutes' walk down Whiteladies Road, and just beyond it Naysmith found Starbucks. He went in and ordered a coffee. Standing at the counter, he casually glanced around the tables, but he knew she wouldn't be there. Not now. Not today.

And yet she had bought a coffee from here, then walked up to the park with it – walked that same road he'd just been on.

He was getting warmer.

★   ★   ★

He folded his newspaper and looked out of the window as the train pulled into Salisbury. Getting to his feet, he stretched, then joined the other passengers already huddled around the door, waiting for it to open.

He walked quickly, deftly negotiating the obstacle course of people and luggage to ensure he got a taxi. Instructing the driver in a tone that didn't invite further conversation, he slammed the door and sank back into his seat. The traffic was still slow with the tail end of the rush hour, but they soon broke free of the town. Gazing out at the familiar trees and hedgerows, he distracted himself by calculating his commission on the Merentha deal, and planning what he might do with the money. In the window, his reflection smiled back at him.

He watched the taxi turn and head off back through the village, then made his way to the white front door and, taking a key from his pocket, let himself in.

'Rob?' a woman's voice called down from upstairs as the door slammed. 'Is that you?'

'It's me,' he replied, putting his phone and keys on the table. 'Kim, come down for a minute.'

Kim appeared at the corner of the stairwell, looking at him with a slight frown. Five foot six, with a youthful grace that belied her twenty-eight years . . . and there was something very arousing about her when she was cross.

'I called you today, just before lunch,' she began, toying with her shoulder-length dark hair, 'and you "busied" me.'

'I was with a client,' he sighed. 'Come on, you know how it is.'

'You never called me back.' Her large hazel eyes studied him accusingly from across the room. She was wearing a simple white top and jeans that accentuated her narrow waist and small, slender frame.

'Ah.' He lowered his voice conspiratorially. 'That's because I didn't want to spoil the surprise.'

She walked slowly over to him, more intrigued than suspicious now. 'What surprise?'

'Well, I had some good luck in Bristol,' he smiled. Taking her hand, he pulled her close, enjoying the feel of her against him. She didn't resist.

'Your meetings went well?'

'Very well,' he murmured, leaning forward to smell her hair.

'Don't tease,' she scolded him. 'What surprise?'

'All right,' he laughed. 'I got the deal – the whole thing – and it's going to mean a really good bonus. I thought we might have a long weekend in Rome—'

'Oh Rob, that's perfect!' She hugged him excitedly, then left her arms around his neck as she gazed up at him. 'Sorry . . . you know, if I was a bit moody . . .'

'Forget it.' He smiled. 'Now, run upstairs and put something else on – I'm taking you out to dinner.'

'OK,' she laughed. 'Do you want to come and help me choose what to wear?'

He looked at her for a long, lingering moment.

'Tempting,' he said slowly. 'But if I have to watch you getting dressed, you know what'll happen.'

She turned and gave him a coy look. 'I don't mind . . .'

'I know,' he nodded, 'but first I'm taking you for a meal at Mirabelle's.'

He watched her obediently skipping up the stairs, and sighed quietly. At moments like this, he was genuinely fond of her.

3

Wednesday, 9 May

He had prepared for it as he would for any other appointment. An entry in his work calendar read *Alan Peterson, 9 a.m., Bristol,* and the rest of the day was blocked out. The meeting was to discuss a potential lead for what could be a lucrative software contract – he had the brochures and sales sheets in his bag – but a week after landing the Merentha deal, nobody at the office was particularly concerned about how he spent his time.

Which was just as well, Naysmith thought, as there *was* no Alan Peterson.

Kim was still asleep as he dressed. She looked so innocent, her dark hair tousled from the night before. He gently pulled the duvet up to cover her exposed shoulder and quietly closed the bedroom door behind him.

Time to go to work.

It was a bright, cold morning and he shivered as he carefully hung his jacket in the back of the car to save it from creasing on the journey. He turned on the radio just as the 6 a.m. news started, and listened for the traffic report as he drove out of the slumbering village and made for the main road. Golden sunlight dappled the lane through the overhanging trees, and he found the A36 still quiet enough for him to put his foot down and enjoy the drive. Everything boded well for a productive day.

He made excellent time as far as Bath, then started to run into some early-morning commuter traffic, but he was still in Bristol well before 8 a.m. Threading his way through the city centre as quickly as possible, it wasn't long before he was driving up the hill into Clifton.

It fascinated him to think about his quarry. Where was she at this moment? What was she doing? Perhaps getting ready for work, maybe already on her way. Certainly she had no understanding of her significance, her part in the game. He wondered how far away she was from him, and imagined the distance closing . . .

There were a couple of empty spaces in the station car park. Getting out of the car, he stretched, then grabbed his jacket and hurried up the tarmac slope, past the station entrance on Whiteladies Road. Moments later, he was settled at a table in Starbucks that commanded a good view of the door, savouring his first coffee of the day, and recalling her image in his mind.

Early thirties, average height, slim figure, straight, mousy hair.

He checked his watch, then sent Kim a short text explaining that his meeting had been delayed, before settling himself into his chair.

From experience, he knew that the key to waiting lay in pacing himself. He had never been a particularly patient man, but he had learned – it was part of the game, like everything else. At first he'd struggled with boredom, frustration and all the other unwanted feelings that crept in to fill the vacuum of inactivity. He'd been too eager to progress and it had almost been his undoing in the early days.

Not now though. Now he knew how to sit so that his body

was without tension. He knew how to slow his thoughts and allow his mind the freedom to wander, without ever losing sight of the target.

He had a newspaper in front of him – the *Telegraph*, which he'd picked up from the counter – but today that was just for show. It was something to put on the table in front of him, a prop he could fiddle with from time to time. It was what people would see when they looked at him – just an ordinary person reading the paper. And yet his eyes, though never too eager, kept glancing back at the door.

He didn't react when she came in. Her mousy hair was tied back and she was wearing a dark green coat and black boots, but it was definitely her. She looked a little hurried – it was almost nine – but there were only two people in the queue at the counter and she was soon ordering her coffee. Naysmith finished his drink as she collected hers and calmly followed her out onto the street.

She walked with a quick, determined stride as she made her way up the hill, but it wasn't difficult to stay with her. He allowed her to lead him along the row of shops and through the tempting aroma of fresh bread that drifted from the bakery. He was just a few paces behind her as she crossed the road by the church, but he let the distance between them open up again as they drew nearer to the park. She was some twenty yards ahead of him when she turned off at a terrace of Georgian town houses and hurried up a set of stone steps to a tall, blue door. There she halted to fumble with her handbag, then seemed to think better of it and buzzed the intercom.

Naysmith watched as the door opened and she let herself inside. He was close enough to hear the buzzer click off as he strolled along the pavement, glancing at a small glass plaque by the doorway as he passed: *Goldmund & Hopkins Interior Design*.

He continued on to the top of the street, then paused and thought for a moment. It was just after nine. There was little reason to wait around for her lunch hour – as long as he was back before five.

★   ★   ★

The Internet Café, like so many others he had visited, was a seedy place. A bank of computers sat on trestle tables facing the wall, each with its designated number and a plastic chair. They were all vacant save one, where a studious-looking Indian youth was quietly touch-typing to a distant friend. A sign, printed on sheets of A4 paper taped together, advertised web access for *£5 per hour, £5 minimum*.

Naysmith approached the swarthy man behind the cash desk and wordlessly held out a five-pound note. The man roused himself from his magazine and took the money, placing it quickly into a small cash tin. He then leaned over to his own terminal, tapped a couple of keys and pointed towards the trestle tables.

'Number four,' he rasped, then cleared his throat. 'Any drinks? Tea? Coffee?'

Naysmith looked at the stack of white polystyrene cups and the jar of instant granules. A sheet of paper on the wall behind it read *Hot Drinx – £1*. He shook his head and silently declined the offer.

Sitting at screen number 4, he brought up a web browser and typed 'goldmund hopkins interior' into Google. When he hit Search, a page of entries appeared, but he didn't need to look beyond the top listing:

Homepage – Goldmund & Hopkins Interior Design Ltd.

He followed the link to their website and was greeted by an impressive page displaying stylish, modern spaces filled with glass and light, but his eye was immediately drawn to the 'Who We Are' tab at the top of the screen. Clicking it, he found a section listing the principal members of staff, each with a small photo.

And there she was. Staring out at him from the web page, that same unmistakable face he'd watched in the coffee shop earlier that day, the same face he'd seen in the park a week ago.

Beside the smiling picture, he read her name – Vicky Sutherland.

Naysmith leaned back in his chair and gazed thoughtfully at the screen. He didn't usually know their names until afterwards.

★　　★　　★

At ten past five, the blue door opened and Vicky Sutherland appeared, briefly checking her bag before hurrying down the steps to the pavement. She turned onto Whiteladies Road and set off down the hill, buttoning her dark green coat as she walked. On the other side of the street, Naysmith matched her pace.

He'd spent an uplifting afternoon browsing among the dusty shelves of the second-hand bookshop he'd seen the week before. The proprietor, a small man with a shock of white hair and a threadbare grey cardigan, seemed content to sit and read until closing time, and Naysmith had enjoyed searching through the stacks of unwanted hardbacks. In the end, he'd settled on a slim volume of short stories by

Somerset Maugham that he remembered reading years ago.

He didn't look over too often, just enough to make sure he wasn't getting ahead of that dark green coat. She walked quite quickly, as though she was eager to be away from the office, eager to be home. He wondered where her home was, and what it would be like.

They came to a pedestrian crossing just as the traffic lights were changing to red, halting the long line of cars. Naysmith was about to cross the road when he saw her change direction, stepping off the pavement to come over to his side. He slowed and turned away, pretending to study a shop window. In his mind, he visualised her walking across the road; he counted the steps and the seconds, not turning his head until he was sure she had passed.

The back of her green coat was just a few yards in front of him as they approached the station entrance. It would be easy to lose sight of someone here, but he was careful to stay close and allowed himself a little smile of satisfaction when he saw her turn abruptly off the main road and hurry down the tarmac slope. It seemed they had a train to catch.

A covered footbridge was the only access to the far platform and Naysmith paused, waiting until she was all the way across, before walking onto it and looking out on the station below. There she was, making her way down the long ramp that led to the curved platform, already lined with a number of early-evening commuters.

He checked his wallet for cash – he knew better than to risk using a credit card on a journey like this – when the rattle of an arriving train made him look up.

Mustn't lose her now.

He hurried across the bridge and down the ramp towards

the platform as the other passengers were boarding. It was a short train – only two small coaches – and he just had time to read the destination *Severn Beach* before leaping aboard through the last open doors. She was sitting with her back to him, at the opposite end of the carriage, so he slid quietly into a seat near the door and calmed his breathing as the train began to move. He gazed out of the window as Clifton Down station slipped away and they crept into the darkness of a long tunnel.

The guard appeared through the connecting door from the other carriage and began to make his way along the narrow aisle, checking tickets. In the fluorescent gloom, Naysmith frowned. He didn't know which station she was going to. Taking out his wallet, he fished out a ten-pound note and held it ready for the approaching guard. He remembered the destination he'd read as he ran along the platform.

'Return to Severn Beach, please.'

He could always get off sooner if she was going to an earlier stop.

The guard took his money, tapped a few buttons on a shoulder-slung machine, and printed out two tickets. After counting out the correct change, he walked back towards the other carriage, swaying slightly as the train emerged from the tunnel, daylight bursting in through the windows.

Naysmith blinked and looked out at the bright green foliage whipping by as they joined the river winding its way along the tree-lined Avon Gorge. When they slowed for the first station, he positioned himself so that he could see the back of her head between the seats but she made no move to get up. He settled back into his corner and stared out at the expressionless faces of the people on the platform, then closed his eyes. It had been a long day.

He found himself thinking of all those other faces, still so clear in his memory, each one a challenge, each one a reward. He understood the game now, knew why he played it, what it had given him. Casting his mind back, it was difficult to remember how he'd felt before it all began. He was different now. The game had changed him, altering something deep inside so that he couldn't empathise with his former self. But there was no regret in that.

He felt the train begin to move. There was a change in tone as they rumbled over a bridge and he opened his eyes again. To the left, the Avon was broader, its sloping banks silted with grey mud. He wondered how far they had to go.

Nobody got off at the next station, but as the train pulled into Avonmouth most of the passengers began to get to their feet and collect their bags. From his vantage point, Naysmith watched intently, but she stayed in her seat, gazing out at the sheltered platform, its back wall decorated by a huge children's mural.

The doors closed and they began to move once more, clattering slowly over a level crossing and following the single track as it curved steeply round to the right. The train passed in the shadow of an imposing old flour mill that towered like a derelict monument above the other industrial buildings lining the side of the track. There were no more houses now, but vast wind turbines could be glimpsed in the distance, along with cranes and mountainous piles of coal.

'Any passengers for St Andrews Road?' the guard called

from the connecting door. 'Request stop only, St Andrews Road.'

A request stop? Naysmith craned his head to peer between the seats. He hoped she wasn't getting off here. Any station that operated by request didn't sound as though it saw many passengers, and it would complicate things if he was the only other person to alight there.

He peered between the seats again but she sat still and quiet as the train coasted through a bleak area of warehouses and railway sidings. They rolled through the deserted station without stopping. Sinister-looking chimney towers belched pale fumes into the sky, but eventually even the industrial buildings became less frequent, and Naysmith felt slightly surprised as he realised he was gazing out at one of the Severn Bridges and, across the dark water, the Welsh coastline. Where *did* this girl live?

And then he felt the train slowing. The remaining passengers began to move, gathering their bags and getting to their feet as the guard called, 'Severn Beach. Last stop.'

She was standing by the doors at the far end of the carriage, staring out of the window with the unseeing eyes of a tired commuter. Naysmith waited until the doors opened, letting her disembark before he got to his feet and followed.

A chill breeze greeted him as he stepped off the train and he thought he could smell the sea, a faint tang of salt on the air. Severn Beach station was little more than a single long platform between two tracks, one side almost lost in a tangle of overgrown weeds. He walked slowly by the solitary metal shelter and passed the corroded buffers that marked the end of the track, the idling hum of the train dwindling behind him. Ahead, he saw her walking down to the road and turning left. He quickened his pace a little. The platform opened out onto a quiet residential street – old and new houses huddled close to the pavement – a bleak little village on the edge of nowhere.

He turned left and walked along thoughtfully, some fifty yards behind her. It felt like somewhere that old people would come to – a quaint little tea room on one side of the street, bungalows with immaculate gardens, Neighbourhood Watch signs in windows. Ahead, he could see a steep tarmac slope that climbed to what looked like a seaside promenade, but his attention was on the figure in the dark green coat as she followed the road round to the left and disappeared from view.

When he reached the end of the road, he caught sight of her again, but elected to walk up the slope rather than follow her along the pavement. He quickly climbed the few steps up onto the top of the sea wall, and was suddenly buffeted by the wind. Before him, the vast grey expanse of the Severn rippled out towards the horizon, the bridge stretching away into the distance on his right. He turned away from it, pulling his jacket close around him against the cold as he walked along the promenade, his eyes following the figure on the street below as she made her way along the line of waterfront houses and turned down a small cul-de-sac. He watched as she unlocked her front door and went inside. It was a nice house – small, like most modern houses, but with its own driveway and a little patch of lawn. Smiling to himself, Naysmith walked on and followed the path down onto the beach.

The train back to Clifton Down was almost empty. He hadn't realised how dark it was getting until he stepped aboard, the harsh interior lighting making it almost impossible to see anything outside. His eyelids were suddenly heavy, and he yawned before settling back into the seat.

There was still a long drive ahead of him, but it had been a rewarding day.

He'd walked past her house on his way back to the station. There was a light on upstairs, and the hallway was illuminated, but otherwise the place was in darkness. He'd noted the small car on the driveway, the cheerful lace curtains, the plaster animals arranged on the doorstep . . .

. . . *but nothing to indicate she lived with a man – good.*

He had been about to move on when he'd noticed a pair of muddy women's running shoes, neatly placed on the mat in the small front porch. And that had given him the beginnings of an idea.

He'd done enough for one day though. Satisfied, he pulled the Somerset Maugham book from his jacket pocket, and began leafing through the familiar pages as the train rumbled out of the station.

4

Naysmith stared down into Kim's deep brown eyes, enjoying the way she lowered her gaze demurely. Those long lashes looked dark against her pale skin. He carefully swept an errant curl of hair away from her face onto the pillow, then placed a gentle kiss on her forehead.

'Come on,' he grinned, rolling off her onto his back and looking up at the ceiling, 'you'll be late.'

'I would have been ready hours ago if you hadn't been here,' she smiled, sitting up and tentatively lowering her small, bare feet onto the polished wooden floor.

'Maybe, but you're glad I decided to work at home this morning.'

He stretched his arms out across the bed as she looked back over her shoulder at him.

'Of course I am.' She stuck her tongue out playfully, then squealed as he tried to grab her. Jumping up, she put her hands on her hips and adopted a mock-serious expression. 'Not again. I'll be late.'

He watched her scamper naked into the bathroom, then sank back into the pillows for a moment. His hand found the watch on the bedside table and he held it up, squinting as sunlight from the window glinted on the bezel: 12.49 p.m. It was time to get ready.

★ ★ ★

Naysmith put the suitcase down on the tarmac and closed the car boot.

'Say hi to your sister for me.' He smiled.

'I will.' She checked her bag, then turned to him. 'Are you sure you don't mind me going?'

'It was my idea,' he reminded her.

'You'll be all right on your own, won't you?'

'For goodness' sake . . .'

He rolled his eyes, and she flinched. Very slightly, but he saw it – one of those nervous little tells that drew him to her, like a flame to a moth.

'It's only till Sunday,' he said in a gentler voice. 'Now go on, before you miss your train.'

She extended the handle from the case, then turned and stood on tiptoes to kiss him.

'Call me tonight?'

'I'll call you tonight.'

He waved to her, watching her bump the wheeled suitcase through the doors and disappear into the station building. Then, sighing to himself, he got back into the car and leaned forward to rest his head on the steering wheel for a moment. He closed his eyes and drew a deep breath.

Time to focus.

He filled the car with petrol on his way out of Salisbury. Every forecourt had CCTV – that was unavoidable – but he deliberately paid in cash. Credit cards left permanent records that were simple to collate. Patterns and coincidences stood out too easily, and at this stage in the game he always disciplined himself to leave as little trace as possible. Tomorrow, he would refill the car somewhere else.

He didn't take the turning for the village but drove on along the main road for a mile and a half before pulling off onto a narrow lane that led along the edge of a small copse. Leaving the car in the overgrown gateway to an empty field, he walked the short distance to the trees, pausing now and again to admire the rolling Wiltshire landscape, and to ensure there was nobody else around. Pushing on into the wood, he left the faint path and picked his way up a gentle incline, stopping when he came to a heap of rubble covered in ivy. He looked around, then stood very still, holding his breath and listening intently for a moment, but there was no sound other than the gentle rustle of the leaves above. Satisfied that he was alone, he crouched down and carefully pulled the undergrowth away from a small section of collapsed brick wall. Leaning forward, he reached into the gap underneath, searching with his fingers. It was further back than he remembered, but it was there, and he felt a tiny spark of excitement as he gained a grip on the plastic. Carefully, he drew out the long, flat parcel, wrapped in layer upon layer of black refuse sacks. He stood up, brushing the dirt and insects from it, and pushed the ivy back into place with his foot. Resisting the temptation to open it, he took his prize and started back down the slope towards the car.

It was almost five o'clock when he got home. Getting out of the car, he went straight into the garage, closing the door quietly behind him before turning on the light. It was a cramped space, cluttered with old packing cases and tools, and he had to step round the two bicycles to reach the cardboard boxes stacked along the back wall. One of them lacked the film of dust that covered the others. Opening it, he drew out two plastic bags and checked the contents.

Dark hooded top, anorak, jogging bottoms, black trainers, plain T-shirt, socks, gloves, cheap wristwatch . . .

To these he added a bottle of thin bleach, a roll of refuse sacks and a travel pack of hand-wipes. Every eventuality prepared for. Everything bought from the local supermarket, paid for with cash – anonymous items that could have come from any town.

He transferred the bags into a single refuse sack, which he carried out to the car, then went into the house.

A little before midnight, he called Kim, smiling as she struggled to hear him over the background noise of the bar she was in.

'What was that?'

'I *said*, tell your sister I can hear that screeching laugh from here.'

'Rob, don't be so mean.'

'You're right. She has a lovely screech.'

'Stop it!' Kim laughed. 'So have you had a nice evening? You haven't been too bored, have you?'

'I've got a bottle of Bombay Sapphire and I'm watching *The Godfather* DVDs you got me,' Naysmith lied. 'I decided I was due a lazy night in.'

'That's good,' Kim shouted. 'Look, I can hardly hear you. I'll call you tomorrow, OK?'

'Not too early.'

'All right. Miss you.'

''Night.'

He stood up and walked into the living room. Pulling the box of *The Godfather* from the shelf, he took one of the discs and put it into the DVD player, then moved through to the kitchen. Opening the cupboard, he took out the large blue bottle and poured three-quarters of the Bombay Sapphire down the sink.

Details mattered.

The warm water felt good on his skin as he leaned back under the shower nozzle, energising him. It was part of the ritual that he went through every time, helping him to prepare physically and mentally for the challenge. He wrapped a towel around himself and padded through to the bedroom, where he clipped his fingernails short. All jewellery, along with his watch, his wallet and his mobile phone were left neatly on the bedside table – personal items were an unacceptable risk. He needed nothing but his keys and some cash.

Once dry, he dressed himself quickly and went downstairs. After switching on the TV and the sitting-room lights, he slipped quietly out into the cool night air.

The Warminster Road was deserted but he took no chances. He chose a quiet farm track, screened by tall hedges, and drove some distance before pulling over. Stepping out into the darkness, he went round to the back of the car and opened the boot. Carefully undoing the black plastic bags, he unwrapped the flat parcel to reveal a pair of car number plates and a small white envelope.

It had taken him time to source those plates. He'd noted the registrations of several cars the same colour and model as his own, eventually settling on one he saw in Basingstoke. Blank plates and self-adhesive letters were relatively simple to obtain, and after an evening's work in the garage and some carefully applied grime, he had a pair of passable fakes. They weren't perfect, but they were enough to give his own vehicle a different identity for all the watchful CCTV cameras – a legitimate identity that would attract no attention, and which had no connection to him if it was ever spotted. Time well spent.

Crouching down, with a torch gripped between his knees, he worked quickly to tape the plates securely over his own, ensuring a perfect fit. Once he was satisfied, he stowed the torch and took the white envelope in his hand, feeling the contents between his fingers before carefully slipping it into his pocket.

Moments later, his car rejoined the main road and he accelerated away, the route now very familiar to him. This would be his fourth visit to Severn Beach – he'd made two preparatory trips in the weeks since he'd tracked her there – and it would be his last.

He cruised past Warminster and drove on into the night, enjoying the long, clear road as it snaked towards him out of the darkness. Bath was asleep, a succession of empty streets and glaring traffic lights, soon left behind as he pressed on towards the orange glow of Bristol on the horizon. There was a little more traffic here, but it was quiet enough as he swept down towards the city centre and round to Hotwells. The Clifton Bridge hung like a strip of fairy lights above the gorge, and he found himself leaning forward to gaze up as he passed beneath it.

Not far now . . .

Avonmouth was a ghost town, and he was suddenly conscious of being alone – conspicuously alone – on the silent roads. This close to his destination, a local police car would present too great a risk. He would have no choice but to postpone and drive on. The thought irked him as he came to the roundabout by the towering old mill and turned off onto the broad, straight length of St Andrews Road. He was watchful now, checking each side turning as it slipped by, glancing up at the mirror to see anyone behind him, but there was nobody else. He was alone.

A little before Severn Beach, there was a turning for a single-track access road that led down towards the water – he'd found it on his second visit and it seemed the ideal place. He drove a short distance along it, then switched off the headlights and looked behind him for other cars.

Nothing.

He waited a few moments, allowing his eyes to grow used to the darkness, then cautiously eased the car forward along the narrow tarmac. It was difficult without lights, especially negotiating the low bridge where the road passed under the railway line. The shore side of the tracks was a dead end, hidden from the main road by the embankment – probably the local lovers' lane but now, just after 3 a.m., it was empty. He turned the car so that it was facing out, ready to leave, then switched off the engine and got out.

A chill wind whipped along the shoreline, rippling the tall reeds like waves. Naysmith stretched and yawned, savouring the bite of the cold after the soporific warmth of the car journey. The Second Severn Crossing dominated the night horizon, a ribbon of motorway lights cast out across the miles of dark water, its reflection glittering on the river below. He shivered and went back to the car, opening the boot and drawing out the refuse sack containing his new clothes. After one last check to ensure he had everything, he locked the car and set off into the wind, trudging along the swathe of rough grass that divided the railway from the beach.

He made his way on into the darkness until he came to a solitary tree and the large group of bushes gathered about it. Pausing for a moment, he looked around, then carried the plastic sack into the midst of the bushes and laid it carefully on the ground. Beside it, he placed the white envelope – an incongruous pale square in the gloom. Removing the keys and cash from his pocket, he took a new refuse sack and began methodically undressing, placing each item of clothing into the sack. It was cold, but it would be folly to rush – he had to make sure that everything was accounted for. At last, naked, he gathered the top of the sack and twisted it shut, before opening the other bag and taking out his anonymous new clothes.

A few minutes later, shivering but dressed, he pulled his gloves on before pushing the black sack deep into the bushes. Shoving his keys and cash into empty pockets, he stared down at the envelope for a moment, then scooped it up and made his way out onto the beach.

The grass gave way to small stones that crunched underfoot as he drew closer to the shore, an endless strip of shingle and debris that marked the uncertain boundary between the land and the estuary. The first houses were visible now, less than a mile ahead, the outermost arm of the village stretching out towards him.

He walked on as the sky began to brighten, the pre-dawn light giving form to dark, heavy clouds. He hoped it might rain, but not until later. Not until afterwards. Water washed away a multitude of sins.

There was one more thing to attend to. Picking his way along the beach, he began to study the larger stones that lay here and there among the pebbles.

Something round and heavy that would fit well in the hand . . .

He stooped to examine several river-smoothed rocks before he found what he was looking for. It felt right as he picked it up, testing the weight and swinging it experimentally. It also had the beauty of coming from this shoreline – he could drop it anywhere and even if it was discovered, it would only reinforce the idea that the whole thing was opportunistic rather than planned. Nodding to himself, he slipped the stone into one of his large anorak pockets and walked on towards the Severn bridges.

As the ground fell away before him, he came to the start of the sea wall that protected the low-lying houses beyond. He walked along the beach below it, keeping close to shield himself from the worst of the wind, and to stay out of sight. Finding a sheltered spot, he sat down on the stepped concrete at the base of the wall and checked his cheap watch. All he had to do now was wait.

5

She appeared at roughly 6.45 a.m. – slightly earlier than he had expected – a solitary figure, running at an easy pace out of her street and turning to follow the coastal path that led along the top of the beach. From his vantage point, Naysmith studied her, taking in the white T-shirt, the blue shorts. Her hair was tied back, bouncing in time with her stride. Absently, he wondered how fast she could run.

Standing up, he shook his arms and legs to loosen them, then set off at a leisurely pace after the receding figure. There was no need to hurry. Let her enjoy her run . . . he would meet her on her way back.

The early-morning light was breaking through the furthest clouds, dappling the distant reaches of the coastline and spinning thin strips of glistening silver across the water of the estuary. He gazed out at the towering wind turbines, visible even though they must be some five miles away, their immense blades gently turning in the seemingly permanent gale that blew along this part of the Severn. Walking on, his eye was drawn to the industrial buildings that punctuated the gently curving coastline towards Avonmouth, the tall chimneys pouring out long, slow streams of smoke. It was a bleak place, but there was an odd sort of beauty in it as well . . .

Fifteen minutes later, he caught sight of her again, a still distant figure, jogging steadily back towards him. She would be fatigued now, breathing fast to get the oxygen to her weary muscles. He knew how it felt to be tired after exercise, the body working in an almost automatic way, the mind already thinking of home and a relaxing bath.

He carefully checked his walk, making all his movements deliberately slow and lazy, despite being wound tight with readiness. Everything about him must be ordinary, unthreatening, irrelevant to the approaching runner. He glanced over his shoulder but there was no one else around.

Green light.

His gloved right hand slipped gently into the anorak pocket and drew out the heavy, round stone, concealing it by letting his arm hang close to his side. He began to adjust his course so that she would be on his right – the side nearest the water – when they met.

She was less than a hundred yards away now and he allowed himself the brief, intoxicating thought of choice. He could change things, right now, at the last moment. He could allow her to live. He felt the authority in that choice, the ultimate level of control. In this instant, he wielded the power of life and death and the thought electrified him.

Fifty yards to go. He noticed that she was wearing earphones, the thin wire dancing loosely as it ran down to her pocket . . .

Twenty yards. Satisfied that she would pass on his right, he lowered his head, muscles taut, as she drew level . . .

. . . and he exploded, swinging the stone fiercely up into her stomach, lending all his might to the blow that smashed the air from her lungs and bent her over, staggering to her knees.

She had no breath to shout.

Immediately, he was there, bundling her off the path, down

a grassy slope towards the beach, moving her as fast and as far as he could before she understood what was happening, before she fought, before she became deadweight.

And then, as she began to panic, he tried to swing the stone round, to connect with the side of her head, to end it quickly, but his gloved fingers lost their purchase and he felt his weapon slip away, thudding into the shingle nearby.

Damnation!

It was too late to stop – he was committed now. As she desperately tried to get air, he allowed his weight to knock her to the ground, dropping onto her to deflate her lungs still further as his hands took hold of her throat.

She made terrible little choking sounds, the worst he had ever heard, and he flinched as her struggling became desperate, turning his head away to avoid her flailing arms.

And to avoid seeing her.

It became unbearable, and he started to feel nausea rising through his adrenalin. Ten seconds . . . fifteen . . . *for fuck's sake!* And then, mercifully, she began to fail, the movements becoming intermittent, weaker, until finally she sagged beneath him and was still.

He realised he was shaking.

Taking a deep breath, he forced his fingers to relax, releasing their grip on her. Straightening up, he anxiously glanced back over his shoulder towards the path and the houses beyond, but he was alone. Utterly alone.

And now he began to sense the onset of exhilaration, the terrible rush building inside, but he pushed it away, closed his mind to it.

Not yet.

He scrambled quickly to his feet and looked around, his thoughts racing through the mental checklist that he had prepared for this moment. Gloves and clothing were intact, keys still in his pocket . . . He'd dropped the stone coming down the slope but he'd left nothing else behind.

Move . . .

She was lying in a crumpled heap, terribly exposed on the open beach, but the tall reeds were just a short distance away. Grunting with determination, he grabbed her ankles and started to drag her towards the water. Moving down across the swathe of small stones was quite easy, but it became harder as he went from shingle to mud. He battled on, straining to pull her as his new trainers sank into the grey ooze, but after a final burst of effort he was able to drop to his knees, the body safely nestled between two large clumps of reeds.

After taking a moment to calm his breathing, he rolled her over onto her back, finding her eyes thankfully closed.

He squatted down again, noting that her T-shirt had ridden up as he'd dragged her, exposing her pale stomach and the base of her bra. Gently, he tugged the edge of her T-shirt down to cover her again, to allow her a little dignity. Then he rocked back on his heels, studying her, looking for something small, something that wouldn't be missed. His eyes settled on her earphones, now a tangled mess after being trailed through the mud. He followed the wire back to her pocket and pulled. Carefully, he revealed the music player she'd been listening to. Deeper in her pocket, he discovered her keys.

Taking them in his hand, he considered for a moment, then reached into his jacket and fished out the white envelope. Opening it, he withdrew a small key, which he placed on her stomach. Disconnecting the earphones, he slid her MP3 player into the envelope, which he stuffed back into his jacket, zipping the pocket shut. Then, hindered by his gloves, he picked up the key and carefully started working it onto her key chain. It took a moment, but finally it was done, and he carefully returned the keys to their place in the pocket of her shorts.

He glanced back up the beach, then lifted her wrist to look at the sports watch that was still clocking up the seconds since she'd started her run: *37 minutes and counting . . .* There was no reason to give the police any help with the time of death, so he removed the watch and deliberately smashed it against a nearby rock, repeatedly hitting it until it was in pieces.

For a moment, he gazed down at her, checking to make sure she wasn't still breathing. Frowning, he crouched beside the body and rolled it over, pressing her face down into the wet mud.

Better to be sure.

When he was satisfied, he reached over to lift the tangled earphones, balling them into a muddy mass and standing up to throw them out into the water. Then, with one final glance down at the body, he picked his way back onto the shingle before turning and walking away along the shore.

The excitement he'd been fighting suddenly welled up inside and now, as he gazed out at the broad, bleak horizon, with its low clouds and distant smokestacks, he finally let it wash over him – a rapture of such sickening intensity that he almost wanted to cry out. The power, the utterly addictive thrill of power, so profound he could scarcely comprehend it. He shook with the cold, dark joy of his own supremacy. There was *nothing* he couldn't do.

He saw nobody as he walked back, but the houses were far behind him and the weather was closing in again – it wasn't a morning for the beach. He found the plastic bag just where he'd left it and, screened by the bushes, he began to strip off his clothes. Everything, from his shoes to his watch, was removed and placed in a second refuse sack before he retrieved his own clothes and started to dress.

Ten minutes later, he was back at the car. From habit, he had double-bagged everything he'd worn on the beach, but in the event he needn't have worried. There had been no blood, and he hadn't needed to clean himself up. He placed the bulging refuse sack in the boot and climbed into the car as the first spots of rain began to appear on the windscreen.

Perfect.

He drove cautiously under the railway bridge. Nobody saw him turn left and join the main road, keeping his speed just under the 50 mph limit. He came to the junction – a signpost pointed left to Severn Beach – but he went straight on, following the road inland, passing over the motorway and accelerating as he came to the dual carriageway. In minutes, he had reached the roundabout where he joined the M48, one anonymous car disappearing into the relentless flow of traffic from the Severn Bridge.

★ ★ ★

It was a little after ten when he arrived back at home. He'd changed the number plates as soon as he left the motorway – emerging from a quiet country lane with his own registration again – but he was tired and in no mood to rush the rest of the clean-up. He had the whole day to dispose of the clothes in one of the charity recycling bins outside the local supermarket, to drop the wristwatch into the river and to stuff the refuse sacks into a lay-by rubbish bin. Right now he wanted sleep.

His eyes had grown heavy, and the mood of elation that normally carried him for days and weeks was already starting to ebb away. He'd started to wonder about it as he'd driven back through Devizes and on along the winding road that led back to Salisbury. Somehow, everything had been just a little too straightforward, had happened just a little too quickly for him. So much of the reward came from the scale of the challenge, but this time? This had been one of the simplest yet. He felt a gnawing sense of dissatisfaction that began to trouble him, but he didn't want to think about it now.

Get some sleep . . .

Perhaps it *was* just lack of sleep – he knew he could be irritable when he was tired. Better that than the alternative – that it *had* been too easy. Damn, what a waste that would have been . . .

Feeling unsettled, he went upstairs and checked his phone. Kim hadn't called yet, which was good. He lay down on the bed, staring up with unseeing eyes before drifting into a troubled sleep.

6

Derek eased the front door shut behind him, not wanting to wake anyone. He felt the soft click of the lock and wearily turned to face the still-sleeping street. Toby was wagging his tail and pulling at the lead, eager as always. Derek yawned.

He felt the warmth evaporating from his anorak as he stepped out of the porch. Hunching his shoulders against the grey morning, he let the excited Labrador drag him down the path. They walked as they did most Sundays, down to the end of the street, bearing right onto Station Road. It was getting light when he climbed the steep tarmac slope to the footpath.

The wind battered him as soon as he reached the top, whipping his hood against the side of his face, finding a way up the back of his anorak while he stooped to let the dog off its lead, struggling with the catch.

He stood up stiffly and watched as Toby bounded away, down onto the beach, then turned his face into the wind to gaze out at the Second Severn Crossing, a snaking ribbon of lights cast across the cold grey water. Tiny vehicles crawled along it, high above the dark waves, their noise lost in the gale.

Eyes watering from the cold, he dug his hands deep into his pockets, turning away from the bridge to make his way along the promenade to the beach. The wind was less violent in the shadow of the sea wall, and Derek could now hear the crunch of his shoes on the shingle. In the distance Toby started barking.

Sheltered beneath the wall, Derek took out a cigarette. It took him a moment to light it, but he relished the first drag of smoke, his small compensation for these early walks.

Toby was still barking.

Frowning, Derek started to pick his way carefully down the beach, skirting the dark patches of mud and debris as he followed the sound towards a broad bank of reeds.

'Toby?' he called out, irritated. 'Toby!' But a sudden gust stole his voice away from him.

What had got the stupid dog in such a state this morning?

He paused for a moment, reluctant to get his shoes too muddy.

'Toby! Come here!'

But it was no good. Bracing himself against the relentless wind, he moved closer. The wet stones became more treacherous as he approached the water's edge and he had to watch where he was putting his feet.

Only when he was a few yards away did he look up to see what Toby had found.

She was dead – had to be, lying face down in the mud. The white T-shirt was soaked through, and water glistened on the back of her legs below her blue shorts. He hesitated, uncertain whether to run for help or to check her pulse and make sure. Taking a step forward, he wavered for a moment, then gingerly reached down, nervous fingers hovering over her pale wrist. A flutter of panic rose in him as he touched her cold, stiff flesh, and he jerked his hand back violently, almost losing his footing as he retreated from the body. She was definitely dead.

He stood for a moment, trying to gather himself, trying to tear his eyes away from the sprawling limbs, the bedraggled ponytail, the sodden running shoes . . .

Why the hell had he touched her? He cursed his stupidity. Mustn't touch anything – everybody knew that! And he'd been walking all around, leaving footprints in the mud!

Breathing fast, he turned and stumbled back up the beach. He was halfway to the sea wall before he remembered the mobile phone in his pocket and, hands shaking, dialled 999.

He didn't know how long he'd been waiting there before the first police car appeared, a sleek BMW that raced down Station Road. It pulled over beside him at the approach to the beach, the flashing lights throwing shivers of blue across the walls of the nearby houses. Two officers – a serious-looking woman and a tall man – got out.

'Mr Wells?' the female officer asked him.

'Yes.' Derek went over to them. 'It was me who called you . . .'

'I'm PC Firth and this is PC Gregg. Could you show us what you found, please?'

They made their way up over the promenade. Derek tied Toby's lead to the railings at the base of the slope, then led the others down to the beach. The wind was dropping now but Firth still had to raise her voice to be heard as they neared the water.

'I need you to stay here with my colleague,' she explained, then picked her way carefully over towards the bedraggled figure in the mud.

'My dog found her,' Derek said, half to himself. He found it difficult, but managed to pull his eyes away from what the female officer was doing. 'I didn't touch anything, except to check if she was . . .'

He paused, remembering how wrong her skin had felt. That horrible lifeless cold that he could still sense in his fingertips. He shuddered.

'It's okay, sir.' PC Gregg looked past him towards the water where his colleague was coming back over to them. She shook her head grimly as she approached, then turned to Derek.

'Mr Wells, I'm going to ask you to go back to the car with PC Gregg . . .' She caught his expression of panic and quickly added, 'It's very cold out here and we don't want you freezing. I think it's best that we get you off this beach, then once the other officers arrive we can see about getting you a cup of tea and having a chat. All right?'

Derek nodded numbly, and took one last look in the direction of the body before allowing himself to be led back up the beach. As he trudged over the shingle slope he wondered who she was.

'Okay.' Firth pressed the phone to her ear, turning to shield it from the wind. 'How long do we have?'

She beckoned to the other figures making their way down the beach.

'Okay, thanks for that.' She finished her call and walked over to meet the three approaching officers.

'What's it look like, Sue?' one of the younger constables asked.

'Like a dead woman, Josh.' She sighed, then addressed them all. 'Body seems to have been here for a while – maybe a day – but I've just spoken to Control and they reckon the tide is on its way out. That probably gives us six hours so we'll need to get a move on.'

She gestured towards the body behind her. 'Let's get the immediate area taped off for starters. There's been enough people through the scene already – we don't need any more.'

She turned and indicated the sea wall, and the line of houses beyond.

'And we'll want someone up there to keep people off the beach.'

Her phone started ringing and she turned away to answer it.

'PC Firth?' She listened for a moment and nodded. 'Okay, sir . . . yes. See you when you get here.'

She stared at the handset, her expression softening for a moment, then turned back to the others.

'One of you tell Gregg to keep the dog walker here. The DI's on his way.'

★   ★   ★

Plumes of steam billowed up from the steel chimneys, pale against the dark sky, to drift out across the Severn. Detective Inspector Graham Harland scowled at the blighted landscape as he drove; the towering chemical works, the wretched structures choked with pollution and rust. Everything along this road was as bleak and joyless as he was.

He indicated left at the sign for Severn Beach and threaded his way through the village, past the miserable caravan park and on to the end of Station Road, where the other cars were waiting. There was a space beside the wire-mesh fence of a small utility building and he nosed into it, parking in front of the padlocked gates.

Serious eyes stared back at him as he caught an unwelcome sight of his reflection in the rear-view mirror. Physically it was the same, good-looking face – high cheekbones, angular jaw – but overshadowed by experience. Lines around the straight mouth that had once been laughter lines, dark hair with a chipped-in fringe, cropped short at the sides to hide the first traces of grey. The same face, just a different person staring out from behind it.

He switched off the engine and leaned slowly back in his seat, listening to the bluster of the wind outside. His thumb gently turned the plain gold wedding ring that he still wore – that he would always wear – as he sat gazing out at the road.

Such a godforsaken place. The only silver lining was that Sergeant Pope wouldn't be here. Taking comfort in that thought, he got out, grabbed a heavy overcoat from the back seat and made his way towards the promenade, a tall, gaunt figure, shoulders hunched against the cold.

The wind hit him as he reached the top of the slope. He gazed out at the broad, flat expanse of the beach, the yellow jackets of the officers working further down where an area had been cordoned off, and the restless grey water beyond. How he hated this place.

Turning left along the sea wall, he approached the young PC who stood shivering at the end of the path.

'Morning, Josh.'

'Morning, sir.'

'Is Firth still down there?'

'Yes, sir.'

'And the witness?'

'PC Gregg has him in the area car.'

'Okay.' Harland yawned. 'Thanks.'

He trudged down onto the beach and walked slowly across the rough grass, his eyes routinely scanning the ground for anything significant, but there were only bleached crisp packets and old plastic bottles. What a dismal place for anyone to finish up. A ragged line of seaweed and other debris marked the upper reach of recent tides and he stepped over it carefully, leaving the grass behind as his shoes crunched across the shingle. The breeze was getting stronger again as he approached the fluttering tape line and he waved to PC Firth as she hurried over to meet him. Her round face was tense, and the wind had teased strands of her dark hair out from under her hat.

'Morning, sir.'

'Morning,' he nodded. 'Been here long, have you?'

'Not long, no, sir,' she replied. 'You were quick.'

'Got the call on my way in.' He shrugged. 'Anything interesting?'

'We haven't touched the body yet.' Firth indicated the area behind her. 'Control says the tide'll be in again by midday so we've just tried to contain things until the SOCOs get here.'

'But it looks like a strangulation?'

'Yes, sir,' Firth agreed. 'Can't see much more without moving her, but there's definitely some nasty-looking bruising around the neck.'

'No sign of a rope or anything?' Harland asked.

'Not yet,' Firth frowned, 'but I actually thought it looked more like—'

She raised her hands to her own throat in a choking motion.

'Okay,' Harland nodded thoughtfully. 'Any idea how long the body's been on the beach?'

'Hard to say, but she seems to be totally stiff. That makes it twelve to eighteen hours or more?'

'Something like that.'

Harland turned and studied the high-water line behind him, then gestured to the taped-off area.

'If it's eighteen hours that means we've had two full tides – more if she's been dead longer . . .'

He looked out at the distant waves that swept along the side of the estuary, waves that could easily move a body or wash a crime scene clean.

'So, did you want to come and have a look?' Firth asked.

She lifted the tape and Harland stooped under it, treading carefully as the ground became more slippery. They made their way down towards the water until they could see the body, lying between several large clumps of reeds.

Harland stepped slowly, studying the ground, then paused.

'These are your footprints?' he asked, indicating the tracks that led over to the dead woman.

'Yes, just mine and the dog walker's as far as I could see.' PC Firth indicated the prints in the mud. 'I tried to follow alongside his tracks when I went to check the body – did my best not to disturb the ground.'

Harland nodded thoughtfully, then picked his way over to the corpse, carefully stepping in Firth's footprints. He quickly noted the runner's clothing and the ugly marks on the side of the neck, but his eye was drawn to the smooth pattern of the mud that had swirled around the head and feet, partly submerging them. The pose of the limbs looked odd too – not quite the same as other bodies he remembered seeing washed up on beaches.

'Firth?' he called.

'Yes, sir?'

'Look at the way the mud's banked up smoothly against the side of her head, and here around her shoes.' He crouched down and studied the undisturbed silt. 'There's a chance this is where it happened.'

'What about the tides?' Firth asked. 'Wouldn't they have moved the body?'

Harland got to his feet and pointed at the reeds.

'These clumps may have done enough to keep her in one place,' he mused, 'and we're far enough up the beach to avoid the worst of the waves.'

'But not far enough to have preserved much evidence.'

'True,' Harland admitted. He took one last look, then turned to find Firth watching him, her expression unreadable before she quickly looked away. He stared at her for a moment, then dismissed the thought and began stepping awkwardly across the mud. 'Let's see what the SOCOs find when they lift her.'

He walked back onto the shingle and tried to scuff his shoes clean.

'Now, tell me about this dog walker . . .'

7

There was an air of hushed expectancy in the station briefing room at Portishead, and everyone looked up as Harland walked in, his phone ringing as he tried to fish it out of his pocket. PC Firth warmed her hands on a large mug of tea and smiled to herself, her eyes following Harland as he studied the name on the screen then turned away from them slightly, speaking quietly into his phone.

'Can I call you back?' he frowned. 'Great, thanks.'

Ending the call, he turned back towards them, careful fingers pushing the hair from his forehead as his eyes flickered up to sweep the room.

'Phones on silent everyone,' he sighed, sinking into his chair.

DS Mendel was sitting across from him, studying a report. His broad frame loomed over the pages spread before him, the fingers of his free hand drumming softly on the table. He'd been busy this week, with DS Pope away on holiday, and things looked like they were about to get busier still.

'Right then.' Harland muted his phone and slipped it back into his pocket before addressing the room. 'James, perhaps you can get us started.'

Mendel looked up from his papers and cleared his throat.

'Thanks, sir. The body was discovered by a Derek Wells – local dog walker – who found her sometime after six. He phoned it in at six twenty-seven a.m. and the area car was on the scene about twenty minutes later, right Sue?'

'Yes,' Firth confirmed. 'We were there about quarter to seven.'

'PC Gregg took an initial statement from Mr Wells, and I've since interviewed him. He's a bit spooked but everything he says seems to stack up . . .' Mendel glanced across at Harland, who nodded in silent agreement. Derek Wells had been on the verge of going into shock when they'd spoken to him, but there was nothing in his demeanour to suggest he was involved.

'So, we'll want to take a look at him, but I really wouldn't peg him as a likely candidate,' Mendel concluded. He rubbed his square jaw with a large hand. 'Moving on to the victim, we still need to arrange a formal ID but we've unofficially identified her as Vicky Sutherland. Single, twenty-eight years old, office administrator for some interior design firm in Bristol. She lived in one of those cul-de-sacs just back from the beach . . .' He consulted his notes for the street name. 'Riverside Park, isn't it?'

He glanced at Gregg, who nodded.

'We're pretty sure she lived alone,' Mendel continued. 'Certainly nobody's reported her missing and she's been dead for a couple of days.'

PC Gregg stood up and carefully refilled his glass from a large bottle of water on a side table.

'How *did* we identify her in the end?' he asked.

'Supermarket loyalty card on her key chain,' Harland explained. 'One of those little key-fob ones. She didn't have any other ID on her – that's to be expected if she was out for a run when it happened – but she would have needed door keys, particularly if there was nobody at home to let her in.'

'Her going for a run certainly fits with what she was wearing: white T-shirt, blue shorts, decent trainers . . .' Mendel turned a page and read on. 'Preliminary medical report shows no water in her lungs, so she didn't drown. Cause of death looks like strangulation and the marks on her throat are consistent with it. No evidence of a rope or anything else being used, so chances are our killer did it with his hands. Some other bruising to her abdomen and arms – no evidence of sexual assault.'

'Any hope of getting prints?' Gregg asked.

'Maybe, but I doubt we'll be that lucky.' Mendel sighed. 'And the tide partially submerged the body at least twice, which won't have helped. No footprints, either.'

There was a pause as the room took this in. Harland leaned back against his chair, a distant expression on his face.

'Sir?' Firth asked. 'Any signs of a boyfriend at her house? Strangulation often has a personal or sexual connection.'

'Good point,' Harland agreed. 'We've got people going over the place now, but I've not heard anything yet. I'll chase them.'

Firth smiled. Mendel turned another page and looked up.

'Very little in the way of personal effects,' he noted. 'She had her keys, as we've mentioned, but nothing else on her person. The SOCOs found bits of broken watch when they lifted her. It's a sports one – assuming it's hers, she may have been using it to time herself running.'

'One more thing on that.' Harland looked up at them. 'When they lifted the body, they found fragments *underneath* her. There were other bits in the mud around the scene – all unweathered – so it's possible they were left there at the same time as she was.'

He rubbed his eyes, suddenly weary, before continuing.

'The pieces that we've recovered so far have all been very small, and there's been a few of them. If this *was* her watch, then it didn't just fall and get broken – it appears to have been deliberately smashed.'

'That's all I've got here.' Mendel shrugged. He stacked his papers together and reached for his coffee, scowling when he found it had gone cold.

'What about CCTV?' Harland asked Firth.

'We've retrieved everything we can for now,' she explained. 'Coverage round there is far from comprehensive but we'll work through it and see if anything jumps out.'

'All right.' Harland got to his feet again and walked slowly over to the window. 'Let's start pulling together a picture of who our victim was. Friends, family, co-workers. We particularly want to know about any relationships she might have been having, or anything else of a personal nature that could fit with strangulation as a cause of death.'

He turned to face them and offered a thin smile. 'That's all for now. Thanks.'

There was a general scraping of chairs as everyone stood up and made their way out of the room. Harland remained, staring out into the street with unseeing eyes.

A violent murder – without the usual tiresome hallmarks of drugs, gangs or deprivation – and it had fallen to him. Deep inside, he felt a quiet euphoria that he didn't like.

★　　★　　★

The call, when it came, was as unwelcome as it was predictable. The momentum and energy of a developing case was like the warming glow that came from physical exercise – an endorphin rush that masked all former pains while it lasted.

Interrupting this state made the summons even more frustrating, but Harland faced it with a resigned stillness. Dealing with superiors was like holding your breath underwater – struggling only made it worse. Wearily, he stood up and made his way out into the corridor.

Superintendent Alasdair Blake was a small, fastidious man, with prematurely white hair and rimless glasses. His usual expression was one of mild disapproval, etched deep into his face over the years, and he sat stiffly as he studied the report.

'Yes,' he called in answer to the knock on the door, and looked up to greet Harland with a doubtful smile. 'Come in, Graham. Take a chair.'

Blake had never felt quite at ease with Harland. Even now, watching him enter the room and sit down, something just didn't seem *right* about the man. Nothing wrong with his work, certainly. He was diligent and clever, a good combination in any career officer. Well presented and well spoken. But why had he, of all people, stopped chasing promotion? Maybe the death of his wife had somehow robbed him of ambition, but that *was* a year ago now . . . Whatever it was, Blake didn't want it getting in the way of this case.

'I've read your report,' he began, indicating the pages in front of him. 'Sounds like we were fortunate to find the body when we did.'

'That's right,' Harland nodded. 'The consensus is that she was either killed there or dumped there. We're almost certain that she wasn't washed-up or moved by the tides – the condition of the body looks too good for that. And if we're lucky, it means we might even have a small area of the crime scene that wasn't disturbed by the water.'

'Really?' Blake looked up. 'I thought the whole area was submerged.'

'It was, but not underneath the body,' Harland explained. 'She was lying face down, and the tide seems to have washed right over her. The ground directly below her might be very significant.'

'Where you found the fragments from a watch?'

'Exactly. And Forensics think they might get something off the front of her clothing where it was protected by the mud.'

Blake sat back in his chair, nodding thoughtfully as he reread the report. The wall behind him, like the rest of his office, was bare and impersonal, save for three large certificates in matching cheap plastic frames.

'Strangulation,' he noted after a moment. 'I assume you're checking for boyfriends?'

'Yes, and we're going through the database to see if there are any locals with a profile that fits.'

Blake studied him for a moment.

'I'm glad you're on this, Graham,' he said. 'It's a nasty business, and practically on our doorstep. We really need to get a result on this one.'

Harland recognised the tone of voice and sat quietly, knowing what was coming. His face remained impassive as he withdrew into himself, away from the meaningless pep talk.

'I mean,' Blake was saying, 'a brutal murder, just a couple of miles down the road from headquarters . . .'

He placed the report on his desk and tapped it meaningfully.

'This will attract a lot of interest from upstairs, so we have to resolve it quickly and cleanly.'

For a moment, Harland's distaste flickered across his face, but he got hold of it. *Too close to headquarters.* Pity the tide hadn't dragged her corpse a bit further along the damned coast.

'Of course,' he said, then added, 'sir.'

Blake caught his eye, misreading the expression. Had this woman's death stirred up painful memories? Hopefully not. He didn't want someone who wouldn't be able to see the job through . . .

'Everything all right?' he asked, reluctantly adding, 'Personally, that is?'

An empty smile creased Harland's mouth.

'Everything's fine, sir.'

'Good,' Blake said quickly, relieved not to have to explore any awkward territory. 'Well, I'll be expecting regular updates on this. And do let me know if there's anything I can do to help move things along.'

Harland got to his feet.

'Thanks,' he said. 'I will.'

He opened the door to leave. Behind him, Blake tapped the report again.

'Quickly and cleanly, Graham.'

8

Mendel was waiting for him outside the interview room. Harland looked up at the flickering fluorescent light that disturbed the stillness of the empty corridor.

'So who is she?' he asked, nodding towards the door.

'Claire Downing, victim's best friend,' Mendel replied. 'I've been over the basics with her but when I heard you were here I thought you might want to sit in for a few minutes.'

'Thanks,' said Harland. 'How's she doing?'

Mendel shrugged. 'A bit emotional, but nothing serious.'

'Did you ask about boyfriends?'

'I thought *you* might want to do that.'

'Fine.'

Harland opened the door and walked into the cramped little room. Claire was sitting at the small table – late twenties, red hair in a bob, a blue jacket that looked a size too tight for her build. He made himself smile as she stared up at him, and extended his hand.

'Good afternoon, Claire. I'm Detective Inspector Harland.'

'Hi.' She took his hand uncertainly and shook it.

'We appreciate you taking the time to come over.' He noticed the cup of tea, untouched, on the table in front of her. 'Did you want another drink?'

'No, I'm fine thanks.'

Harland sat down next to Mendel.

'So, my sergeant tells me that you and Vicky knew each other well?'

Claire's expression softened and she looked down.

'Yeah, that's right.' She was gently twisting the strap of her handbag around her fingers. 'We used to share a house together in Montpelier.'

'Really?' There was no hurry. Allow her to settle into the conversation with something comfortable. The past was an easier place to begin.

'It was in Purton Road. One of the old houses with massive high ceilings . . .' A faint smile as she recalled it. 'We were only there eighteen months but we've been mates for ages.'

'When did you meet?'

'Six or seven years ago. I'd signed up for this dance class and she started the same night as me. We got on really well right from the beginning.'

'But it was a while before you actually shared a place together?'

'Yeah. We talked about it loads of times before we actually did it.'

'When did she move out of Purton Road?'

'Oh, that was about . . .' Claire considered for a moment, then shook her head in mild surprise. 'It must be almost two years ago now. Doesn't seem that long . . .'

Harland gave an understanding nod.

'And then did she move in with a boyfriend or . . . ?' He left it hanging.

'No, it was her mum.' Claire raised her head. 'The place in Severn Beach belonged to Vicky's mum and she left it to her when she died. It was really sad. Cancer.'

'Sorry to hear that.'

'Yeah, her mum wasn't even that old. Vicky was ever so good with her, looking after her and all that . . . *and* she was doing the marathon this year, raising money for breast cancer . . .'

She trailed off, eyes focused on something far away. Harland steered her gently back from the edge.

'So, there wasn't a boyfriend?'

'Oh yeah,' Claire nodded. 'She was seeing a guy called Simon. He was all right at first – Vicky really liked him – but I don't reckon he was all that supportive when her mum died. People need looking after when they lose someone, you know?'

Harland knew. For a moment he was in a different place, wrapped in a darkness too deep for tears, but he managed to keep his face steady as he struggled back to the surface.

'So she ended it?'

'Not sure. They just saw less and less of each other, and then after a while she said it was over.' Claire frowned. 'I don't reckon she dumped him, though – she was really gutted about him for a while. He probably just couldn't cope with all the upset after her mum died.'

Harland understood. He remembered the friends who became more and more insistent (*'If there's anything we can do, Graham . . .'*) but spent less and less time with him. When the numbness had gone, he found he was alone. Nobody wanted to endure the awkward atmosphere that clung to him, to the house where they'd lived. Sympathy was easier than support.

'It must have been a difficult time,' he said quietly. Then, gathering himself, 'What was Simon's last name?'

'Matthews, I think . . .' She looked thoughtful, then her eyes widened a little. 'But you don't think he did it, do you? Not Simon!'

Harland held up his hand in a calming gesture.

'I simply want to know Vicky a bit better so I can find out what happened to her, that's all. These are just the standard questions that we ask – right, Sergeant?'

Mendel looked up and agreed with an earnest nod. Claire looked wary but settled slowly back into her chair.

'So, *after* Simon, did she see anyone else?'

'No. Well, I think she quite liked one of the guys at work for a while, but he was married. And anyway, she was concentrating on fixing the house up, always painting and stuff. She wanted to sell it and move back into Bristol, but it needed a lot doing to it first.'

'Did she enjoy her work?'

'Oh yeah, she loved it. She joined them ages ago – before we moved in together – working her way up the ladder. I've had three different jobs in that time but she was happy where she was. A really nice bunch of people by the sound of things.'

Harland maintained an encouraging smile as he listened to her, slowly piecing together the picture, first of Vicky, then of Claire – work, friends, family – but nothing stood out. Eventually, with the room becoming claustrophobic, he decided to bring the session to an end.

'And when did you last see Vicky?'

'We had coffee together last Thursday.' Claire began toying with her handbag again. 'We'd often do that – meet up at Starbucks near the station, or go and sit in the park at lunchtime if the weather was nice . . .'

'And how did she seem to you? Anything unusual?'

'She just seemed really happy.' Her voice was plaintive now. 'Everything was going well for her at work, and we were making plans to go out this weekend.'

Her shoulders sagged and she sat, staring down into her lap, murmuring, 'She was really looking forward to it . . .'

Harland caught Mendel's eye, then deliberately pushed his chair back from the table.

'You've been a great help, Claire,' he said softly. 'It's been really useful for me to learn more about Vicky, and I appreciate it.'

Claire sniffed and smiled at him.

Mendel pulled the door closed and stood under the flickering light.

'Well?' he said after a moment. 'What do you reckon?'

'I think we're further away now than when we started.' Harland sighed.

'What about the ex-boyfriend?'

'Let's track him down and see where he was at the relevant time, but he doesn't seem too likely, does he?'

Mendel shrugged. 'Who else is there?'

'Speak to the people at her work,' Harland replied. 'Find out about this married guy she liked, and see if there's anything that jumps out – you know what to look for.'

'What are you going to do?'

'I'll see if there's anything new from Forensics, and then I'm done for the day.'

'Yeah.' Mendel grinned. 'Firth said you were in early this morning. Go home and put your feet up, eh?'

'That's the plan,' Harland smiled. But it wasn't. His smile faded as he turned and stalked away down the corridor.

* * *

Harland parked two streets away and walked. Dennel Road was mercifully quiet but he still hesitated as he approached the building. He checked his watch, but he wasn't early – it was time. Taking one last look around, he mounted the steps quickly and pushed open the heavy door.

There was an oppressive stillness about the empty waiting room. He sifted through the pile of women's magazines on the table until he found the token men's car monthly, then retired to a chair to wait.

He thumbed through the dog-eared pages for a moment, vaguely taking in the same pictures he'd glanced at last time. One of the adverts mentioned a forthcoming motor show and he realised that it was three years out of date.

He tossed the magazine back onto the table in disgust. Posters on the opposite wall made accusing references to a range of mental illnesses. He was thinking of walking out – just for a cigarette perhaps – when the sound of footsteps brought him back to his surroundings.

Jean stood in the doorway, holding open the glass door.

'Graham.' The usual professional smile. 'Would you like to come through?'

Just a rhetorical question to begin with, he thought as he rose to his feet, willing his body language to be calm. They hadn't started yet. It didn't start until they were in the room.

The sound of her heels echoed along the bare corridor as he followed her, silently admiring the movement of her hips. Any distraction was welcome, however brief. All too soon, she was pushing a brass key into a lock, opening the door marked 'Private'.

He followed her into the small room. She sat down by the window, leaving him to close the door behind them.

'Take a seat,' she said, unnecessarily.

'Thank you.'

He sat down carefully, trying to relax but unable to find

a comfortable position. At least he'd avoided folding his arms
or crossing his legs this time. There was a box of coloured
tissues on the small table beside him. For other people.

He forced himself to meet her steady gaze, catching her
assessing him from behind her dark-framed glasses for just
a moment before she smiled again and asked the first
question.

'How have you been this week?'

Always that same opening gambit.

He shuffled slightly in his seat.

'It's been quite good.'

He knew that he was expected to say more, that she would
sit patiently, quietly, until he did.

'I've been keeping myself busy,' he began. 'Putting in some
extra hours at work. We're investigating a new case and that's
occupied my mind. I think that's helped.'

'Helped in what way?' she asked.

He hesitated.

'Well, it's given me something to focus on, to distract myself
. . . And I haven't lost my temper with anyone this week . . .'
He smiled, looking up to find her staring at him impassively.
How quickly she diverted him from what he'd planned to
say.

'I've been sleeping better too,' he admitted.

'That's good,' she said. 'No unwanted dreams?'

'None.' That, at least, was a relief. Long hours, enforced
by the dread of an empty house, were taking their toll. He
looked up again, found her gaze on him.

'Really,' he shrugged. 'No dreams at all.'

She nodded and gave a slight smile.

Light from the window behind illuminated her hair. She
was wearing it down this week. He preferred it down. She
had to be in her late thirties, early forties – close enough to

his own age – an age when too many women embraced the lie that shorter hair would make them look younger.

'As your sleep pattern improves, you'll start to feel better, more in control,' Jean assured him.

She was wearing the same tight sweater she'd had on the first time he'd come here. He remembered the disappointment when he'd initially noticed her wedding ring, the abstract resentment towards a husband he'd never met.

Someone for everyone . . . except him.

Still, it was probably better this way. He could hardly be honest with her if there was any possibility of them getting together . . . and if he couldn't be honest with *her*, what was the point?

'Have you been getting enough exercise?' she asked.

'Doesn't it show?' He made a joke out of it but they both knew she wouldn't respond to questions, only answers. 'I've been swimming. There's a pool just down the road from the station. I went twice this week.'

In truth he'd enjoyed the water. Physically he was in good shape, not athletic but fit, with no excess weight on his six-foot-two frame. The exertion of lane swimming had helped to clear his head and leave him mentally calmer.

'Very good,' she nodded. 'Regular exercise can be most beneficial to a person's mood.'

'It's a good way to unwind after work,' he agreed.

She sat back in her chair and regarded him thoughtfully.

'So, you enjoyed work more this week?' A leading question.

'I'm not sure that "enjoyed" is the right word.' Harland paused, remembering the eerie eagerness he'd felt as the case started to unfold in front of him. Nobody in their right mind would enjoy that. And yet . . .

'It's been a better week,' he admitted.

She nodded very slightly. 'How have you found things when dealing with your colleagues?'

'That's been fine.'

'And what about . . .' she glanced down at her notes '. . . what about Pope?'

He forced a thin smile.

'No problems with DS Pope this week,' he answered honestly.

No problems at all. The little shit was on holiday.

'Okay.' She studied him for a moment. He felt an uneasy sort of excitement, caught in her gaze, both worried and aroused by what she might see in his face.

'So,' she broke the spell, 'no incidents at all since our last session?'

He looked away and sighed.

'No incidents. But there was a moment this morning where I found it . . . hard to keep everything together.'

He glanced back to see her sit up a little in the chair – her ready-to-listen pose – then looked past her out of the window. He needed a cigarette.

'Maybe you could tell me about it,' she prompted.

He bowed his head.

'Things have been relatively stable recently. It's not that the feelings have *gone* – they're never gone – but they were . . . less painful somehow.'

She nodded. 'Go on . . .'

'It felt . . .' He frowned for a moment, struggling to clarify the intangible. 'It felt as though I was sort of removed from it – as though it was *someone else's* pain and I was watching it; sympathetic but not really part of it. And then I was interviewing a woman at Portishead, and something she said must have caught me off guard. All those emotions, all the pain . . . it all washed right over me, like the tide on that damned beach . . .'

He shook his head, the words becoming difficult.

'And then it wasn't distant any more,' he continued. 'It was happening to me again. I felt like I was right back . . .'

He paused, but she allowed him the moment. In his pocket, his fingers traced the edges of the cigarette packet. Just a few more minutes . . .

'I was right back at the time when I lost her,' he said at last.

Jean's eyes held him for a long moment.

'And what happened next?' she said quietly.

He allowed himself to recall the crisis, experiencing yet again the crushing weight of loss, the chasm of despair opening up in front of him.

'Graham?'

He focused on the room – the beige carpet beneath them, the badly painted skirting boards, the small table – dragging himself back from the darkness.

'I managed to hold on, I suppose. Until the worst of it passed.'

'And now?'

'Now?' He stared out of the window for a moment before meeting her gaze again. 'Now I'm extremely tired.'

She looked at him thoughtfully for a time.

'I think it's encouraging that you were able to deal with the situation, and emerge from it in control. I think this shows real progress, that you're growing stronger.'

'Thanks,' Harland shrugged.

But he didn't feel strong – just the opposite. He wondered how much strength he had left.

9

Monday, 4 June

Harland stared at the rain as it hit the windscreen, slowly melting his view of the car park into a shifting mosaic of indistinct shapes. With a relentless *tip tap* on the glass, one drop ran into another and began snaking down in long erratic trickles, new drops quickly falling to replace those that were lost. He leaned forward and switched off the engine, the sound of the rain swelling to fill the silence, then took his coffee from the drink-holder and warmed his palms on the cardboard cup.

It was strange for him to arrive at this time – he was usually early in, late out, stretching the hours away at both ends of the shift – but he wasn't looking forward to work today. And unless Forensics came up with something significant, he had nothing good for his pointless daily report.

The hot coffee was burning his hands.

It had started so well – a challenging case to distract and occupy his mind, the opportunity to work with Mendel again – but now Blake's interest meant it was becoming political. He had seen the signs already, but today . . . Today, things would be worse.

The pain in his hands was agonising, but he forced himself to wait.

Outside, the downpour continued. It wasn't going to ease.

Slowly, he peeled his scalded palms away from the cup, supporting it between the tips of his fingers, breathing through the discomfort, mastering it. He could endure it. He could endure the coming hours.

Rain blew in as he opened the door and climbed out.

PC Gregg looked up as Harland stalked in.

'Morning, sir,' he smiled.

'Morning, Stuart.' Harland frowned, shaking his arms irritably, water dripping from his sleeves onto the floor. 'Did you finish going over that CCTV footage from Avonmouth?'

'Should finish it this morning. Nothing useful so far, though. Sorry,' he said apologetically.

Harland shook his head. *Another dead end for the report.*

'Worth a try,' he shrugged. 'Anyway, with a bit of luck Forensics will get something off the body.'

He prowled down the corridor to his office and shut the door behind him. It was a small room, dominated by a large desk and two huge filing cabinets that made the limited space seem even more cramped. The walls were off-white, bare except for a pair of laminated fire-safety notices by the door and a print of an Alpine lake in a simple wooden frame. A coat stand in the corner displayed a spare pair of trousers, as well as a new shirt, still in its cellophane bag.

Water was already seeping through his jacket as he slipped it off and draped it over the radiator to dry. Slumping down into the chair, he switched on his screen and took a careful sip of coffee. There were a few new emails but nothing urgent and, more importantly, nothing from the lab. He slid a printed sheet of paper from under the phone and ran his finger down the list of names until he found what he was looking for and dialled the number.

He sat back in his chair, rubbing tired eyes as he waited for an answer.

'Good morning, this is DI Harland from Portishead. Has Doctor Brennan come in yet?'

He leaned forward, pulling a notepad and pen towards him.

'No, I can hold on . . .'

His eye fell on the tiny, gold-framed photo of Alice beside his screen. Blonde hair, demure expression and mischievous eyes . . . For a long time after he returned to work he'd kept that picture in the drawer, unable to look at it. This morning he felt a renewed sense of loss as her face smiled out at him from years ago. He'd tried to bury his feelings, but the part of him that cried out for her rose starkly in his mind once more.

'Hello?'

The quiet voice on the other end of the line snapped him back to the present.

'Morning, Charles . . . Tell me you've got some good news.'

'Patience is a virtue, Graham. We've only done the preliminary workup and there's still a lot to go over.'

'That doesn't sound encouraging.'

'It is what it is. Want me to run through the headlines?'

'Please.'

'Okay . . .' Brennan started reading through his notes. 'Cause of death was asphyxia – she was strangled, and it was hands-on-the-throat as you said. Killer was probably male, judging by the force used and the size of his hands. Oh, and I can't be sure yet but I think he may have worn gloves.'

'Really?' Harland scribbled in his notebook. In warm weather, gloves suggested something premeditated.

'Yes, thought you'd like that,' Brennan said. 'We've narrowed the time of death to somewhere between three a.m. and nine a.m. the day before, so the body had probably been out there for twenty-four hours or so when it was discovered. It'll be hard to get more specific – the tides haven't done us any favours.'

'Do you think she may have been washed up from somewhere else?'

'No. Her lungs were absolutely dry, and there was a clog of undissolved mud in her mouth. It looks as though she was killed right there where you found her.'

'That's what we thought,' Harland agreed. 'Anything else on the body?'

'She appears to have taken a serious blow to the stomach. Did you see the bruising?'

'No . . .'

The door opened and DS Pope wandered into the room. Harland's shoulders sagged. Somehow Russell Pope just didn't look like an officer – below average height, slightly chubby figure, with glasses that made his eyes appear small.

'Morning, sir,' he mouthed, with a bland smile. His thick hair seemed lighter since the holiday and he was undoubtedly pleased with his tan.

'Something hit her very hard,' Brennan was saying. 'It looks like there was a bit of a struggle but this blow was much worse than the usual knocks and grazes you'd expect to find – one of her ribs was pushed right back into the abdomen.'

Harland nodded and continued to make notes, aware of Pope hovering in front of his desk.

'I'd say that it happened just before she was killed,' Brennan continued. 'But there's no sign of any interference with the body after death, sexual or otherwise.'

'Sorry, Charles, just a moment.' Harland put his hand over the mouthpiece and stared up at Pope. 'I'm on the phone.'

Pope just nodded.

'No rush,' he shrugged, oblivious.

Harland glared at him for a moment, then turned his attention back to the call.

'So, no DNA then?' He sighed.

'Nothing so far.'

'And the fragments of plastic?'

'They're all consistent with the type of sports watch a runner might wear,' Brennan said. 'The pieces under the body suggest there may be a small patch of ground that wasn't swept clean by the waves but we've not found anything else in it yet.'

'Keep looking, will you?' Harland continued to make notes but his eyes were following Pope around the room.

'Don't worry,' Brennan replied. 'Look, I have another call waiting, can I get back to you on the rest of it?'

'Of course.' Harland put his pen on the desk. 'Thanks, Charles. Bye.'

He put the phone down as Pope turned to face him with his usual watery smile.

'Things going badly?' he asked, with a monotonous contentment that Harland had learned to detest.

'Today hasn't started that well,' Harland answered truthfully, but the irony was wasted on Pope. 'Was there something you wanted?'

'Well, first day back after two weeks lying in the sun . . .' he gave a knowing nod '. . . I thought I'd better roll my sleeves up and help you out.'

Harland stared at him coldly but said nothing.

'The murder on Severn Beach?' Pope prompted him. 'I've been hearing all about it ever since I got in this morning.'

'I'm not sure that would be the best use of your time,' Harland began. 'Mendel's up to speed on it already and the team are making progress.'

'Didn't sound like it from that phone call,' Pope said. 'Strangulation, wasn't it?'

'That's right.'

'It's probably a sexual assault gone wrong,' Pope decided. 'They had something similar happen over in Newport a few years back – although I think they caught the guy who did that, I'll have to check – but this'll turn out to be either a boyfriend or most likely an opportunist pervert, you'll see.'

Harland put down his pen again.

'I think Mendel can manage for now,' he said, firmly. 'Go and see what else he had on before this cropped up; see if there's anything you can take off his plate.'

Pope assumed a puzzled frown.

'Well, it's up to you, I suppose—'

'That's quite correct,' said Harland.

Pope gave him an appraising nod then shrugged and turned to the door.

'If it *is* a failed sexual assault, we should be trawling through the database, looking for someone who fits the profile—' He caught Harland's eye. 'But I'll go and check if there's anything that Mendel needs me to wrap up for him.'

Harland waited until the door closed, then looked down and sighed. Staring at his notes, he wondered what he could scrape together for yet another unsatisfactory report.

★   ★   ★

The photographs of the scene told him nothing new – just that same ghostly silhouette sprawled on the dark mud. He'd been there, seen the body *in situ*, studied the ground around her, and walked the beach. Nothing. He turned his attention to the list of clothing and personal effects: T-shirt, shorts, sports bra, briefs, sports socks and trainers – proper running

ones apparently – and a few keys on a key chain. They'd
retrieved several pieces of what seemed to be a cheap digital
watch – the kind with a stopwatch timer, ideal for runners.
He pondered the pictures of each item, willing something to
jump out at him, haunted by a feeling that there was something there but he lacked the wit to see it.

A little after midday, there was a knock on the door and
Mendel leaned into the office.

'You sent Pope to tidy up after me?' he asked, with a grin.

Harland smiled. 'Have you eaten yet?'

'I was going to grab something in a minute.'

'Come on.' Harland stood up. 'Let's go across the road
and I'll get you a drink.'

The light drizzle eased as they walked along Wyndham Way,
but the pub was still quiet when they entered. Harland set a
half-pint of beer in front of Mendel, then eased himself in
at the table, sipping from a tall glass of Coke as he did so.

'So, you tracked down the former boyfriend then?' he asked.

'That's right,' Mendel nodded. 'Simon Matthews. He's a
lucky boy actually. Turns out he was away on a stag weekend
in Amsterdam – flew out of Heathrow early on the Friday,
back late on Sunday – so he's got a whole group of lads plus
the Passport Control people as his alibi.'

'Oh well,' Harland reflected, 'I wasn't really expecting a
signed confession from him. If he's not in the picture he
might as well be *completely* out of it. What about that guy she
liked at her work, the married one?'

'That'd be Phil Teyson – he's the only married bloke there
under fifty – although we spoke to everyone in the firm. Same
reaction from all of them – *can't believe it*, tearful – just what
you'd expect. We did a bit of digging, and I got Sue to have
a quiet word with one or two of the girls in the office to see

if she could pick up any gossip, but there's nothing there, I'm sure of it.' Mendel shrugged, then raised his glass. 'Cheers.'

Harland nodded slowly, turning a beer mat between his fingers.

'How did we get on with the neighbours?' he asked, suddenly.

'As it happens, we had a very nice chat with the woman who lives next door to Vicky.' Mendel sat back and smiled. 'She's great. Says she doesn't like to pry, keeps herself to herself, but she knows every bloody thing that goes on in that close – spends a lot of time at the net curtains, I reckon.'

'Neighbourhood Watch.' Harland smiled.

'Exactly. She seemed pretty sure that Vicky didn't have a bloke – said it was a shame really, a nice girl like that needed to get out and enjoy herself after all she'd been through . . .'

Mendel paused and looked at Harland, trying to read his expression.

'You okay?' he asked.

'Sorry.' Harland put the beer mat down. 'The more dead ends we find, the more I'm worried about missing something. You know me . . . By the way, Charles says our killer wore gloves, which might hint at something . . . *planned.*'

He sipped his drink, then stared at the glass for a moment.

'It feels too . . . *tidy.* You know? In the spur of the moment, the heat of passion, people make mistakes, they're seen, they leave things behind.'

'But not this guy,' Mendel said.

'Not this guy,' Harland agreed. A faint smile crossed his face. 'Pope told me it was a sexual assault gone bad.'

'Pope's an idiot,' Mendel scowled.

Harland's phone was ringing as he strode back into his office. Pulling off his jacket, he grabbed the receiver as he walked round the desk.

'DI Harland?'

'It's Charles,' said a voice. 'I just thought I'd give you a call, let you know how we're getting on with the analysis on that mud.'

'Get to the point,' Harland scolded, draping his jacket over the back of the chair. 'What have you found?'

'Fibres,' Charles replied. 'We've picked up several strands of dark blue nylon from the mud under the victim's chest – anywhere else and it would have been washed away, but this is new, comparatively clean, with no sign of exposure to the elements.'

'That's good.' Harland scribbled the details on his notepad. 'Do you think the killer was wearing a dark blue top or jacket?'

'Well, it doesn't match anything the victim was wearing,' Charles agreed. 'No guarantees, of course, but it's something.'

'It is.'

'Anyway, that's all I've got for you at the moment, but we'll see if we can work out what sort of clothing we're dealing with. I'll let you know.'

'Thanks, Charles.'

He put the phone down. It wasn't much, but it was a start. And, he thought as he switched on his screen, it was something new to put in his report. Smiling grimly to himself, he started to type.

★   ★   ★

As usual, the kettle was empty. Scowling, Harland moved across to the sink and turned on the tap. How hard was it to refill the damn thing when you used the last of the water? He clicked the switch down hard, then wandered out of the kitchen while he waited for the water to boil.

Moving into the main office, he found PC Gregg leaning back on a chair, drinking a cup of tea. Harland frowned.

'Nothing to do, Stuart?'

'Sorry, sir.' The young officer tipped his chair forward and looked up. 'Is there something you need?'

'Finished those statements?'

'Yes, sir,' Gregg nodded, reaching for a folder.

'Then I'd like you to check the victim's effects. Start with that key chain.'

'Sir?'

Harland sighed.

'She had three keys on it,' he explained. 'Two will be her front-door keys, but I'd like to know what the third one was for. It's probably for a door at her office. Find out for me, will you?'

Gregg shrugged. 'Okay.'

'And Stuart?'

'Yes, sir?'

'Fill up the bloody kettle when you empty it.'

He strode back to the kitchen to find the water had boiled. Rummaging in the cupboard, he found his mug, then reached over to take a tea bag from the box.

'Sir?'

Harland turned to find Firth behind him.

'What is it, Sue?' he asked.

'Blake wants you,' she said, with an apologetic little smile.

Harland gave a quiet sigh and returned the tea bag to its box.

'Dark blue nylon fibres . . .' Blake spoke the words slowly, as though pondering their significance. He glanced up with a flat expression. 'Is there anything specific about them? Any indication as to what kind of clothing they might come from?'

Harland shook his head. 'Not yet, sir. Forensics only picked up on them this morning.'

'Pity.' Blake returned his attention to the report. 'Of course, it's good to see *some* progress, as far as it goes, but I was hoping for rather more.'

Harland said nothing. He sat still, his face carefully neutral as he waited to be told how important the case was. As if he didn't appreciate that. As if he wasn't fucking trying.

'There's a lot of interest in this case, you know,' Blake was saying. 'I want to be certain that we're exploring all avenues, making the most of our resources.'

Harland's head snapped up as an unwelcome idea began to form in his mind. This didn't sound good at all.

'I believe we're covering the ground fairly quickly,' he said, 'building a picture of the woman and her circumstances. We've been able to rule out a number of angles already—'

'That's all very well,' Blake interrupted, 'but I still feel we might move things along with a bit more urgency.'

He sat back in his chair, eyes fixed on a point high on the wall behind Harland.

'It's important that we're seen to be doing all we can,' he said. 'Do you think you have enough manpower on this?'

'I think the manpower is appropriate, yes.'

Blake paused, then tried a different approach.

'It wouldn't do any harm to rattle the cages of a few undesirables,' he observed. 'It shows we're not standing still, and if it *is* a failed sexual assault, we might get a break that bit sooner.'

There it was: *failed sexual assault*. Harland felt the tension wash down through his body as his suspicions were confirmed. Pope had gone behind his back and talked directly to Blake. The bastard.

'I assume you've had someone take a look through the database, pulling up any similar cases,' Blake continued. 'There's bound to be a few people with previous form in this area – it might be worth taking a look at them, seeing who can account for their movements and who can't, that sort of thing.'

Harland sat in silence, his body taut with anger. He stared out at Blake, biting his lip for fear of giving voice to the thoughts that boiled inside him, able only to nod in mute agreement.

'Well, I mustn't keep you, Graham.'

He was dimly aware that their interview was at an end and, masking his emotions, got carefully to his feet.

'Oh, and I see Russell Pope is back . . .'

Harland froze.

'Let's get him onto this along with Mendel and the others. I'm sure he'll have some ideas to contribute, and an extra man should get things done that little bit faster.'

Harland shut the door and stumbled along the corridor. He veered off into the toilets and stood over the washbasins, breathing quickly.

The little shit had gone around him and spoken to Blake directly. Made him look bad. Made him look weak.

He gripped the edges of the sink and screwed his eyes shut for a moment, but he couldn't shake off the terrible fury that seemed to be smothering him, boring into his skull. His eyes snapped open, glittering with rage as his pale reflection snarled back at him from the mirror. He wanted it to stop but he knew it wouldn't.

Pope was doing it on purpose – *had* to be. Manipulative little bastard.

His fingers clawed at the soap dispenser on the wall in front of him, the joints whitening.

Made him look weak.

He lashed out at the dispenser, suddenly needing to hit it,

to hurt it even though it was a lifeless object. Again, harder now, his hand swept down, splintering the plastic housing with a loud crack . . .

. . . and then he was himself again, looking at the broken bits of plastic in the sink. His hand felt numb as he turned it over and studied it. For a moment it was fine, then painful red lines bloomed out across his palm and blood began to ooze from the beaten skin.

There was no anger now, just a profound weariness as he ducked into one of the cubicles, grabbing wads of toilet paper to staunch the bleeding. Nobody had seen him. He'd be able to slip out, make some excuse, go home and bandage himself up properly. He ought to be glad.

Huddled there in the toilet cubicle, shivering, he waited for the bleeding to stop.

10

Harland stood by the window, tracing a line of condensation with his finger as he listened to the voice on the phone. Shoulders tense, he nodded wearily in response to what he heard.

'No, I understand,' he sighed. 'Thanks for trying.'

He ended the call and slipped the phone into his pocket, still gazing out at the rain. The droplet under his finger trickled down and seeped into the gap beneath the window frame.

'Bad news?' Pope had a talent for the obvious.

Harland's head drooped and he slowly turned round.

'Forensics didn't get anything off those blue fibres,' he said. 'They're from a common fabric used in about a hundred generic clothing lines. It's just another dead end.'

'Oh dear,' Pope said. 'That's not much help.'

Harland shot him a withering look, then walked slowly over to the table.

'No,' he admitted after a moment, 'it's not.'

'Still,' Pope continued undeterred, 'I've just been speaking to Gwent Police about that murder over in Newport. You know, the one I was telling you about before? They never got the guy who did that so it might be worth getting a list of any suspects they had and start checking up on them?'

Harland looked at him for a moment, then nodded.

'I suppose so,' he shrugged. 'What have we got to lose?'

He gathered his notebook and his coffee from the table and trudged back to his office.

Vicky's ex-boyfriend had been out of the country. One by one, her male work colleagues had been looked into and then ruled out. She wasn't exactly the sort to have enemies – indeed it seemed nobody had so much as a bad word for her – but she was still dead.

And now he was running out of leads. Even their searches on the database had failed to produce any likely suspects, though he'd not been particularly surprised at that. Without a motive – and despite Pope's theories, he couldn't see one – it was difficult to know what they were looking for, or how to proceed.

He entered his barren little office and closed the door. Moving slowly round the desk, he sank into his chair and gazed up at the ceiling for a moment. He wanted a cigarette but the blustering rain that spattered against the window made the idea less appealing.

Leaning forward he switched on his screen. Typing was difficult – he'd bound the injured hand himself, perhaps too tightly – and it hurt to use the mouse. And yet he sensed there was still something out there to look for, to dig into, if he only knew where to start. Something he could get a hold on and trace back through the fog that surrounded him. Sighing, working slowly to spare his hand, he began to sift through the records of unsolved cases, praying that he wasn't about to add to its number.

It was almost noon when there was a brisk knock on the door and Mendel looked in.

'You look like you could use cheering up,' he said.

Harland sat back in his chair and shook his head.

'I've got a case that's turning out to be nothing but dead ends,' he sighed.

Mendel stepped in and closed the door.

'They're not *all* dead ends,' he said quietly.

Harland stared at him. 'What are you saying?'

Mendel gave him a grim smile. 'Remember the key chain?'

Harland nodded.

'Well,' Mendel said, 'we never did find a match for that third key. Until now.'

'What was it? Something at her work?'

Mendel shook his head as he sat down.

'Couldn't find anything that fitted. But there was a decent thumbprint on it, so in the end we ran it through the system to check. Turns out it wasn't from Vicky Sutherland at all.'

Harland frowned.

'Whose was it then?'

'The print belongs to a Ronald Erskine, and that key will most likely be the front-door key to his flat.'

'Okay,' Harland nodded. 'We'll need to speak to him, figure out any connection to the victim.'

'Ronald Erskine's body turned up four months ago in Oxford,' Mendel said. 'He'd been beaten to death.'

Harland sat back in his chair, his mind suddenly racing. His whole perspective on the murder had shifted.

'This isn't the first time our man has killed,' he said after a moment.

Mendel looked at him, then nodded.

'Changes things a bit, doesn't it?'

'Oh yes,' Harland got to his feet, 'this changes everything.'

I I

Harland was humming to himself as he turned off the roundabout and drove out of Portishead. He accelerated down the
long straight road that led towards the motorway, enjoying
the feel of the car. Over the trees, the towering red cranes at
Portbury loomed up against a steel grey sky, dwarfing the
thin stains of smoke that rose from the buildings at their feet.

The investigation would take on a different shape now.
Someone from the Major Crime team would be over to see
him tomorrow, and there'd be a whole new set of protocols
and time-wasting. But he was still looking forward to it.

He allowed the car to coast up onto the flyover, overtaking
a slow-moving lorry before turning onto the Bristol road and
powering up the hill.

Blake's face had been ashen when he'd told him. Finding
a definite connection to another unsolved murder raised the
stakes uncomfortably high. Neither of them had mentioned
the words – serial killer – but the thought had been there,
unspoken between them. Nobody wanted that sort of thing
creeping onto his patch. But Harland felt the cold eagerness
in his stomach, the guilt-laden thrill that he disliked so much.
He needed this.

There was very little traffic this evening. He was making
good time, and had to remind himself to slow down for the

speed camera in Leigh Woods, changing down a gear and letting the car leap forward as soon as the wretched thing was behind him.

He would have to speak with Thames Valley CID, maybe go to Oxford, compare notes with the officers who'd worked the Erskine case . . . and then what? How far might this trail lead?

He flung the car through the steep bends on the hill down into Bristol, making the most of the road being so quiet.

Two bodies, almost a hundred miles apart. Two bodies that they knew of *so far*. No wonder Blake looked worried – this wasn't petty politics any more, this was something serious.

His mood lasted until he hit the outskirts, but he began to feel the familiar gloom descending as he drew closer to home. The traffic slowed as he emerged from the underpass, gently imprisoning him again in the unhappy rhythm of the city. Driving up Coronation Road, he considered letting it carry him straight on along the river – he could go into town, maybe get something to eat – but it would only be postponing the inevitable. He had to go home sometime.

Sighing, he turned right into the warren of quiet residential streets and wound his way between the parked cars to Stackpool Road.

He pushed the front door shut and chained it behind him. Keys dropped in the bowl on the hall stand, jacket draped over the banister, then immediately through to the lounge to switch on the TV, driving the lurking silence away. He paused, willing his shoulders to relax, before wandering through to the kitchen.

It had been fish yesterday evening so tonight would be pasta – eating the same meal on consecutive nights made him feel uncomfortable about himself. He turned the oven on and slid in a piece of French bread to warm, then placed a pan of water on the stove. Even when his appetite deserted him, he made himself go through the ritual – cooking passed valuable time.

When it was ready, he sat at the kitchen table with his food, a book and a single glass of wine – he knew better than to risk more when he was in this sort of mood – reading until the light from the windows began to fail.

After the washing-up was done, he took what was left in his glass and stood in the back garden to smoke: Alice had never liked the smell of smoke in the house. It was dark now, and over the distant rumble of the city he could hear a girl laughing in the next street. Frowning, he went inside.

By eleven, it was becoming difficult to stay awake. Wearily he climbed the stairs and went to the bathroom, then walked along the landing, past the closed bedroom door and on into the spare room. He hung his jacket in the single wardrobe and dropped his clothes in the wicker basket, then gathered up the duvet and pillows and went downstairs.

The sofa bed opened out with a metallic creak and he arranged his bedding in the usual way before turning off the main lights. Settling down, he made himself comfortable, put the TV on timer and concentrated on the programme even though his eyelids were heavy. There was nothing on, just a documentary about architecture, but it didn't matter. Anything, so long as his mind didn't wander. This was how he survived, forcing himself to watch until, eventually, sleep claimed him and granted him peace.

part 2
SOUTH DOWNS

12

It was difficult to see over the dashboard so he lay back into the seat, gazing up and out of the windscreen, watching sunlight flicker down through the trees. The motion of the car was comforting, with the steady rumble of the road beneath them as tall buildings slid gently by. And then they were slowing down, the *tick tick* of the indicator sounding as they pulled in to the side of the road.

They had stopped again. He looked up at his father sitting beside him, staring straight ahead with a blank expression. For a long moment they sat in dreadful silence, until a motorbike roared by, breaking the spell. With a deep breath, his father got out of the car and came round to open the passenger door.

It was a warm day and the pavement looked pale and dusty as they walked along. A cat was sitting in the sun, just a few steps into someone's driveway, but his father hurried him on down the street – there was no time for stroking cats today. No time for anything.

They came to another telegraph pole – the same splintered grey wood as all the others. His father pulled out a piece of white paper, carefully covered in polythene, and began fixing it to the pole with drawing pins, his face an unfamiliar mask of fear as he smoothed down the clear film and pressed home the last pin.

Another one done. Large, uneven capital letters at the top of the sheet, telephone number along the bottom . . . and the dark, photocopied face in the middle.

He stared up at the face smiling out through the polythene in clean school uniform and smartly combed hair. It was the same photo that usually sat on the shelf above the fireplace at home. It was a photo of his big brother.

'Come on.'

A large hand reached down to take his and led him back towards the car. The door was held open for him and he climbed in, settling back in the seat once more. A moment later, his father got in and wearily reached across him, grasping the seat belt and pulling it over. It felt tight, pinning him down into his seat. There was a click as the belt clip snapped into the slot, and he looked up. His father was staring at him, the expression slowly changing from worry to puzzlement . . .

'Sir?'

Naysmith opened his eyes. Everything was suddenly very bright and very loud, and he became aware of a low rumble all around him. He blinked a couple of times and found himself looking up at a pretty blonde flight attendant in a smart red uniform.

'We'll be landing at Southampton in just a few minutes. I need you to put your seat back up for me, please.'

She had nice eyes.

'Thanks for waking me,' he smiled as he pressed the button to raise his seat. 'I hate it when I sleep through my stop.'

She laughed and turned to walk back up the aisle. Naysmith watched her go, then rubbed his eyes and yawned. He checked his watch – 7.20 p.m. – before turning his attention to the window. A green patchwork of fields drifted up into view as the aircraft banked, occasional wisps of cloud whipping past the wing. Everything looked different from up here, bathed in the golden light of early evening. He leaned over, trying to identify the landscape that slid below them, searching for the coastline, motorways, rivers – anything he might recognise – straining at his seat belt to see better. It felt tight, pinning him down into his seat . . .

. . . and suddenly he remembered the dream, that familiar dream he'd not had for years. Was it all beginning again, those memories of another life encroaching on his sleep? He stared out at the tilting horizon and wondered what it meant.

A chime came over the public address system, followed by the captain's voice saying, 'Cabin crew, seats for landing please.'

Naysmith stretched and let himself sink back into the headrest. An omen, or simply a dream? Either way, there was nothing to do now but enjoy the ride.

He liked small airports. Everything was close together and the queues were short. Ten minutes after stepping off the plane and onto the tarmac, he was walking through the double doors into the main terminal concourse. Kim was waiting by the coffee bar, wearing a long charcoal jacket and jeans, her hair up. Her face broke into an excited smile when she spotted him and she ran over, greeting him with a long kiss.

'Hey,' he grinned after she let him go, 'I've only been away three days.'

'Well . . . I missed you.' She gave a bashful smile, then brightened. 'How was Amsterdam? How was your presentation?'

'Bloody tiresome.' He yawned. 'The conference went well – picked up several new clients – but I had to sit through so many boring meetings. The Belgians were the worst – I took a couple of them out to dinner and it was the longest evening of my life. I almost pushed one of them into a canal, they were so dull.'

'You poor thing.' She slipped her tiny hand into his as they walked out of the building. 'Sounds like you had no fun at all.'

'I wish.'

'Well, I'm glad to hear you behaved yourself.'

Two ambiguous statements. He slowed, searching her face and reading the glimmer of guilt that betrayed her meaning.

Other women.

'Don't start that again, Kim.'

She faltered, then looked down, long lashes hiding her eyes.

'Sorry,' she said quietly.

They crossed the road. Kim paid for the ticket and led him into the car park.

'You've had a long day,' she said as she opened the boot for his bag. 'Can I drive us back?'

'Only if you drive fast,' he smiled, lifting his bag into the car. 'I just want to get home, open a bottle of wine and curl up with you.'

'I'll drive fast,' she promised.

He opened the passenger door and slid into the seat, yawning as he did so. Pulling the door closed, he reached up for the seat belt . . .

. . . and paused as his fingers touched it. His thoughts returned to the dream, to what it meant, to the game. Ideas began to form, a blur of exciting possibilities and challenges . . .

. . . but not tonight. For now it was still just a whisper, and he could push it away, force it to the back of his mind. Tonight he simply wanted to enjoy Kim.

He reached across and caressed her thigh as they pulled out of the car park and drove off into the evening.

★   ★   ★

Wrapped in a warm white bathrobe, Naysmith made his way slowly down the stairs. He yawned and pushed his hand through his hair as he walked through to the kitchen where the flagstone floor was cold and invigorating beneath his bare feet.

He switched on the kettle and took out a tin of fresh coffee, inhaling the dark aroma before scooping a few spoonfuls into the tall cafetière. Life was too short to drink instant coffee. Opening the bread bin, he took out a crusty loaf and cut four thick slices, dropping them into the toaster. Padding across to the fridge, he gathered up butter, marmalade and orange juice and placed them on the large wooden table. Then, yawning again, he picked up his phone and checked his email while he waited for the toast.

Kim wandered in, rubbing her eyes.

'Morning, you.' She tilted her head to one side, tangles of long brown hair spilling down over the shoulders of her baggy T-shirt. She wore a pair of white socks to protect her feet from the chill of the floor.

'Hey, sleepyhead,' Naysmith smiled. 'Coffee's on. Sit down. I'll get it for you.'

'Mmm, thanks.' She shuffled over, gave him a drowsy hug and then sat at the table, propping up her head with her hands. 'What time is your meeting?'

'Ten,' he replied. 'There's plenty of time.'

He plunged the filter down slowly and carefully through the coffee and poured two cups. Adding a splash of cream to hers, he placed it on the table, then moved behind her chair to massage her shoulders. She felt delicate and pliable in his hands, her skin pale and smooth to the touch.

'Mmmm,' Kim sighed, as she reached up and put her small hand on his forearm. 'It's nice to have you back.'

Naysmith smiled and turned back to the counter to put the toast on a plate.

'Any news from Jemma?' he asked as he sat down. 'Did she make it over here in the end?'

'Yes, she came round on Tuesday to keep me company. Actually, that reminds me: she invited us to have dinner with her tomorrow night. John will be there. I didn't want to say anything until I'd checked with you . . .'

Naysmith poured a glass of orange juice for her, then one for himself.

'That's fine,' he nodded. 'Tomorrow's quiet for me – just a few calls to make, and I can do that from here. Today's the only proper meeting.'

Kim sipped her coffee.

'What is it today?' she asked.

'Monthly operations meeting at Woking,' he replied, without enthusiasm.

'Are you driving or taking the train?'

'Driving.'

She was quiet for a moment, studying him with those large hazel eyes.

'I wish you weren't,' she said at last.

Naysmith glanced up at her.

'You must be tired from Amsterdam,' she continued. 'I don't want you having an accident or anything.'

He looked at her for a moment, surprised by the note of concern in her voice. It was oddly pleasing.

'Nothing's going to happen to me,' he said, taking her hand, 'I'm much too careful.'

He held her gaze for a long moment, then, smiling quietly to himself, continued his breakfast.

Kim ran her finger round the top of her glass.

'Well, I still think it's unfair that you have to go out today,' she frowned.

'That's enough.' The stern edge in his voice silenced her, and she looked down, biting her lip nervously. There was something about seeing her like this – suddenly timid and vulnerable – that quickened his pulse.

Naysmith swallowed the last of his coffee and stood up. Leaning over her, he kissed the top of her head, then gently lifted her chin so that she was looking up into his eyes.

'We each do what we have to do,' he smiled.

13

The heavy steel shutters shivered for a moment before crawling back up into the darkness. Naysmith eased the car under them and down the short ramp that led to the basement parking. As he pulled into his space, he noted the other cars lined up in the gloom beside him.

The rest of them were already here. Good. He disliked people being late.

He got out, smoothing down his shirt before retrieving his jacket from the hook in the back. Then, taking his bag from the front seat, he walked quickly across the low-ceilinged space beneath the office building. A magnetic fob on his key ring made a featureless grey door click open and he hurried up the stairwell.

'Hello, Amy.' He smiled as he breezed into the sunlit reception and dropped his bag onto the newspapers that covered the waiting-area table. 'How's your week been?'

'Oh hi.' She looked up from behind a curved wooden desk and returned the smile. 'It's been okay, thanks. You're just back from Holland, aren't you?'

'Last night,' he shrugged, 'but you know I can't keep away from this place.'

Amy laughed. She was a little quiet, but intelligent and very organised. Today she was wearing a smart cream blouse and had taken some trouble over her hair. Not particularly attractive but always well dressed, always professional – he admired that.

'The others are already here?' he asked, glancing up at the clocks behind her desk. There were three of them, each showing a different time, with 'Woking', 'Hamburg' or 'Boston' written below. Naysmith thought they were pretentious.

'Yes,' she nodded. 'I think they're in the boardroom.'

'Okay.' He picked up his bag. 'I'm going to grab a coffee before I go in – would you like one?'

Her face lit up. Clearly it had been a while since anyone else had offered.

'I've got one here,' she smiled, pointing to a cup hidden behind her screen, 'but thanks for asking.'

'No problem,' he grinned, opening the office door. 'See you later.'

Coffee in hand, he pushed open the heavy door and walked into the boardroom. There was a polished oak table that ran the length of the room, with high-back chairs on three sides and a large video conference screen at the opposite end. As he walked in and took a coaster for his cup, the three people already seated greeted him. On the screen, a man wearing rimless spectacles waved and called, 'Hey, Rob!'

'*Morgen*, Andreas.' Naysmith raised a hand in acknowledgement. 'Are you running Hamburg on your own today? I don't see Christof.'

'No, but he will soon join us I think.' Andreas smiled. 'Everyone is there in England now?'

'Yes, we're all here.' Naysmith took his seat and looked round the table. Fraser and Gina, the two directors, sat opposite him, while Alec, the permanently miserable project manager, was to his left.

Gina finished typing and closed her laptop. She was immaculately dressed as always, in a navy blue jacket, her dark hair in a smart bob.

'I think we'll get started.' She smiled. 'Rob, would you like to begin?'

Naysmith's presentation went smoothly. He ran through the new opportunities from his visit to Amsterdam, then gave an update on existing clients and sales projections.

'Looks like we're going to hit our numbers for the quarter.' Fraser nodded approvingly as he looked at the spreadsheet in front of him. He was a lean man in his early fifties, with short greying hair and a likeable manner. Naysmith got on well with him.

The morning ebbed away as the meeting dragged on. Andreas and Christof discussed business from the German office and then, after the arrival of a tray of sandwiches and cold drinks, Alec launched into a monotonous report on the status of the various projects that his team was working on.

Naysmith found his mind wandering. He began to think about his next game, anticipating the thrill of finding a new target. He yearned to be out of this room, out in the streets waiting for fate to present that next challenge. But it couldn't be anywhere round here. Finding someone too close to his work or home would be foolish. He had to be patient.

Alec was still talking. The report he was giving sounded very much like the report he had given last month.

Naysmith wondered what sort of person his next target would be. He or she was out there now, the path of their life meandering blindly towards that instant when they would meet him and the game would begin. It fascinated him to think of them, being so unaware that they were on a count-down to such a significant moment.

He glanced at his watch and willed the meeting to end.

        ★   ★   ★

By three o'clock, he had escaped. Emerging into the strong sunlight from the underground car park, he at once felt invigorated and threaded his way out of the town centre before speeding north towards the motorway. Gina was always a difficult one to impress, but she'd been pleased by the numbers he'd presented today. She and Fraser would both give him a free hand now, which was ideal. Especially if he wanted to dedicate time to a new game.

Leaving Woking behind, he cut across country and soon joined the motorway. Pulling into the outside lane, he could feel the desire growing steadily inside him. He was wound tight with expectation and impatience, rebelling at the monot-onous miles of green and grey sliding by. He yearned for that terrible rush, the heightened sense of awareness that flowed through him when he hunted. It was so strong in him now, he could barely contain himself.

A road sign indicated 'Winchester', next junction.

Winchester.

He felt a sudden calm, as though something inevitable had slotted into place. Smiling, he moved into the left-hand lane and turned off the motorway.

Winchester was somewhere he'd rarely visited, but as he approached the city centre he found himself warming to the place. Old buildings and narrow streets, trees and stone, not yet wholly overcome by the wretched creep of bland town planning.

He drove for some time without purpose through a knot of

unfamiliar one-way streets. After a while, the road began to climb and he found himself breaking free of the city centre. Crossing a bridge, he instinctively turned right up a steep hill lined with a terrace of elegant town houses on one side and tall trees on the other. It was quieter here, away from the traffic, and he slowed down. Cresting the rise, a small swathe of green park opened up on his left – a tranquil oasis above the shops and offices. He drove on until he found a place to leave the car, then parked and walked back along the leafy road.

Tall trees cast long shadows in the afternoon sun and he strolled thoughtfully across the grass towards an old wooden bench. He sat down, running his fingers along the rough grey planks of the seat. A faint breeze stirred the dust around his feet and he leaned back, enjoying the cool air on his face as he gazed up at the cloudless blue sky.

It was perfect.

He shut his eyes, feeling the warmth of the sun through his clothes. The rustle of wind in the trees mingled with snatches of birdsong, but there were also voices in the distance. *People.*

The familiar wave of excitement washed over him as he prepared himself for the start of a new game. In a moment, he would open his eyes and walk back to the road, then on down the hill. As ever, the first person to make eye contact would be the one.

He smiled, listening to the distant voices for a moment longer, then opened his eyes, squinting for a moment under the sudden glare of the afternoon sunlight . . .

A child stared back at him.

Naysmith blinked. A little boy, clutching a brightly coloured ball, was standing there, some twenty yards across the grass, staring quietly at him. For a long, dreadful moment, every-thing stopped, the child's unwavering gaze holding them together in frozen fascination.

No!

Three years old. Blond curls framed a round face. Large eyes and a small mouth. He wore a blue top with a picture of a hippo on it, jeans and tiny trainers.

'Jack?'

Naysmith glanced round. Nearby, a woman with a push-chair had stopped and was calling to the child. Early thirties, five foot six, with a natural figure. She had straight brown hair pulled back into a simple ponytail, and a sleepy smile as she called to her son.

'Come on, Jack.'

The little boy turned and scurried away across the sunlit grass, his mother already moving on along the path at an easy pace, unaware and unconcerned.

Naysmith watched them dwindle into the distance, unable to look away. Somewhere, beyond the trees, a clock struck four.

He sat there for some time. Nothing like this had happened before – it was something he'd never even considered. And yet, there were rules to his game, and they could not be taken lightly. The choice *had* to be random, which meant he *had* to accept the targets he was given. His fingers gripped the wood of the bench beneath him, nails digging into the rough underside of the plank as he struggled silently, alone in the quiet of the park.

No!

Suddenly getting to his feet, he strode away over the grass, his face contorting in an involuntary snarl.

Beyond the park, the road fell away sharply. On the right, a line of three-storey houses stood on a raised pavement reached via worn stone steps, looking out across the city in grand permanence. Naysmith walked quickly in the shadow of the trees on the other side of the street, a steep drop to a railway cutting visible through the bushes on his left. At the foot of the slope, a busy main road halted him and he stood for a moment, glancing around, looking up at the buildings on the corner as he waited for a lull in the traffic. His restless eye caught a road sign – Clifton Terrace. He thought back to where he'd found his last victim . . .

Clifton.

The coincidence set his teeth on edge. Everything he did was artfully random, without pattern or repetition. He played a serious game, controlling the situation, seeking out coincidence and eliminating it.

And yet, here it was. Fate was mocking him.

No!

His breath came faster now, and he found that he was clenching his fists so hard that it hurt his palms.

Fight back!

He looked around hurriedly for a moment, taking in the street, the bridge, the steep slope down to the railway line below . . .

Do something. Don't cower like a startled animal – embrace the fear. Rush out and meet it head-on. Do something. Now!

He was staring down at the railway tracks. And then, placing a hand on the wall, he sprang up and over the rough brick-work. Muscles taut and pulse racing, he scrambled down the embankment, through the sickly aroma of nettles and ivy, turning his body sideways so that he could lean back into the slope and steady himself with his hand. The descent was surprisingly easy and he ran the last few yards to stop, panting, at the base of the cutting.

Do it.

Forcing himself to walk slowly, calmly, he made his way back under the shadow of the bridge, stepped up onto the oily bed of stones and over the first heavy rail. The rusted sides contrasted with the gleaming top surface, the corrosion ground away by the wheels of the speeding trains. Standing on a huge concrete sleeper between the two rails, Naysmith crouched down and bowed his head. Holding his watch, he waited for the second hand to sweep up to the top of the dial.

Five minutes. He would not move, for five minutes, no matter what. Come on . . .

He stared at the watch face as the second hand crawled past the twelve. It moved so slowly, taking an eternity to reach the one.

Five seconds gone. Six . . . seven . . . eight . . .

He wondered how many trains passed through here in an hour. How many minutes apart were they? He had heard none as he walked down from the park.

Ten seconds . . .

It was no good thinking about it. A train would come or it wouldn't. But he would not move until it was time. He continued to stare at the watch.

Fifteen seconds . . .

A car horn sounded on the bridge above, the noise echoing oddly along the cutting. He closed his eyes, tapping out the seconds with his fingers on the ground. He pictured the watch face in his mind, tracking the progress of the thin second hand as it laboured on.

Thirty seconds?

What if he was counting too quickly? Or too slowly? He promised himself he would look when he got to that first minute. The count shouldn't be too far out by then. He focused on the rhythm he was tapping out, forcing himself not to speed up, whispering each number in his head, keeping a smooth and regular pace.

Fifty-seven . . . fifty-eight . . . fifty-nine . . . sixty! Sixty-one . . .

He opened his eyes briefly and focused on the watch. He was counting in perfect time. Satisfied, he shut them again and began the long journey to the next sixty.

Steady rhythm, fingers on the ground, just keep it going . . .

In the past he'd vaguely wondered what would happen if he found a target he couldn't pursue. Not one that eluded him – that had happened before and would probably happen again – but one that just shouldn't be part of the game. For some reason he'd never considered the possibility that it might be a child. Now, as he stared into the abyss, he suddenly began to remember why.

Don't think about that now!

A sudden breeze passed through the bushes along the embankment, rustling the leaves, but he didn't look up.

Concentrate. Finish the forfeit.

He continued to tap out the seconds, rocking slightly as he counted.

Fifty-eight . . . fifty-nine . . . Two minutes.

His eyes flickered open, checking his watch once more. His counting was slightly behind – already the second hand was pointing downwards and he stared at it as it inched round towards the bottom of the dial.

Nearly halfway . . .

He willed it past the six, closing his eyes as he picked up the count for this, the third minute.

Thirty-one . . . thirty-two . . . thirty-three . . .

Softly, very softly, the rails began to sing.

At first it was vague – a distant ringing sound that he felt as much as heard. His count faltered and he strained to listen, but now there could be no doubt. Something was coming.

Shit.

Slowly, he opened his eyes, staring down at his watch, refusing the terrible urge to look up.

Fifty-eight . . . fifty-nine . . . Three minutes!

He would not move. His heart rate had spiked and he suddenly felt cold, but he would not move. If fate wanted to play, he would play.

Come on!

The two-tone blare of a train horn echoed along the cutting and reverberated under the bridge. All around him now the noise from the rails was growing, the vibration flowing up through his feet and into the pit of his stomach.

Come the fuck on!

He could hear the train itself now, feel its approach. The horn blared out again, closer this time, much closer. But he wouldn't look up. He wouldn't move.

The second hand seemed almost stationary. It crawled agonisingly towards the four-minute mark but somehow Naysmith knew he didn't have enough time.

Fifty-eight . . . fifty-nine . . . Last minute.

He was counting down now. The oncoming rumble was getting louder and louder, and the horn blared out a third time, deafeningly close. His hand was clammy, shaking so hard that he could hardly read the watch. There was a sudden piercing screech as the train applied its brakes, but it was too late.

Naysmith stopped counting and bowed his head.

A gale swept up and over him, the noise surging to a terrifying crescendo as the train roared through the bridge arch, passing only a few feet away from him on the adjacent track.

Buffeted by the wind, Naysmith braced himself to avoid being sucked under, eyes screwed shut against the dust and debris that swirled in its wake. The sound, deafening for a moment, suddenly relented as the last coach clattered by.

He hadn't moved.

He opened his eyes, struggling to make out the watch face, smiling as he saw the second hand slide up and past the twelve.

Five minutes.

The forfeit was done. Shaking, he got to his feet and looked round, seeing the train for the first time as it slowed a little way further along the track.

He was alive. Perhaps more alive than he'd ever felt before. It was like that first time – the power of absolute control, surging through him. He let out a howl of triumph as he stepped across the rail and down to the side of the cutting, his body strangely light and agile. The hex was broken, fate defeated. Eagerly, he began to pick his way up the slope, climbing back to the top of the high embankment, leaving the last of his fear on the track below.

14

Light flickered in between the trees as the train cut across country. Harland spread his hands on the small table, feeling the warmth of the sun on his skin. He gazed out at the fields and villages slipping by, and frowned.

Linking the Severn Beach murder with this killing in Oxford had shifted everyone's view of the case – even Pope had gone quiet with his idiotic theories. Urged on by Blake, there had been an enthusiastic burst of activity, with a wave of checks done to try and turn up anything that would link the two deaths.

'We're going to find something,' the Superintendent had insisted. '*We're* going to put it together and get a conviction.'

It could be quite the feather in Blake's cap, especially as Thames Valley seemed to be no further along than they were, and Harland suddenly found himself being pushed into a lead role. He wondered how long it would last.

Diagonally opposite him, a smartly dressed woman in her thirties was tapping out a message on her phone. Fine light-brown hair framed a delicate face, and her lips parted slightly as she concentrated. He smiled to himself and turned his head towards the window, ignoring the blur of passing greenery to study her reflection in the glass. Her left hand toyed with a simple gold pendant that glinted as she turned it, and below it her smooth skin glowed in the sunlight. He wondered where she was going, how long she'd be sitting opposite him, what he might say. It couldn't hurt just to speak to her.

In her hand, the phone began to ring, a thin little tune that was abruptly silenced as she quickly answered the call.

'Hello?'

In the glass, Harland saw her face melt into a smile, watched her head tilt to one side and her fingers touch her chest.

'Yeah, I was just thinking about you . . .' The bashful expression, the inviting tone of voice. She was already taken, and he suddenly hated himself for looking.

He slumped back in his seat and sighed to himself, allowing his eyes to focus on the distant horizon. It was less than an hour to Oxford but the journey seemed to be taking a long time.

Detective Inspector King was an athletic-looking man in his forties. Tall, with dark cropped hair and a quick smile, he'd been waiting to meet Harland off the train. They'd shaken hands warily, but King's easy manner seemed to cut through all the awkward formalities.

'It seems we have a common problem,' he noted as they walked out of the station. 'Months of dead ends and all the fun associated with turning up nothing. And now the whole thing's kicking off again.'

'There's certainly a lot of interest in it.'

'Such is life,' King observed. 'I just hope I can spare you some of the grief that we've been getting.'

He spoke – and dressed – like someone who didn't have any political aspirations. Harland found him immediately likeable.

They made their way past several long lines of parked

bicycles and down towards the road. King paused at the kerb and looked at Harland.

'Did you want to see where it happened first? It's close enough to walk . . .'

The bridge was quite short, rising only slightly as it carried the main road across a meandering stretch of river. An old brown-brick pub sat at one corner, and foliage from trees on the riverbank shone in the sunlight.

'The body was found down there,' King explained, leaning over the metal railings and indicating the dark green water that swirled silently below. 'You've seen the photos I assume?'

'Yes.' Harland stared down at the rippling reflections. He remembered the glistening grey skin, the sodden clothing, the misshapen head . . . 'But I always like to get a feel for the place, see the geography for real.'

'I know what you mean.' King straightened up and pointed along the pavement. 'Anyway, it's fairly clear what happened. Ronald Erskine was walking home from a bar in the city centre, a little before midnight. As he came down here towards the bridge, someone smashed in the side of his skull with a metal bar – we found the weapon when we dragged the riverbed. Not much sign of a struggle – first blow probably put him down – but there were several strikes to the head before he was moved down there to the bank.'

They made their way across to the north side of the bridge, where there was an opening in the railings. A paved footpath led down to the grassy riverbank and on along the water's edge.

'Where does this lead?' Harland asked, peering along the path that curved away into the distance, overhung with trees.

'It's the old canal towpath. There's nothing much down there, except a few barges and some playing fields.'

'Anyone live on those barges?'

'There's a few people, yes.'

'And nobody saw anything, or heard anything?'

'Nobody ever does.'

They stood for a moment in the shadow of the bridge, gazing out at the water where the body had been dumped. Some ducks swam slowly towards them before passing on along the bank.

'It's a good spot for it,' Harland said thoughtfully.

'I suppose. Not many people come down here at night.'

'And there's water to dump the body into.'

Harland made his way to the water's edge and looked up as the muted sound of a motorbike engine echoed from above.

'It's also well hidden from any traffic passing over the bridge, which is important if you need to spend any time doing things to your victim . . .'

'Doing things?' King walked over to stand beside him. 'There was no sign of anything sexual.'

'No, I meant searching his pockets, taking one of his keys,' Harland suggested. 'That all takes time and you wouldn't want to do it up there where you could be seen.'

'No, you wouldn't,' King agreed. He stared down at the water and sighed. 'Strange about that key though.'

'Strange?' Harland glanced across at him.

'The victim lived alone,' King explained. 'He'd been out for the evening, and was on his way home. But although he had five or six keys on a key ring, he *didn't* have the one for the deadlock on his front door.'

'Which the killer took.'

'Yes. But there were *two* locks on that door, and the key to the second one was still on the victim when we found him.' King paused. 'It doesn't make sense. One key's not much use without the other. So why did he take it?'

Harland looked at him for a long moment, then shrugged his shoulders.

'I don't know,' he said. 'I can only think that there has to be some connection between the two victims, something we haven't spotted yet.'

They made their way back up onto the bridge. Harland paused as he reached the top of the slope, turning to look over his shoulder at the towpath. Then, waiting to let a car pass, he stalked across the road and peered over the low wall at the broad, open-air car park on the other side.

'There's a lot of ways to get out of here,' he noted. 'It really is a very good spot.'

'You're thinking this was planned?' King asked.

Harland stared into the distance.

'No witnesses, no evidence, no mistakes . . .' he said slowly. 'I think this was planned extremely carefully.'

15

The meeting-room table was strewn with photographs and papers burning bright in the rays of morning sun that streamed in from the windows. On one side, Mendel sat quietly thinking, his face in shadow, one large hand absently stroking his chin. Sitting opposite him, Pope was hunched forward, scribbling something down in a notebook. Harland rubbed his eyes and turned back to the whiteboard.

'So we've got two victims,' he mused, tapping the board with his pen, 'one in Oxford and one in Severn Beach. Nothing to link them except a key that we now know was lifted during the Oxford murder and planted during the Severn Beach one.'

He paused again, staring at the two names in front of him. *Ronald Erskine. Vicky Sutherland.* Two people with nothing in common.

'What about a link between the two places?' Mendel asked. 'At first we thought the killer might be from somewhere round here – Bristol area or maybe from the other side of the Severn. But now we know there's a link with Oxford, it suggests we look further afield. Our guy might be from Oxford itself, or perhaps somewhere between the two places, like Swindon.'

Pope nodded. 'It's right on the M4, less than an hour from

here and roughly the same distance from Oxford. There's also Gloucester. Or Cheltenham. They're all conveniently between the two sites.'

'Maybe,' Harland said slowly. 'Let's check for any similar cases along the M4 corridor and see if anything turns up.'

He picked up his mug and took a bitter sip of cold coffee.

'I'm not sure we're going to find our killer sitting in the middle of the map, though.'

'How's that?' Pope asked.

'Well, he's not made many mistakes yet, has he?' Harland said, taking a photo of the Oxford crime scene from the table and sliding it across to Pope. 'Look at the location he chose there – and I do believe it was chosen, not random. The more we learn about him, the more things seem carefully planned out.'

'So he's probably too smart to live in a dump like Swindon then,' Mendel grinned ruefully.

Harland smiled. 'I'm not trying to burst your bubble. I just don't believe our man would do something as obvious as that. He dumped both bodies in water and managed to avoid being spotted or leaving anything of himself at the scenes . . . I think he's probably quite clever.'

'Clever people make mistakes too,' Mendel said.

'We live in hope.' Harland paused for a moment, then looked up. 'I do think there might be something in the location of the murders, though. Let's say for a moment that the two killings weren't opportunistic – they were premeditated. If that's true, then the killer probably knows both areas fairly well, or has spent a bit of time in each place, planning how he was going to do things.'

'Why wouldn't they be opportunistic killings?' Pope asked.

'On its own, the Oxford one might have been,' Mendel said, 'but you wouldn't choose a freezing cold morning on

Severn Beach unless you knew someone was going to be there.'

'Exactly.' Harland walked over to the window and looked out at the bright blue sky over Portishead, wisps of silver cloud blowing in across the town. 'DI King thought that Erskine's killer was probably someone local to Oxford because they seemed to know the place. We thought the same about the murder here. Now we've connected both deaths, perhaps we need to change our thinking about how the killer knows the two sites.'

'He might live near one, and work near the other,' Mendel suggested.

'Severn Beach is a small place,' Pope said. 'It'll be easier to find someone there than somewhere like Oxford.'

Harland considered this. They had to be seen to be doing something.

'It's somewhere to start,' he said, walking slowly back to the whiteboard. 'We certainly need to find something besides that house key to link the victims.'

'Did Thames Valley have any theories about the key?' Mendel asked.

'No.' Harland shook his head. 'It was such an innocuous thing. With the other door key still on the body, King said they didn't really attach too much importance to it, at least until we contacted them.'

'Not exactly their finest hour,' Pope muttered under his breath.

Harland was suddenly angry, turning to say something, to put Pope in his fucking place, but a thought stopped him dead.

'What is it?' Mendel asked.

'Something innocuous, something you wouldn't spot unless you were looking for it.' Harland frowned, leafing through his papers until he found what he was searching for. He quickly scanned the list of personal effects, then turned to the others. 'What if there was something on Erskine's body that didn't belong to him? Maybe not a key, but something small, ordinary . . .'

'Something planted there by the killer,' Mendel nodded.

'That would mean there's a third body out there somewhere,' Pope said. 'We need to call Thames Valley, get them to check through Erskine's personal effects.'

'Agreed.' Harland picked up his papers, paused and looked at Mendel. 'What about Vicky Sutherland?'

Mendel sat back in his chair.

'That could be tricky,' he said quietly.

'What are you talking about?' Pope asked.

'Finding something that isn't there,' Mendel replied. 'If we find something from a previous murder planted on Erskine, it follows that something may have been taken from Vicky.'

'For the next victim,' Harland explained. Adrenalin coursed through him, no longer driven by anger, but excitement. They were just scratching the surface, and what they were uncovering might be bigger than anyone thought.

Blake beckoned Harland into his office, his expression a blend of determined optimism and unease.

'Take a seat, Graham.' He walked round the desk and slid into his own chair. There was an unpleasant eagerness about him at the moment. Ever the politician, he was always keen for news, for progress, for a chance to take credit, but just as ready to push the whole mess back onto Thames Valley if it looked like it was turning sour.

'Thank you, sir,' Harland said, keeping his voice and his body language neutral, difficult to read. He wasn't going to make anything easy for the white-haired Superintendent.

'I understand that DI King's been assisting you with details of the Oxford murder.' It wasn't a question. Blake was keeping a close eye on this one. 'I trust that's proved useful . . .'

He left it hanging, using the silence to underline the severity of the situation. It was a tiresome game, but Harland didn't want to drag things out.

'Any information is useful,' he said. 'This victim was male, so we know it's not someone who simply hates women. There are certain similarities in the two attacks – both inflicting fatal injuries to the head, both disposing of the body in water. And we're now convinced the killings are planned in advance.'

'Motive?'

'Nothing yet. But the body in Oxford makes it less likely that the killer is local to *this* area. We've started looking for similar attacks along the M4 corridor.'

'Good.' Blake nodded slowly for a moment.

Harland glanced up at him. Good? The second body had done virtually nothing for the investigation other than reset-ting it to square one. What was the Superintendent thinking?

Blake stared thoughtfully at his desk for a moment, then sat back in his chair and looked at a point on the wall above Harland's head.

'I think we need to be seen to pursue every avenue, Graham,' he began.

This didn't sound good . . .

'The media is an essential tool in the fight against crime, and I believe it's time we used it. We're going to do a TV reconstruction, see if it turns up any new leads.'

Harland rubbed his weary eyes, with a sudden dread of where the conversation was going.

'I want you to help with this, present the relevant facts and make sure we're properly represented on the programme.'

Not me. Anyone but me.

He thought back to the media training course he'd been forced to attend – his dread of reporters with their cameras and their microphones ready to ensnare him – and shuddered.

'Wouldn't it be better to have someone else do it? I'm not really cut out for this sort of thing—'

Give it to someone else. Give it to Pope – he'd love the attention.

'Nonsense.' Blake was already on his feet, moving round the desk to open the door for him. 'I've told the media team to expect you. It's all arranged.'

Harland stood up. His mouth suddenly felt dry and he was numb with frustration, but he wouldn't let it show.

'Thank you, sir,' he murmured and stalked out of the room.

16

Sunday, 24 June

Sunday had dawned grey and overcast, and they spent a lazy morning in bed with the papers. By eleven, the sun had begun to peep in, illuminating the pale linen curtains and casting a golden strip of light across the crumpled duvet. Stretching sleepily, Kim got up and disappeared into the shower while Naysmith wandered downstairs.

They enjoyed a relaxed brunch at the kitchen table, music drifting through from the living room, easing themselves into the day.

'It's brightened up,' Kim said, gazing out into the garden. 'Did you want to go for a walk?'

Naysmith looked up from his magazine.

'Okay.' He smiled. 'Where would you like to go?'

'I don't mind,' Kim shrugged. 'We can just see where the afternoon takes us.'

They left the house and walked slowly through the village, strolling along the narrow pavements, stopping to listen to the burble of water from the culvert streams that meandered between the old houses. They had planned to stop at the pub, but the weather was fine and they found themselves going further than intended.

'It's not that I don't want the responsibility,' Kim was

saying, 'but they can't keep taking on more and more work, then expect it to get done in the same time. We were short-staffed *before* Harvey left, and now there are only four of us doing everything.'

Naysmith considered this as they turned off the lane onto a narrow farm track that climbed up across the fields.

'I thought they were going to replace him,' he said after a moment.

'They told us they would but that was months ago.'

A warm breeze ruffled Kim's hair as she walked beside him. The track led up to a hilltop crowned by a stand of trees and commanded a wonderful view of the rolling countryside beyond it.

'It's not as though they're short of money,' Naysmith reasoned. 'Has anyone spoken to them about this?'

'Well, Marcus is the most senior so he should really be the one to raise it . . .'

'But?'

'He doesn't want to.' Kim made a face. 'I think he's looking around for another job – probably doesn't want to upset anyone in case it jeopardises his references.'

Naysmith shook his head.

'I don't like them taking you for granted. Perhaps it's time you looked for something else too.'

Kim walked beside him, her free hand brushing against the long grass at the edge of the path, lost in thought.

'Maybe you're right,' she said at last, 'but there aren't too many other firms around Salisbury. It's easier for Marcus; he has no ties . . .'

Whereas you have me, Naysmith thought, oddly intrigued by the notion.

It was strange to think of them as 'tied' to one another. When had that happened? Over the last two years they had certainly become closer than he'd ever expected, but when had they become a proper couple? There wasn't a specific moment he could put his finger on. Was it when they'd started living together? No, she'd moved in by instalments; technically she still had her house in Taunton, but really that was her sister's place now. When had everything changed?

As they walked on in silence, he caught her glancing shyly up at him and he thought he saw that same realisation in her eyes – that awareness of how entwined their lives had become.

'Rob,' she said slowly, 'can I ask you something?'

She hesitated, and for an uneasy moment he wondered what she was going to say. He stopped and looked at her as the wind teased at her hair.

'Where do you see yourself in five years' time?' She gazed up at the trees ahead of them, then turned to him, 'You know . . . what do you want out of life?'

'Five years is a long time,' he answered carefully. 'I'm not following a timetable, but you know what I'm like – I just want to feel alive, to be happy, keep challenging myself.'

She lowered her eyes. They had been talking about work, but suddenly he knew this walk was about something else.

'And what about me?' she asked.

Ah. Here it comes . . .

She looked up at him, searching his face.

'I'm not a challenge,' she said quietly.

Unbidden, he found that his hand was outstretched, caressing her face. He stepped forward, gazing into her eyes as the breeze swirled the long grass around them.

Had he wanted her more back then, before things had changed? When she was still pretending? Still playing hard to get?

He smiled. Perhaps, but her gradual surrender to him – both physically and emotionally – had been so complete that he'd become drawn to her in a profoundly different way. There was a strange blend of enjoyment and responsibility – holding her on the knife-edge of total submission – that he found intensely compelling.

She wasn't stupid. He knew she must sense the hunter in him – the sexual predator at least – and yet she chose not to believe it.

Because you don't want to believe it.

'Listen,' he said, studying her upturned face, 'I don't want *every* part of my life to be . . . competitive. Yes, I need to challenge myself, test myself, but that's not all I need.'

His fingers pushed a wisp of hair away from her anxious eyes.

'You're not a challenge,' he said softly. 'You're the *balance* in my life; the one person who I'm *not* trying to get the better of.'

Because now there was no resistance left, so utterly had she submitted to him.

Kim held his gaze for a moment, then leaned her head on his shoulder.

'But Rob—'

'Shhh,' he interrupted her. 'Trust me. I want you just as you are.'

And in a way it was actually the truth. Struck by this, he took her hand and, giving it a reassuring squeeze, led her on towards the hilltop.

'Come on,' he laughed, as she began to smile, 'let's go and look down on the world together.'

17

The meeting had been a complete waste of time and Naysmith was in a filthy mood. He pulled the car door hard, slamming it to shut out the sounds of the people and the traffic, then gazed out through the windscreen with unseeing eyes.

He could respect companies who wanted to negotiate hard, or who had no choice because their budgets weren't enough, but this lot just didn't have a clue. Two directors who couldn't agree what they were doing and ended up arguing in front of him.

Fucking amateurs.

He sighed and unclenched his hands from the steering wheel. Closing his eyes, he stretched out his fingers and placed the palms flat on his thighs, allowing his shoulders to drop. A slow breath in, then out, willing his muscles to relax . . .

It wasn't important. It was irrelevant.

He opened his eyes . . .

. . . and smiled as a thought came to him. He'd been putting it off, dwelling on other things, but no more. Perhaps it was because of what had happened last time, but there was no reason for him to wait any longer – in fact, today would be the perfect day to begin a new game.

As he drove out of Farnham, he already knew where he

was going. He'd seen the road signs for Winchester on the way up here, silently calling to him, luring him back, and now he responded, ignoring the motorway and cutting directly across country. It would be a pleasant detour and he sensed that the city was drawing him back for a reason.

It was another bright afternoon in Winchester, and he could feel the touch of the sun on his back, warming the skin through his shirt. He walked over to the wall beside the bridge, pausing to run his fingers lightly across the rough bricks before leaning against it and gazing down the ivy-covered embankment to the railway tracks below. How small he must have looked down there, kneeling between the rails, head bowed . . .

For several minutes he stood there, lost in thought, until the noise of a train roused him. Smiling to himself, he turned away. He was free of the curse, free to start a new game, with a new target. Right here.

He considered the road in front of him, and the footpath leading away on the other side of it. It would do nicely. The first person to make eye contact once he crossed over would be the one. He waited for a lull in the traffic, then stepped off the kerb.

Across the road, the paved footpath climbed steadily, following the trees and bushes that lined the top of the railway cutting. Passing under the shadow of the foliage, Naysmith walked along slowly, admiring the white painted town houses with their brightly coloured doors and their beautiful little gardens. Everything neat, everything pleasing. There was a sense of peace here that touched him, infusing him with calm, clear purpose.

He was in control. He was ready.

On his right, the town houses gave way to an endless flint wall, eight foot high and topped with old ivy and trailing branches. Sunlight dappled the footpath here and there through the leafy canopy above, but still there was nobody to be seen. On his left, a train clattered along the cutting some-where below, leaving a still deeper silence in its wake. Ahead of him there was a heavy gate set deep into the wall, and he could see that the path beyond it started to drop away.

The sense of anticipation was palpable now. It was a powerful feeling, moving quietly through the world, so deadly but so anonymous.

And then there was movement.

Coming up into view over the rise, a figure was walking briskly towards him. It was an older man, perhaps in his fifties, wearing a beige shirt and one of the worst jackets that Naysmith had ever seen. He walked with a determined gait, head up and staring straight ahead. For a moment, it seemed as though he would pass without a glance but then, just a few yards before they drew level, the man shot him a brief, disapproving look and their eyes met.

He would be the one.

And now, as the gap between them closed, Naysmith studied the man, taking in each detail of his appearance and locking it into his memory.

He was about five foot ten, a little overweight, but not too much for his age, with a sparse covering of light brown hair above a slightly puffy face. The awful jacket was brown, and he wore dark trousers over the sort of shoes that are bought for comfort rather than style.

Another step and they would be past each other . . .

Large, prominent ears, downturned mouth, and a pair of steel-rimmed glasses framing small, hooded eyes . . .

And then, with a final look of disdain, the man had passed on his way, his pace never slowing.

Naysmith walked steadily on, listening to the footsteps receding behind him, picturing the man in his mind, until the sounds faded away. After a few moments, he slowed, then halted to check his watch. It was a couple of minutes before three and his target's twenty-four hours' grace had begun.

He closed his eyes and smiled to himself – it was exhilarating to be in the game again.

⋆   ⋆   ⋆

It was an eerily familiar image. The long, curving beach, the swathe of coarse grass, the shingle strip and the glistening grey mud. He remembered that same bleak sky and the dark water of the Severn whipped along by the relentless wind.

But the woman on the screen was different. Similar – mousy hair, white T-shirt, blue shorts – but not the same. As she jogged towards the camera, it was clear that her build was a little too athletic, her face a little too broad. Naysmith smiled as he noticed they'd given the actress no earphones – no MP3 player. *But of course – they didn't know she'd worn one.*

'Vicky went running along this path most mornings.'

A gaunt man in his forties, presumably the investigating officer, was pictured by the sea wall. He wore a dark coat, and spoke in quiet, measured tones, but there was something about his eyes . . .

'We believe she may have been attacked up here and then dragged down onto the beach where her body was later found.'

The camera panned across to the beach, and Naysmith felt another shiver of recognition as he remembered those difficult last moments as she'd struggled against him before finally lying still.

The reconstruction ended with a view of the Second Severn Crossing, curving away against a dark sky. The police officer appeared once more.

'Were you near Severn Beach on Friday the twenty-fifth or Saturday the twenty-sixth of May? Did you see anyone acting suspiciously? Or did you notice any unfamiliar people or cars in the area?'

Naysmith stared intently at the face on the screen, taking in the slightly greying hair, the lean frame, the angular features. And those haunted eyes.

'Rob?' Kim called through from the kitchen, disturbing his thoughts. 'I'm making coffee. Do you want one?'

'Please,' he replied, turning back to the TV.

The detective was now seated in a studio. A caption below him read: *DI Harland. Avon and Somerset Constabulary.*

'A tragic and brutal murder,' the presenter was saying. 'Do the police think that Vicky was killed by someone who lived locally? Maybe even someone she knew?'

'We're pursuing several different lines of enquiry.' Harland remained impassive. 'But we believe her killer may also have had ties to the Oxford area.'

Oxford.

Naysmith sank back into his chair as the significance of the remark hit him. He pictured that single house key, his gloved fingers carefully removing it from one key fob and later adding it to another. The little ripples, drifting out across the water below the bridge . . .

And now the police had finally connected two of the killings. It had taken a long time – he'd almost begun to think that his work would never be recognised – but now that was changing, and the game would surely be more interesting as a result.

He picked up the remote control and switched the channel as Kim came through with his coffee. This DI Harland had been smart enough to find the link. As he reached over to take his cup, Naysmith found himself wondering what the man was like, what he knew, and what lay behind that haunted expression.

18

Harland awoke. There was an indistinct voice talking nearby. Raising his head slowly from the warm pillow, he sat up blearily, rubbed his eyes open and looked across the darkened living room. On the TV, a woman continued to read the news. He had fallen asleep without setting the timer again.

Sighing, he sank back into the sofa bed, but he was awake now. After a long moment, he pushed himself up and rolled his feet down onto the cold floor. Stooping to pick up his wristwatch, he checked the time: 5.40 a.m. Damn. Yawning, he got unsteadily to his feet and trudged upstairs to the bathroom.

When the kettle finally boiled, he poured water into the filter and inhaled the aroma of the coffee, letting it stir his senses. Leaning forward, the sleeves of his bathrobe on the kitchen counter, he closed his eyes and yawned again. So fucking tired – no matter how much sleep he got, it didn't seem to touch the weariness inside him, the bottomless pit that sucked the strength from him. Sometimes he felt as though the only energy he had was when he got angry . . .

He picked up his cup and carried it over to the other side of the kitchen. A firm wrench slid the top bolt back and he opened the door to the chill of the small garden. Shivering, his bare feet flinching from the cold step, he fumbled a cigarette into his mouth and carefully lit it. There was a light touch of rain, so he stood inside the doorway, gazing out at the grey morning light on the ivy that covered next door's wall. There suddenly seemed so much of it, as though it was slowly consuming the brickwork of both houses. Alice used to cut it back, keep it in check – now it would engulf everything.

He frowned and took a last drag, exhaling slowly. He didn't want those thoughts, not just now. Stubbing the cigarette out into a butt-filled flowerpot, he turned and went inside, shutting the door behind him against the cold. Thankfully, he had work to do.

Mendel was mashing a tea bag against the side of his mug. He looked up and smiled as Harland walked into the station kitchen.

'Can I have your autograph?' he asked, opening the fridge and taking out a pint of milk.

'What?' Harland stared before realising: 'They showed the reconstruction on TV last night . . .'

'And you didn't fluff your lines or anything,' Mendel commended him. 'Mind you, don't let the stardom go to your head.'

'No risk of that.' Harland took a mug from the cupboard and reached for the coffee. 'The whole business leaves me cold.'

'There are some silver linings, though.'

'Such as?'

'Well, Pope's been spitting feathers this morning,' Mendel said quietly. 'I reckon he's gutted that Blake had you do the big TV thing. You know how much he likes the sound of his own voice.'

Harland smiled and took a sip of coffee.

'Did you get anywhere with that list of Vicky Sutherland's effects?'

'I've got it on my desk. Want to run through it?'

'Give me five minutes,' Harland said, turning towards his office. 'I've got to call somebody back.'

The phone rang five times, six, seven, then there was a rattle as it was picked up.

'DI King speaking.' He sounded out of breath.

'It's Harland.'

'Ah yes, the famous detective. Saw you on TV last night.'

'Don't you start,' Harland warned him. 'Apparently it's already a hot topic around here.'

'Jealousy makes people say terrible things,' King laughed. 'Any responses to the show yet?'

'Nobody's mentioned anything, so I assume not.'

'Can't say I'm surprised. That beach looked a miserable place from what they showed of it.'

'You have no idea,' Harland sighed, lifting his coffee.

'Anyway,' King continued, 'I've got something that I thought might interest you.'

'Go on . . .'

'Remember you asked about Erskine's personal effects?'

'Yes?'

'Well, we went back over the list, checking everything out, just to make sure that everything was legit, nothing was out of place.'

'And?'

'As far as we could tell, nothing else was missing. We went through all the usual personal items, wallet, cash, credit cards, and nothing seems to have been taken.'

He paused.

'But something seems to have been added.'

'I knew it.' Harland put his cup down on the desk and leaned forward. 'What did you find?'

'There was a video library card,' King replied. 'No name on it, but we checked the number and it turns out it doesn't belong to our Mr Erskine.'

'Whose is it?'

'It belonged to a Khalid Ashfar. Thirty-seven-year-old Asian man from Brighton.'

Belonged.

Harland sat back in his chair. It was just as they'd thought.

'I'm guessing that Mr Ashfar is no longer with us?' he asked quietly.

'His body washed up on a beach six months ago – multiple stab wounds. At first, the Sussex boys thought it might have been racially motivated, but they never turned up anything specific in that direction.'

Harland turned his chair, gazing out through the rain-streaked window. Dark clouds were rolling in along the skyline.

'Well, that's three,' he said after a moment. 'Three that we know of.'

'It looks that way.'

Harland reached across his desk for a pen and flipped open his notebook.

'What was the victim's name again?' he asked.

'Ashfar. Khalid Ashfar.'

Harland scribbled it down, frowning to himself.

'And who are you speaking to in Sussex?'

'Investigating officer was DI Charlotte Bensk. Want her number?'

'Please.'

His mind was racing as he copied the number down. How far back would this series of killings go? And how far forward?

19

Naysmith walked out of the car park, crossed the road and cut down an alley to the High Street. Shoppers drifted lazily across his path as he made his way up the slope, past the carved-stone Buttercross monument, admiring the white plaster and black beams of the Tudor buildings above the storefronts. There was a lot to like about Winchester.

Things had been unusually busy in the week since his initial encounter, affording the target several days' grace beyond the minimum twenty-four hours that his rules demanded. The opportunity to pitch some major new clients had meant a lot of unexpected work, with an endless series of presentations and conference calls. On top of that, Kim had been upset after falling out with one of her friends and he'd decided to make a fuss of her yesterday – a romantic meal and some quality time in her favourite shops – to stop her dwelling on things.

But today was clear. The clients had everything they required, Kim was working in London, and he had the whole afternoon to himself. It was warm again, and he sipped an iced coffee drink as he climbed the hill towards the railway station, his thoughts fixed on the man he was searching for.

Who was he? And, more importantly, where was he?

So many people were victims of habit – living lives of dull

repetition, doing the same things at the same times every day or every week. When he first started to play the game, he'd been amazed how many of his targets he'd found by simply returning to the same spot a day or a week later. Such dreary lives to end – they were practically mercy killings – but there was little challenge in those cases, and little satisfaction. And yet it was the logical place to begin and, as he had the opportunity, he resolved to retrace his steps and start with the narrow lane where he'd first spotted his target.

Beyond the pedestrian precinct, the hill became steeper, with narrow pavements edging their way up past bars and small shops. He continued his ascent to the wonderful old stone buildings of the Castle, where he crossed over to bear left up Romsey Road.

Now he could see the railway bridge before him and, coming into view, the familiar town houses of Clifton Terrace. Alert, his eyes studied every passer-by, looking for that particular brisk stride, that portly frame . . .

Once over the bridge, he stopped to check his watch – it was almost three o'clock, the same time he'd been here seven days earlier. He paused for a moment, his gaze following the footpath as it curved up under the trees. A young couple were strolling down the slope towards him, talking and laughing together. Naysmith waited for them to pass before he set off up the path. The girl had short hair that highlighted a slender and elegant neck; her boyfriend was broad and blond, with an easy manner. Absently, Naysmith wondered where they had come from and where they were heading . . .

When they were gone, he began to make his way slowly up the incline, taking his time to think as he went. A quiet little footpath like this wasn't an obvious thoroughfare – it was a route for people who were familiar with the area, who lived or worked locally.

A smoky-grey cat with white boots and bib sat beside a small wrought-iron gate. Naysmith stooped to stroke it, looking through the half-open gate to the town house beyond it. Did his target live in this terrace? He paused and considered the welcoming facades with their doors painted red, blue or green, their gardens full of character. He looked at the rambling hedges, the romantic little pergolas woven with wild flowers. The cat rubbed itself happily against his hand. No, these places had a joyous charm that he had not sensed in those disdainful glances. He stood and continued up the hill.

Near its highest point, the footpath crossed the end of a quiet residential street. Naysmith paused there for a moment, standing quietly, trying to hear those receding footsteps from days before. It was possible that the man had been going that way, but once again something made him doubt it. His eyes lingered on the houses for a moment longer, then he turned and continued along the path. There seemed to be no CCTV cameras around here.

Now, the trees on his left cast out their branches to brush the high wall on the right, closing over him like a shimmering tunnel in the sunlight. He slowed as he approached the point where he'd made eye contact, stretching out his hand to caress the rough surface of the wall, his fingers sliding across the exposed pieces of flint, then dragging on rough mortar. It was pleasing to the touch, old and solid.

He glanced back over his shoulder. A silver-haired old woman was walking along the path, some way behind him. No sign of his target.

The path began to drop more steeply now, the wall arcing down with it. Above the weathered stones, he could see the tops of fruit trees and the upper storeys of a grand old house, faded red brick against the bright sky. He pondered it for a moment, then shook his head. Too expensive for his target.

At the bottom of the path, Naysmith walked out from the shade of the trees and stood, shielding his eyes from the bright sun. He had emerged on a quiet road that swept down a long, straight slope before a narrow bridge carried it over the railway line below. On the other side of the road, an old cemetery stretched out along the side of the hill, tall iron gates set into a towering stone archway at its entrance.

He crossed over, gazing between the railings with their flaking black paint, smiling at the single cobweb strands catching the light, staring at the forgotten headstones in the grass beyond.

Which way had his target come from?

He turned and looked at the road, trying to visualise the man approaching from each direction. That rounded figure, the brisk stride and the dreadful jacket . . .

Naysmith looked one way, then the other. His eye settled on a small signpost, pointing up the hill, bearing a single word.

University.

He gazed thoughtfully at it for a moment, then set off up the road.

20

Tuesday, 10 July

Naysmith stepped down onto the platform and adjusted his jacket before allowing himself to be carried along in the current of passengers that streamed towards the ticket barriers. Indistinct station announcements echoed high above in the glass canopies, train motors idled noisily, and all around him came the insistent murmur of voices as people hurried along, ready for the grey London morning.

He glanced down at his watch and considered for a moment. Time enough. He could walk rather than suffer the tube.

Threading his way across the busy Waterloo concourse, he looked at the unseeing faces that slipped past on either side. Serious or smiling, bored or confused – so many people, all unaware of his passing. They had no idea who was in their midst; here in the crowd he was truly invisible.

Veering right, he passed under the arched entrance and emerged into the daylight, trotting briskly down the broad stone steps towards the steady growl of traffic on York Road. A walk would give him time to clear his head.

The last couple of weeks had certainly been challenging. This latest game was becoming a real test of his instinct and, to some extent, his determination. He'd now spent a good deal of time in Winchester and clocked up several hours walking the streets around the university. The cemetery, which lay adjacent to it, provided a useful focal point for his journeys. He'd identified a suitable grave to visit – one that commanded a good view of the main university entrance across the road – and chose different places to park on each trip so that he could walk down different streets. As he'd come to know the area, he occasionally thought about the large hospital that stood a little way further up the hill, but something told him that he was looking for an academic and he'd decided to play his hunch for a while longer . . .

'*Standard*, sir?'

Naysmith blinked, then realised that a street vendor was offering him a free newspaper. Shaking his head, he ascended the flight of steps by Mandela's statue on the South Bank, smiling as he noted the traffic cone perched on the great carved head. Sidestepping an erratic group of schoolchildren, he walked along the side of the Festival Hall and up to the Jubilee footbridge.

Music wafted down to him as he climbed, and he found a weather-beaten old man playing a clarinet at the top of the steps, a thin but uplifting melody cast out over the Thames against the dull rumble of the city. Pausing to drop a coin into the upturned hat at his feet, Naysmith strolled slowly onto the bridge.

There was no wind today, but the water below was a sullen grey to match the overcast sky. Here and there, knots of tourists took photos of each other leaning against the handrail, or pointed at St Paul's. On the adjacent railway bridge, a train crept slowly towards him, the metallic groan and squeal of its wheels against the rails drowning out the music as it passed.

At first, he'd imagined that his target might have been going for a train. The footpath where they'd made eye contact wasn't far from Winchester station, and the man had been walking in that direction.

He'd studied the timetables, and sat watching the station entrance from his car. He'd tried an hour earlier, and an hour later. Once, he'd actually come by train so that he could wait in the station itself – there were only two platforms and it was possible to wait on one and see passengers on both sides of the tracks.

But his target hadn't appeared.

Sitting there, searching the faces of the commuters without success, he'd resigned himself to the idea that the target either lived locally or had travelled by car. Perhaps it was the way the man had been dressed, with that dreadful jacket. There was a certain stuffy formality in his clothes – however poorly chosen they were – that didn't seem consistent with someone popping out for a walk.

Of course, this raised a new problem. Parking was scarce in that part of the city. Sticking with his academic theory just a little longer, he decided to focus on the university car parks.

Once across the Thames, Naysmith wandered slowly past the leafy entrance to the Embankment Gardens and up the narrow chasm of Villiers Street as it climbed between the looming buildings. There was a quiet bustle here, amid the cafés and the aromatic coffee shops. Restaurants and bars were having their tables set out on the pavement, ready for lunchtime, while a delivery van unloaded crates of bottled water for a local gym.

At the top of the incline, he checked his watch once more before turning right onto the Strand. It was busier here, with a steady stream of people weaving through each other as they hurried along. Seeing a break in the traffic, he stepped out

from the broad pavement and made his way across the road
to the quieter north side. A tailor's shop window caught his
attention for a moment before he turned left and made his
way up towards Covent Garden.

Winchester University had a number of car parks spread
over a large campus, so he had decided to play the odds and
watch the main entrance on Sparkford Road. He had considered watching from his car, but in the end he'd been annoyed
by his own timidity and elected to take a much bolder
approach. It was a warm day, so he'd taken his laptop and
sat on a bench near the main entrance. Nobody questioned
someone typing on a laptop.

At first, he'd felt optimistic, but after an hour, the doubts
had begun to creep in. How much did he really know about
his target? Everything thus far had been guesswork – intelligent
and considered, but guesswork nonetheless. The man might
just as easily have come from the nearby hospital, or even the
cemetery. Sitting here could be a complete waste of time.

And yet he had stayed there. Something stubborn inside
had kept him in place, looking out over the screen of his
laptop even as the traffic slowed and a silver car coming
down the hill stopped to let a delivery truck pull out of the
campus entrance.

It was him.

He was wearing a different jacket, but it was unmistakably
him, impatiently waving at the truck driver to get out of his
way.

Naysmith calmly typed out the car's registration, then
closed his laptop.

That had been yesterday. Now he stood on a narrow street
just off Covent Garden and paused to check the address

before pushing on a heavy glass door that swung open onto a bright, airy foyer. Walking across the polished marble floor to the broad reception desk, he put his bag down and smiled.

'Robert Naysmith, here to see Christina Valdares.'

The receptionist, a thin, effeminate man with immaculately spiked hair, glanced up at him, then tapped a number into a console and spoke quietly into his headset.

Naysmith checked his watch. He was a few minutes early.

'Please take a seat over there.' The receptionist pointed with a slender hand. 'Someone will be right down for you.'

'Thanks.'

He wandered slowly over to a group of burgundy leather sofas and sat down. Artfully scattered on a low glass table were a couple of broadsheets and a selection of dreary trade magazines – nothing he cared to read. He sat back and gazed out at the street.

It was a Silver Honda Accord, registration number K347 GMX. Now that he knew what he was looking for, it wouldn't be hard to find where his target parked. Smiling, Naysmith opened his diary and checked when he would be free to return to Winchester.

21

Thursday, 12 July

Naysmith put down the phone and stared out of the small window, taking in the bright expanse of sunlit grass and the village beyond. His biggest client was on holiday and, having chased up all the current leads in his diary, he was at a loose end. Closing his laptop, he turned slowly in his chair, got to his feet and took his empty mug down to the kitchen.

A restless energy coursed through him as he waited for the kettle to heat up, and the quiet stillness of the house became oppressive. He looked at the clock above the stove – 11.45. Not even lunchtime yet.

His eyes fell on Kim's fur-trimmed gilet, hanging over the back of a chair. After staring at it for a moment, he turned, switched off the kettle and went to find his car keys.

Half an hour later, walking along a narrow street in Salisbury, he dialled Kim's number.

'It's me. I'm in town . . . yeah, right now. Can you take an early lunch?'

He paused, then smiled and nodded.

'Good. See you at the pub by the river in a few minutes.'

Ending the call he looked around. Light sparkled on the rippling water below him as a swan glided silently by. He walked slowly past the pub, along the riverbank in the direction of

Kim's office, stopping by a narrow side street. It was quiet, just as he'd hoped.

Perfect.

He waited there for her, anticipation building inside as he peered along the footpath. Far from dull, the day now seemed vibrant and exciting, charged with power.

Come on . . .

And there she was, walking along the riverbank towards him, long dark hair catching the sun, a smart blue jacket over a simple white blouse, a short skirt accentuating her legs. He smiled and waited for her to come to him.

'Rob.' She beamed as she reached him, but he put a finger to his lips and hushed her with a smile. Taking her hand, he led her wordlessly into the shadow of the side street. She looked puzzled, but he reassured her with his eyes as they moved a short distance from the river and stopped by an alcove between two buildings.

Now, he turned towards her, gathering her in his arms and kissing her as he pushed her gently back against the rough brick wall. He could feel her surprise, and she started to say some-thing, but as their lips met she closed her eyes and put her arms around his neck. For a long moment, they stood there, until he moved, untangling himself from her enough to slide a hand inside her blouse as he bent forward to kiss her again. He loved the warm softness of her skin, the wonderful uncertainty in her movements, the way she felt so unprepared for him.

Her breathing had quickened but she slowly relaxed her arms and allowed her hands to drop to her sides.

Good. She knew what was going to happen.

People were walking by just a few yards away, but it didn't seem to matter any more, and she yielded to him as he touched her. Head upturned, she kissed him deeply, then gasped as his hand slid down between her legs. Her eyes flickered open nervously but he stared down into her face as he moved, holding her gaze from looking round, smiling as he felt her body beginning to respond.

He knew her well, could sense how the surprise melted into an excited abandonment. As the urgency grew, she lowered her eyes and half turned her head, but he gently touched her chin and drew her back so that she was looking up at him again. He wanted eye contact.

His fingers moved quickly now, teasing her relentlessly until she couldn't help herself any longer. This was what he wanted from her. Staring down, he watched her bite her lip, saw the slight widening of her eyes as her body tensed and felt her squirm against his hand for a moment.

Then, blushing deeply, she gasped and sagged. He released her and she leaned back against the wall, beads of perspiration visible below her neck.

'Hello,' he grinned.

'Rob!' she whispered, as she smoothed the front of her skirt down, then gave him a bashful half-smile. 'I can't believe you just did that . . .'

He kissed her lightly on her forehead.

Glancing left and right along the alley, she seemed to steel herself, then looked up at him.

'Do you want me to . . . ?' She placed her small hand on his crotch.

It was intoxicating. She would probably kneel down in front of him right here if he told her to. He smiled and shook his head.

'This isn't the place, and I'd hate for us to be arrested.'

She adjusted her jacket and smiled back, her face flushed. He pushed a strand of hair away from her face, then reached down to fasten the open button on her blouse.

'I've got a meeting this afternoon, but I shouldn't be too late,' he explained. 'When I get home . . .'

She nodded shyly and leaned her head against his shoulder, so obedient, so vulnerable. Unfamiliar emotions glimmered briefly within him and he put his arm around her.

'Come on,' he said softly. 'I promised you lunch.'

He took her hand and led her back out into the sunlight.

★   ★   ★

Naysmith indicated left and turned off the road, wheels crunching on the loose stones as he entered the car park. He drove forward slowly, casually, pretending to look for a space. This was the third car park he'd checked. He pulled the wheel round hard, turning into the next row, his eye scanning the noses of the parked cars.

There was another silver one, about two-thirds of the way along. He crept down the line until he could see it better . . .

K347 GMX. There it was, the target's car, sitting partly hidden behind a blue people carrier.

Got you.

Craning to look over his shoulder, Naysmith reversed back up the row and turned his car round. There was only one exit from this car park, but, looking up and down the road, there seemed to be nowhere that he could sit and wait without attracting suspicion, or being given a parking ticket.

He checked his watch.

If their previous encounter was anything to go by, the target should be leaving just after five – less than an hour from now – and would probably go down Sparkford Road.

Better to go ahead and wait for him.

It was a bit of a gamble, but he could easily find that silver Honda again, now that he knew where it would be. Satisfied, he pulled out of the car park and drove down the hill. Peering out, he considered the turnings on the left and right, but they all seemed to be side roads, little residential cul-de-sacs. He allowed himself to go a bit further until, coming round a sharp bend, he found what he was looking for. Here, there were houses on either side of him and the street broadened out slightly, with just enough room to pull over and park. A little way ahead, the road passed beneath the railway embankment via a short tunnel. It was too narrow for vehicles to pass side by side, and a set of traffic lights controlled access – two cars were waiting at a red light as he looked – it was a natural bottleneck.

The perfect place to wait.

He angled the car in to the kerb and parked. Switching off the engine, he adjusted the rear-view mirror so he could watch the road behind him, then glanced at the dashboard clock. Just over half an hour to go.

Leaning back, he adjusted his seat to make himself more comfortable, and turned on the radio.

It was nearly half past five, a little later than he'd expected, when he spotted the silver car approaching. He already had the engine running as it passed, and pulled out behind it as it slowed for the traffic lights.

So close . . .

The light changed to green and they passed under the railway, emerging onto a wider street with larger houses on either side. Driving carefully, he followed the silver car down towards the main road.

It was important to keep the distance between them right – too close, and he could end up sitting behind him at the junction long enough to be noticed; too far and he might lose him altogether.

He took it slowly, allowing a slight gap to open up between

them, coasting gently along for a hundred yards, then accelerating as he saw the Honda's brake lights go off. They turned right onto the main road, but swung left down a small side street a moment later.

At least the man used his indicators. That would make the task somewhat easier.

They followed a small road that wound its way down beyond the last of the houses, past wide playing fields and out across a low water meadow. A bridge took them over the calm river that gently meandered between the trees. Naysmith hung back as far as he could, but the road was quiet and the silver Honda was travelling slowly.

They were well outside the city now, and the target was moving faster. At a roundabout, Naysmith decided to let another car slip in between them – there was no point following someone if you weren't going to try to be subtle about it – but after a mile or so the silver Honda turned off onto a smaller road signposted 'Petersfield' and it was just the two of them again.

From a gentle dip, they climbed a broad hill crowned with trees and drove out onto the rolling South Downs. The landscape fell away on either side beneath a vast sky, and the sun gave a golden glow to the clouds on the horizon. It was like journeying into a painting . . .

They had been driving for nearly half an hour when a red car appeared in the rear-view mirror. Naysmith glanced back at it, watching as it steadily closed the distance between them.
Good.

He allowed it to overtake, gently increasing his speed to tuck in close behind it and urge it along. It would be no bad thing to have a car between him and the target again.

The silver Honda was clearly visible up ahead and, slowly, the gap between the three cars closed. Thankfully there were few opportunities to overtake after that – tall hedgerows created blind curves, and oncoming traffic made it impossible when the road did straighten out.

They continued on together, dropping slowly down between the hills until they came to a remote rural crossroads where a red light halted them. There was a large country pub on the far side of the junction, and a small petrol station opposite.

The Honda indicated right but, as the lights changed to green, the other car drove straight on, leaving Naysmith directly behind the target once more.

Where were they going? It had been well over half an hour now – how much longer could he sit behind this car without it becoming suspicious?

Cresting a long hill, the road plunged down through some trees towards another village. The Honda's brake lights came on as they approached the bottom of the hill, but then the left indicator light started flashing as well.

Finally, he was turning off.

As the gap between the two vehicles closed, Naysmith reluctantly decided to drive on. It would be too obvious to continue the pursuit. His eyes followed the silver car as it turned down a narrow lane before being lost from view as he continued on through the village.

West Meon was a quaint little place, with well-kept houses and old flint walls that pressed close to the road winding sharply left and right between them. He took the next turning onto a small side road and pulled over to think.

He must be close now.

The lane that the silver car had disappeared down didn't look as though it led anywhere. In all probability, this was where the target lived. It couldn't hurt to take a quick look along that lane and see what was down there . . .

He waited a few moments, then turned the car round and crept back through the village. There it was; the little lane marked 'High Street'. He smiled as he turned off the main road and drove slowly between the smartly white-washed buildings that huddled close on either side. It was all rather charming – an old-fashioned butcher's with a painted mural that read 'Supreme Sausage Champion', a tiny shop-cum-post-office and, moments later, a very grand-looking pub.

Naysmith glanced left and right, hunting for any sight of the silver car, but without success. He cruised on slowly until the houses thinned out and he suddenly found himself driving under the shadow of thick foliage where the lane passed through some trees.

Emerging from the gloom, he found turn-offs to a couple of narrow lanes that might lead to more houses, but he knew from experience that villagers remembered strange cars. He was driving with his own number plates on, so it was better not to take any risks. In any event, even if he had lost the Honda, he had made good progress. He checked the dash-board clock: 5.52 p.m. It would be easy enough to lie in wait down here on another day.

Satisfied with his afternoon's work, he drove out of the village, looking for a place to turn the car round. There were a couple of houses on the left and he glanced across briefly as he passed.

There!

On a gravel driveway, set back a little from the road, sat the silver car.

K347 GMX.

He didn't stop, just continued up the lane until he came

to a small junction where three ways converged around a triangular patch of rough grass. There, he halted for a moment, suddenly aware of the excitement growing inside him. The game was moving towards its next phase.

Smiling, he drove back through the village and out to the main road. It had been an excellent day.

22

There was a sedate pace that people adopted in this super-market. Everyone slowed down a little, especially the people in front of Naysmith, or so it seemed to him. He was hungry, and he didn't like shopping when he was hungry – it made him buy things he didn't want. Pushing the trolley around the vast store, he tried to focus on just the items he needed, but his mind was elsewhere.

It would have to happen on a Wednesday. He would need an excuse to be out for the evening, perhaps even the whole night. Nothing too specific or too complicated – he didn't want to catch himself out with an over-elaborate lie. At the same time, if he was too vague or evasive it would make Kim suspicious. On some level, she knew he slept with other women – she had to – but as long as he wasn't too obvious about it, he could deny it to her, and she could deny it to herself. In a way, both of them lied to protect the relationship.

Of course, it wasn't always another woman. Sometimes, as Kim fired her tearful accusations at him, when she was so certain that he was cheating on her, he taunted himself with the idea of telling her the truth. Of gently holding her small shoulders, staring down into those wondrous eyes, and telling her where he'd really been, what he'd really been doing. But it was a hollow fantasy. Something like that could never be unsaid. So he'd deny it, and she'd accept it, and they'd end up in bed together, each as dishonest as the other.

He sighed. It was one thing to go through all that when he really *was* screwing someone else, but he didn't want to argue when he wasn't.

The aroma from the bakery aisle tugged at him and he stopped to select a crusty loaf before moving on to find a good bottle of wine.

He would say it was a networking event. There was nothing unusual about that – his work often took him to industry get-togethers – and mentioning a noisy bar in London would explain why he couldn't answer his phone. If he had to stay out all night, he could tell her he'd drunk a little too much. The key was to mention it to her as soon as possible. Last-minute absences were suspicious, but dates on next week's calendar were less spontaneous and somehow more believable.

He put a couple of bottles of Merlot into the trolley and turned towards the checkouts. In front of him, an older man finished placing his items on the conveyor belt and stood, waiting to pay. This man had thicker, darker hair, but there was a definite similarity to the target – five foot ten, same age, same podgy build. Naysmith gazed at him for a moment as he joined the queue. So close now, just inches away, he considered how quickly someone of that build moved, wondered how heavy he was. And then, as he stared at the back of the man's head, he suddenly knew how he would do it.

*   *   *

Friday came, and there was still a lot of preparation to be done. He drove down the hill into West Meon, braking hard just before the '30' speed-limit sign. He knew the road quite well now. Glancing briefly at the turn off for High Street, he continued on through the village, just as he had that first time, eight days ago. The road twisted one way, then the other before he saw the side street he wanted and swung left into Station Road.

It was narrow, with old flint walls and hedgerows pressing close on either side. There were a couple of houses and then the countryside closed in again, with tall trees lining the road as it started to climb. Naysmith slowed and turned onto a gravel track that bent away to the right. Following it round, he emerged into a small car park, deserted save for one other vehicle. He switched off the engine and opened the door, drinking in the quiet, listening to the faint rustle of the leaves above.

This was the northern end of a walking trail that followed the course of a disused railway south along the Meon Valley. At another time it would have been appealing to explore it and see where it went, but today he had something else in mind. He was dressed appropriately in jeans and an anorak – just like any other walker, except that he'd deliberately avoided bright colours. There was no sense in standing out.

Locking the car, he made his way along to the end of the car park, grinding small stones underfoot until he found the muddy path that led into the trees. Snaking through the bushes, it swept down onto the grass-covered remains of the railway line. He halted suddenly, listening. There were faint voices ahead, growing steadily louder. It would have been better to go unseen, but there was no reason why anyone should remember him – he was just another walker. The key was to avoid anything that would attract suspicion. He set off in the direction of the sounds and soon met a grey-haired couple coming back up the path towards him. They nodded and offered a polite 'Good afternoon' as they passed. Naysmith gave them a warm smile and continued to walk on into the trees, listening to their voices gently dwindling in the distance. Slowing now, he glanced over his shoulder, checking that they were out of sight, then turned around and stalked silently back up the track behind them. Ignoring the way that led to the car park, he pushed hurriedly on through the bushes, following the overgrown trackbed. Once he was clear of the path, he paused, listening intently. Not far away, a car started and he heard the tyres bite into the gravel as it slowly drove away.

For a moment, it seemed as though a blanket of silence fell on the woods, but then he became aware of the gentle sigh of the trees as a faint wind drifted through the branches above him. He was alone.

Each footstep was somehow louder in the stillness, his boots swishing through the long grass and crackling down into the undergrowth. He moved quickly but carefully, watching the ground for obstructions. The trackbed seemed lower here, and he suddenly realised that what had looked like earthen banks on either side of him were actually two overgrown platforms wreathed in brambles. Decades ago, this must have been West Meon station. He paused to look around, suddenly seeing the shapes beneath the moss, glimpsing the memory of another time. There were no buildings left, but here and there a piece of crumbling brickwork was visible among the nettles, and a few worn steps led up into a tangle of bushes. In front of him, right where the old steam trains would have passed, a young tree had forced its way up towards the light as the last remnants of the railway were gradually swallowed up by the forest.

Beyond the station, the foliage grew thicker and less light filtered down through the canopy above. The track ran into a deep, overgrown cutting before passing under an arched brick bridge, and the air was heavy with the sickly-sweet smell of nettles.

There was a faint tingle of déjà vu as he stepped forward into the shadow of the bridge, and he found that he was smiling. The memory of that day in Winchester came back to him as he picked his way through the damp darkness, drawing strength from it as he emerged into the light, clean air beyond. Ahead of him, the trackbed curved away, a swathe of grass and leaves, twigs and ivy. The railway had not endured, but he had. There was nothing he couldn't do.

He walked on along the damp ground, stopping for a moment to listen, but there was nothing – just the long flat curve stretching out in front of him. He'd done his homework, studied the maps – he knew that High Street was just a few hundred yards ahead through the trees – but it wasn't real until you walked the route for the first time. It was important to prepare properly.

Now the ground began to fall away on either side, with steep grassy slopes tumbling down to the forest floor and green fields beyond. He found himself almost in the canopy of the trees that lined the foot of the embankment below as it swept on in a gentle arc.

And then, quite suddenly, the trackbed came to an abrupt end. Naysmith stepped forward to the edge and gazed out across the void before him. This was where the bridge had stood, carrying the rails on, high above the road and the meandering river just visible through the foliage below. It must have been a huge construction – he couldn't even see the other side through the trees – but now nothing was left except some ancient, ivy-covered pilings down there in the bushes by the roadside. He sat down slowly, thinking.

This was his third visit to West Meon. It had been chance that had brought him to the village on Wednesday evening, earlier that week. After visiting a client in Sussex, he'd decided to stop here on his way home. It wasn't too much of a detour and it saved him making a special trip.

He'd parked a little way outside the village and walked back along the road, hoping to take a look at the target's house. By the time he got there, it was dusk, with dark clouds closing in across the deep red sky. The lane was deserted, but he walked close to the high hedge, staying in the shadows as he approached the driveway. Gravel was a nuisance – far too noisy. Hopefully there would be another, easier way into the garden. Entering the house itself was not something he favoured. Even if the target lived alone, it still tilted the odds against you, putting them on familiar territory. It also increased the risk of evidence being recovered. He knew the importance of varying his attacks, doing things differently each time, but going into houses seemed amateurish. For now, all he wanted was to look around and learn more about the man he was hunting.

And then, as he'd stood there in the lane considering what to do next, a door had opened, spilling a wedge of light across the garden. Naysmith shrank back into the darkness for a second before turning and walking away, back up the road. Close, much too close, came the crunch of footsteps on gravel behind him, but fortunately the man turned right when he emerged from his driveway, and set off towards the village.

It had been unexpected, but there was also a profound surge of excitement in that moment. He hadn't been spotted – and even if he were, he had done nothing wrong . . . yet. This might be a chance to learn something useful. Quietly, he turned and walked down the lane after the target, straining to see him in the gloom. The light was failing now, and there were no street lights out here. He followed at a distance – far enough that his footsteps wouldn't be heard – but when they reached the trees, he lost sight of the figure in the shadows.

Walking quicker, he'd hurried under those dark branches, padding along the road as it angled slightly to the right. Then, as the cheery lights of the village came into view, he'd spotted the man again, making his way along the road and turning aside at the pub.

It would have been a natural point to turn back – to go and look at the house – but Naysmith had walked a little further. Approaching the sound of conversation and laughter that drifted out from the pub, he stopped and noted the chalkboard sign propped by the roadside: *Pub Quiz Every Wednesday*.

Afterwards, walking back towards his car, he'd passed once more through the lonely tunnel of trees. His eyes had grown accustomed to the darkness and, as he glanced up at the dark branches, he'd noticed the towering railway embankment, silhouetted against the sky.

That was on Wednesday. Now, he sat on top of the embankment, hidden in the foliage, gazing down on that same spot. The man would have to pass through here on his way to the pub, and again on his way home. Those old pilings would offer a place of concealment, right beside the road, and having the river so close was another advantage.

Naysmith remained there for a while, studying the ground below him and fixing it in his mind, noting which point on the embankment commanded the best views of the road. It finally felt right.

Satisfied, he turned and made his way slowly back along the railway line, learning the ground. The next time he came here it would be dark.

23

Wednesday had come, and Naysmith sat at his desk, restless. Since that first encounter in Winchester, this had developed into a challenging hunt and the work he'd put into it heightened his anticipation for the inevitable climax. After exercising so much patience it was now somehow galling to wait even a few hours more. But he forced himself, deciding that he would work through until lunchtime, however difficult it was to concentrate. He sat in on a tiresome conference call, oblivious to the distant voices, watching the clock tick round towards noon. Outside his window, grey clouds gathered slowly in a dark sky. The weather was finally turning and the forecast was for rain that evening. In theory this was a good thing – rain could wash away all sorts of evidence – but working in the wet brought its own risks, especially at night, and that meant he would have to take even greater care than usual.

A little after one o'clock he sent his last email and slowly closed the laptop. It was finally time to get started.

He'd replenished the cardboard box in the garage over the last few weeks – quietly picking up items here and there, always going to different shops, always paying in cash. Although seemingly random, everything had been deliberately selected to mask his identity, from the lined gloves that would pick up no fingerprints on their insides, to the shoes that were not quite his size. Every item had been meticulously wiped clean, and he disciplined himself to wear gloves even here. It was this attention to detail that elevated him above the amateurs, ensuring his continued success in the game.

Stooping, he dragged the cardboard box into the middle of the floor and opened it to inspect the contents – something he hadn't been able to do while Kim was in the house. Carefully, he drew out the bag containing the clothes – all new, all in dark colours, own-brand items bought from the supermarkets. There was a cheap wristwatch – a couple of minutes fast – that he would throw away afterwards and, in light of the weather, a couple of large towels. In a second bag he placed the usual bottle of bleach, travel wipes and spare refuse sacks. Finally, he drew out a large metal wrench, which he hefted thoughtfully in his hand. It was heavy and solid, about eighteen inches long, with a shaped grip that wouldn't slip through his gloves. He considered it for a moment, tightening it up so that the jaws wouldn't rattle, then placed it in with the clothes.

Satisfied, he transferred both bags into a thick black refuse sack that he took outside. Opening the boot of his car, he placed the sack inside, next to the flat parcel containing his alternate number plates, and the white envelope from Severn Beach. He'd retrieved them from their hiding place on his way home the day before – now everything was ready.

Back in the house, he went upstairs and shaved. There was an art to deception – the more you behaved as though something was real, the more real it seemed to others. He wasn't going to a networking event in London, but he was certainly going to get ready as though he was. Rinsing his face, he stared at his reflection in the bathroom mirror, running a hand across his smooth chin. Smart clothes were laid out on the bed next door, including the trousers that Kim had said for him to wear – and he *would* be wearing them when it was done, when he was on his way home. He studied his smiling reflection for a moment, then turned away.

The shower felt hot when he first stepped in, but after a few minutes he was comfortable with the temperature, closing his eyes and breathing in the steam. He washed slowly, allowing the calming water to cascade over him, rinsing away the loose skin cells and hair follicles. There was a purpose to every part of his preparation.

Back in the bedroom, he dried himself and folded his smart clothes into a bag, along with an appropriate pair of shoes. Placing the bag by the bedroom door, he selected some casual clothes and got dressed – tomorrow, these items would be folded and returned to their drawer without Kim ever noticing they'd been worn. It was strange to think how he'd adapted his routine – a routine he'd meticulously followed for years – just to accommodate her. He pulled on a pair of shoes from the back of his wardrobe, then gathered up the bag of clothes and took it downstairs. Satisfied that everything was ready, he went through to the kitchen to make himself a sandwich.

By four o'clock he was driving through Salisbury, following the dual carriageway that skirted the northern edge of the city centre. The cathedral spire loomed bleak and tall against the dark clouds, a grey finger of warning raised against the approaching storm. Naysmith scowled up at the sky – it wasn't raining yet, but the weather wouldn't hold for long. As the A36 climbed out eastward into the Wiltshire country-side, he turned onto a small side road and drove for a mile or so until he found a quiet lane. Stopping the car, he got out and stood on the tarmac, listening.

There was no sound. And he would hear any approaching vehicles before they got close. Satisfied, he retrieved the flat parcel from the boot of the car and crouched down to change his number plates.

The first spots of rain appeared on the windscreen as he joined the motorway. By the time he reached Winchester, it had become torrential. Naysmith pulled over and sat for a moment, listening to the heavy drops drumming on the roof. Hopefully it would ease a little as the evening drew in – he didn't mind getting wet, but it would be very frustrating if the weather stopped the target from going out. He shook his head. There was no sense in worrying about that now. He took out his phone and sent Kim a text telling her not to wait up, then switched off the handset and stowed it in the glove compartment. Everything was in place. He felt the familiar whisper of excitement ripple over him, a fleeting glimpse of the ecstasy to come.

Strange cars stood out in small villages and he'd spent a lot of time thinking about where to park. Stopping outside someone's house would raise suspicion and be remembered when the locals discussed the news in the coming days. He'd briefly considered a pub car park in a neighbouring village – hiding the car in plain sight – but it was just too risky. In the end, he'd identified somewhere suitably remote – a grassy field shielded by a thick hedge, some distance from West Meon. It was off a narrow lane, with an old metal gate that looked as though it hadn't been closed for years. Checking his rear-view mirror to make sure nothing was coming, Naysmith slowed to a crawl and pulled off the road. The ground was slippery but firm. He tucked the car in behind the hedge so that it couldn't be seen from the lane.

The rain was coming down harder now, stinging his face with cold as he got out into the wind and hurried round to open the boot. Taking the bags, he locked the car and set off at a run, splashing along a farm track that led away from the lane across the field. After a few minutes, he came to a heavy iron gate, which he climbed over, then walked quickly along the edge of a ploughed field. He had just over a mile to go, always keeping to the grass to avoid leaving footprints in the furrows, making for the dark line of the woods that lay ahead of him. He really couldn't have chosen a more miserable night.

Eventually, he passed under the outlying trees and stopped to catch his breath, shaking off the worst of the rain as he turned to gaze out at the downpour behind him. Hopefully it would ease a little. Running a hand through his dripping hair, he moved on, pressing deeper into the woods until he found a vast old tree – a natural landmark that would be easy to locate again once the night closed in. Here, almost no rain made it through the dense foliage above, and he gratefully put down the bags.

Taking a deep breath, he slowly peeled off his wet clothes, refusing to hurry despite the cold, placing each item in a neat pile beside the gnarled old trunk. Jeans, underwear and finally his top – everything was accounted for. He couldn't afford to leave anything lying around. Naked, he used one of the towels to dry himself, then placed it into a black bag with his wet clothes. *So damn cold.* Shivering violently in the chill evening air, he opened the other bag and drew out his anonymous supermarket clothing. It was difficult to dress, pulling the new T-shirt across his cold, damp skin, dragging his socks up. Eventually, he slipped on his gloves and stood up, hugging himself to get warm.

After a moment the feeling began to return to his hands, and he stooped to retrieve the wristwatch from the bag, peering down at it as he fumbled with the strap. Ten past six – slightly ahead of schedule.

He jammed the white envelope deep into his pocket and zipped it shut. Then, drawing out the heavy steel wrench, he twisted the tops of the bags and hid them in a hollow beside the tree. With a final check to make sure everything was concealed, he gripped the wrench and set off through the woods.

This *felt* like hunting – searching for his prey, alone in the rain-lashed wilds – and a primal thrill coursed through him. The anticipation, the dreadful eagerness, so intense that he couldn't help but grin as he picked his way through the undergrowth. Suddenly, in that moment, all the preparation made sense, all the effort was justified.

Before long, the ground sloped sharply down and he stepped out onto the flat grass of the trackbed. He was on the walking trail, a little way south of the car park. Although it was getting late, and the weather made it unlikely that anyone else would be out here, he was alert now. It was difficult to hear anything other than rain on the leaves above, so he would periodically crouch down low, his eyes searching for movement below the foliage, but there was nothing other than the steady swaying of the trees.

He walked between the overgrown platforms of the forgotten station and approached the bridge, yawning before him like a cavernous mouth in the gloom. A squall of rain spattered his face as he stepped into the shadow of the arch, and he stood for a moment in the darkness, listening to the rustle of the trees echoing off the brickwork above him. The weather wasn't easing, but he no longer cared – all that mattered was finding the target. He stepped out into the failing light and walked on, following the embankment as it curved round, steadily rising above the forest floor. The rain, heavy now, echoed among the branches with a dull and constant roar. He smiled – at least nobody would hear him approaching.

When he reached the drop where the viaduct had once stood, he halted and positioned himself in a sheltered spot, free from the worst of the rain, staring out through the glistening leaves towards the target's house. As he waited, he kept himself moving, stretching and turning, maintaining the heat in his muscles. He hefted the wrench in his gloved hands, making sure of the grip, reminding himself of the feel of it.

The weather had settled a little but rain was still falling steadily. Surely it wouldn't dissuade his target from coming out . . . although it might mean that he'd be walking faster, hurrying along to get out of the downpour as quickly as possible. Still, even if he was, he'd probably slow down again here, under the relative shelter of the trees. Either way, Naysmith was prepared. And he'd have two opportunities – once on the journey *to* the pub, and once on the journey home.

He glanced at his watch. It wouldn't be long now.

His mind went to the man he was hunting. How strange, for someone to be approaching their final moment, and not to realise it. The target's life, counting down through those last minutes, as it came to a premature climax. It would have been compelling just to observe, but the sense of holding that life in his hands was simply staggering. The power of life and death. And he had the strength to use it, to turn

potential into reality. To overcome the barriers and break the
most fundamental human law. And to do it all without ever
getting caught. The only rules that applied to him were those
he set himself to heighten the challenge.

Drops of water trickled down his neck, making him shiver,
but he ignored them. All that mattered was staying supple
and watching the road. He twisted his upper body left then
right, stretching the muscles.

And then he spotted something. There in the distance . . .
movement. Was it his target?

He stepped over to the very edge of the precipice, leaning
forward, straining to see, but it was impossible to be sure.
Should he wait? No, he had to get closer, had to make certain.

Grasping the wrench, he scrambled down the sheltered
side of the embankment, moving carefully on the slippery
grass and leaves, until he reached the base of the slope.
Moving as quickly as he dared, he crept down through the
trees and crossed the narrow river at a shallow point, all the
time picturing where the target was, visualising his progress
towards the trees.

Scrambling up the bank beside the road, Naysmith tucked
himself in behind the large brick-faced pilings and took a
breath. Nothing could be heard above the splash of rain in
the river, so he peered cautiously around the edge of the
brickwork.

A dark figure was hurrying along towards him, wrapped
in a flapping overcoat, a black umbrella held aloft against the
weather. It was the target all right. That portly shape, the
slight waddle as he tried to move quickly, the same height.
There was no doubt.

Naysmith looked up and down the road. No traffic. No
other people in sight. This was the time to do it.

His pulse was racing now. He waited, pressed against the

wet bricks, until the man hurried past his hiding place, then slipped out from the shadows and vaulted the fence. The wrench, held in his left hand to confuse the forensics people, glistened in the gloom. The figure was just yards ahead but he had to move fast, do it now before they got out of the trees. Rushing forward, running on tiptoes to deaden any sound, he raised the wrench and, as he reached the target, swung it round, under the umbrella and into the side of the man's head.

That sound. The dull, grating thud of metal on bone.

The man's legs buckled under him from the first blow, but Naysmith struck again immediately, bringing the wrench down hard before he fell. The umbrella skittered across the wet tarmac as the figure collapsed to the pavement. The first blow was rarely fatal, usually just fracturing the skull. It was the second or third that killed. He gazed down at the twitching figure on the pavement, then swung the wrench down hard once more. And in that moment, he felt it – felt the terrible give as the side of the head caved in under the impact, felt the life at his feet blink out and cease, felt the unbelievable rush of power surge through him. He controlled life itself.

When he came to himself, he found that he was shaking. The dreadful thrill of ecstasy coursed through him as he straightened up, and looked around. He had to keep to his plan, had to get the body off the road.

Dropping the wrench, he stooped to grab the man's feet, pulling him across to the edge of the pavement. Euphoric, his pulse thumping in his ears, he lifted the body with surprising ease, tipping it over the fence to fall into the grass. Turning, he went back and gathered up the wrench and the umbrella, eyes sweeping the road for anything else he'd missed. Then, he climbed over the fence and half rolled, half dragged the body down the bank, trying not to look when the misshapen head turned face up.

Hidden behind the brick piling, he knelt beside his victim and carefully went through his pockets. Coins, wallet, house keys . . . there was very little to work with. But then, from the depths of the man's inside jacket pocket, he drew out a mobile phone.

Naysmith smiled. He pulled the silver MP3 player out of the white envelope. Placing it in the man's jacket, he took the phone and slipped it into the envelope.

The noise of an approaching car made him freeze, and he flattened himself on the ground beside the corpse. Headlights raked through the trees, lighting up the rain as the vehicle passed, but it didn't slow. Nobody had seen anything.

Naysmith raised himself up slowly. Jamming the envelope into his pocket, he tipped the body so that it rolled over into the river, mercifully face down in the dark water. He collapsed the umbrella and threw it in too, before retrieving the wrench. With a final check to make sure he hadn't left anything behind, he leapt across the river and strode up the sloping side of the railway embankment.

And *now* he allowed himself to feel it, to bask in it – the uncontrollable excitement inside that made him want to scream out and punch the air. He stalked on through the storm, no longer aware of the wind or the rain, laughter echoing as he passed under the arched bridge and disappeared into the darkness.

24

Harland stepped off the uneven pavement and looked up at the trees. There was no sound except the gentle rustling of the leaves above him as he stood, lost in thought, on the quiet country lane. The scent of grass came to him on the warm air and he closed his eyes, enjoying the moment of peace.

They had been due a bit of luck. Days had stretched into weeks with nothing to show for their efforts, just one dead end after another. But this was more than just luck – this was a proper, old-fashioned hunch that had paid off. It had been Mendel who first asked the question: if Vicky regularly went out running, wasn't there a chance that she might have had an iPod, or something, to listen to music?

'Spend a lot of time watching young women jogging?' Pope had teased, and they'd all laughed, seizing any opportunity to lighten the mood that could otherwise become unbearable. But Mendel's idea was a good one. They'd gone back through the list of names, spoken to her family and friends and discreetly poked around.

Yes, poor Vicky loved her music, and come to think of it she had got herself one of those new MP3 players, a little silver one. No, nobody knew where it was now.

It hadn't seemed like much, but it was a new lead to follow. There was a chance that Vicky had been wearing her music player when she met her killer, and a chance that the killer had taken it. But it might just as easily have been swept away by the tides, if it had ever been there at all.

'It's a possibility,' Blake had shrugged when Harland told him. 'But I wouldn't get my hopes up if I were you, Graham. This business is shaping up to be a lot worse than we first imagined. We mustn't allow ourselves to get distracted from the evidence we already have, and we need to be sure that the other forces are all pulling their weight.'

Harland had been angry when he left the Superintendent's office. Stalking out into the corridor, he'd stood there, shaking, struggling to shrug off the rage that gripped him. The man was a fool. He'd made his way down the stairs and out of the building to stand in a sheltered corner, his phone already in his hand. Drawing heavily on a cigarette, he'd called Mendel and told him to pull up any mentions of silver MP3 players on the database. Blake could go to hell.

It had taken Mendel some time. Searching for a commonplace item was never easy, and in this case there was still some uncertainty over the exact make and colour of the device. With so many unrelated pieces of evidence obscuring the one they were hoping to find, there was no guarantee that they'd turn up anything.

But Mendel had been smiling when he put his head round Harland's door.

'Got a minute?' he asked.

Harland beckoned him in.

'You look cheerful,' he said. 'What's brought that on?'

'I found something I think you're going to like.' Mendel eased himself into a chair and gazed across the desk at Harland. 'Vicky Sutherland's missing MP3 player – it was a small, silver one, right?'

'Yes.'

'Well, there are over a thousand possible matches for that on the database, but I had a bit of a think.' He leaned forward. 'We're looking for something that's turned up in the weeks since she was killed, and that narrowed it down quite a bit.'

'What did you find?' Harland asked.

'I found a guy called Morris Eddings,' Mendel said. 'He's a sixty-one-year-old university lecturer, killed near his home in some picture-postcard Hampshire village. Guess what he had in his jacket pocket.'

Harland nodded thoughtfully.

'Can we be sure it wasn't his own MP3 player?' he asked.

Mendel shrugged and spread his large hands wide.

'Too early to say anything for sure – this only just turned up and I thought I'd loop you in right away.' He sat back in his chair. 'Seems a bit out of character though – some old duffer in the counties with a slinky little MP3 in his jacket.'

'It does,' Harland nodded. 'If we can get our hands on the device, we should be able to establish the ownership one way or another.'

'We could just check the tracks.' Mendel grinned. 'If it's all R&B then it probably didn't belong to our lecturer.'

'Bad taste isn't exclusive to the young,' Harland smiled. 'When did this one die?'

'Last month. The Hampshire lot are still pretty warm on it, but they haven't turned anything up yet. So far there seems to be no obvious motive. Sound familiar?'

'Too familiar,' Harland sighed. 'Where did it happen again?'

'I'll send you the reports but it was some little village near Winchester. West Meon I think it was.'

He'd stood up and made his way to the door.

'Picturesque little place by all accounts. Very Agatha Christie.'

And it was. The main street meandered left and right between rustic houses on a wooded slope in the Meon Valley, a charming muddle of thatched roofs and old flint walls draped with colourful bushes. There were pavements that suddenly disappeared where the road grew narrow, five-bar gates across gravel driveways, and hanging baskets everywhere. Harland had turned down a quiet lane, past the old butcher's shop with its hand-painted sign and the tiny village Post Office. He'd parked just beyond the victim's house and walked back along the lane. There was a small 'For Sale' board outside the place now – the only visible reminder of what had happened. How long would the house lie empty?

Now he stood on the narrow pavement, further along the lane, looking down at the bend in the stream where Morris Eddings had been dumped. They were still hunting down the missing MP3 player, but just being here convinced him that this was the work of the same killer. Once again, just as he'd felt in Oxford, he was struck by how good a spot this was for an attack.

There was water nearby, and the body had been left partly submerged, greatly compromising any evidence that the forensics team might otherwise have been able to retrieve. The location was secluded – a sheltered dip beside the stream would be ideal for a killer who needed time to go through his victim's pockets. And there were plenty of different ways in and out of the place. The lane itself was an obvious choice, but Harland had seen signposts for footpaths that struck out through the trees, or the killer could simply have followed the course of the stream.

Thoughtfully, he clambered over the fence and picked his way down towards the bank. This was where it had happened. Just a few yards away – not that far to drag the body but it would have required a bit of physical strength to get the deadweight over the fence. A few moments' respite – plenty of time to exchange souvenirs – and then just roll the remains into the water.

Harland closed his eyes. He could see the photos in his mind – the same stream that lay in front of him, only now there was a body sprawled in it, the back of a broken head gleaming wetly above the dark water . . .

His mobile was ringing.

Opening his eyes, he took the phone from his pocket and glanced at the screen. It was Mendel.

'Hello?'

'It's me. Can you talk?'

'Yeah, just taking a walk in the country,' Harland said. 'What is it?'

'We just had a call from Hampshire Police,' Mendel replied. 'They managed to track down that MP3 player – it was in a box of stuff they'd sent on to Eddings' sister.'

Harland nodded to himself.

'That's good. Once we have that, we'll know if Eddings is another link in the chain.'

'Thought you'd like to know,' Mendel said. 'Anyway, sorry to bother you on your day off.'

'It's okay – I wasn't doing anything.' Harland gazed down at the stream. 'See you tomorrow.'

He slipped the phone into his pocket again, then turned and made his way back up the slope.

25

Some bastard had parked in his space. Harland gripped the steering wheel angrily, revving the engine and lurching the car onward, past his house. Nowhere to park – that was all he needed right now. He eventually found a spot on the opposite side of the street and manoeuvred into the kerb behind a large white van. He switched off the engine and sat for a moment, waiting for his breathing to slow down, for the red mist to pass over. It wasn't a big deal. Not really.

He locked the car and trudged back down Stackpool Road, his eyes taking in a series of front rooms through gaps in curtains, people on sofas and the flickering glow of televisions. Next door's garden looked bright and cheery, with colourful pink flowers neatly bordering a large red-leaved bush. The space in front of his own house was an untidy no-man's-land of cement paving and weeds. With nobody caring for them, the little shrubs had choked and withered, but that had always been Alice's thing. He had neither the understanding nor the inclination to restore them.

He unlocked the door and went inside, irritably tugging a sheaf of flyers from the letterbox and screwing them up in his hand. Somehow they taunted him, reminding him that the house was empty.

Except it wasn't.

She was still here, haunting every room. Usually, he tried to distract himself, thinking of work, staying out late until he was tired, or wretchedly stoking the lustful feelings he had for other women. But her presence was everywhere, joyful and sad, eager and shy, an eternally outstretched hand that he could never hold again.

He sighed and placed his keys in the bowl, the noise of metal on porcelain stark in the silence, then walked through to the kitchen.

They told him that it would get easier, that the pain would diminish with time. But it didn't. Yes, he had developed *coping strategies*, cheap tricks to try and push her from his mind, but he wasn't stupid. It didn't matter what clever names they gave their techniques – at best he was deluding himself, at worst he was betraying her.

He took a beer from the fridge and closed the door. There was a small snapshot of the two of them together that she'd stuck to the door with a magnet. He paused, staring at the image, the two faces smiling out at him from the past. They'd been in Devon when it was taken – a weekend away, walking along a quiet beach, their whole bloody lives ahead of them. He took a deep breath and stared at Alice, her long blonde hair golden in the sunlight, her lips smiling, her eyes full of mischief. And him beside her, his head leaning in against hers, laughing at something she'd said. He envied his former self, and hated who he'd become. She'd be so disappointed.

He turned away from the memories, walking over to the counter and rifling through the drawer for a bottle opener. Even here, so many little utensils that he'd never used, more of her things that had been left behind to torture him. He closed his eyes, knowing that there was no escape from it. Not tonight.

He needed some air. Wrestling with the top bolt, he unlocked the back door and took his beer out into the enclosed garden, where he sank down wearily to sit on the steps. Lighting a cigarette, he slumped against the door frame and fought back the first tears that welled up in his eyes.

Not here. Not yet. A quiet smoke and a drink first, just to calm the nerves.

He sat there, utterly alone, watching the cigarette slowly turn to ash between his fingers. In his darkest moments, he flirted with the thought that it might have been better if they'd never met. It wasn't just that he'd have been spared the pain of loss – it was the fact that his future was suddenly stripped of hope. He'd found the person he was meant to be with, and he'd lost her. Now, the best was behind him, and all that remained was regret. Once again, an appalling sense of guilt washed over him and he pushed the idea away. Such thoughts were beneath him.

The smell of a barbecue came to him from one of the nearby gardens. He could hear voices, but they were some distance away. Sighing, he got to his feet and went indoors to cook.

There seemed little point in eating, but somehow he forced himself. A reluctant concession that he made to her memory – *what she would have wanted.* Some evenings it was a way to pass the time, to distract himself, but that wouldn't work tonight. He settled on a simple microwave meal and switched on the TV while he waited for his food to cool down. The voices from the screen dispelled the oppressive silence, but he was under no illusions. This was going to be a bad night.

Later, when everything was neatly put away, he stood in the hallway, looking up the stairs to the dark landing. He felt so tired, but it was a weariness that sleep couldn't touch.

Reluctantly, he placed a hand on the end of the banister and made his way upstairs. The thick carpet that had once seemed so homely now muffled his footfalls, creating an unwelcome hush as he paused outside the closed bedroom door, then slowly turned the handle.

The door swung silently inward and he followed it into the stillness of their old room. Pale sun streamed in through the lacy net curtains that she'd chosen, the last light of the day glowing on one side of the bed and casting long shadows across the floor.

Everything was just as she'd left it – clothes in the wardrobe, make-up and skincare products on the dressing table, a pretty little jewellery box next to her bedside lamp, on top of the book she'd been reading. He'd resisted every offer of help, every kind suggestion to clear things up. Nothing was different, except for the ugly web of cracks in the mirror he'd made on that first night back here. He'd not slept in this room since.

Her presence was much stronger here, and the terrible sense of loss more intense. When he took flowers to her in the cemetery, it was somehow disconnected and remote, as though it was happening to somebody else. It was different here. This room was where he spoke to her, where he mourned her.

The duvet felt soft and welcoming compared to the sofa bed he slept on downstairs. He eased himself gently onto his side of the bed, reaching out to retrieve the nightshirt from under her pillows. Lying down, he scrunched his face into the soft fabric, eyes tight shut. The smell of her clothes and her hair had always provided a sense of comfort, but even that had faded now, and he was unable to recall her scent. Curling up, he buried his face in the pillow, sliding his arm out across the empty half of the bed.

And wept.

26

'So how have you been, Graham?' Jean asked.

Harland sat with his hands on his knees, staring down at the beige carpet. It felt different coming here today – none of the usual reluctance, just a weary sense of resignation as though all the fight had gone out of him. He glanced up at Jean and managed an empty smile. She was wearing a casual grey jacket with a knee-length skirt and patent-leather shoes, her mousy hair gathered back so that it fell behind her shoulders. Their eyes met for a moment, then he looked at the floor again.

'It's been . . . difficult recently,' he admitted. 'The past few weeks . . .'

She watched him calmly as he faltered, giving him a moment before gently breaking the silence.

'Well, it's been a few weeks since I've seen you,' she said patiently. 'Perhaps you can tell me about what's been happening in that time.'

He took a breath, tried to compose himself a little, then nodded.

'I have missed a couple of appointments,' he said. 'Sorry about that.'

'It's all right,' she nodded. 'How have things been?'

Harland sat back in his chair.

'Up and down,' he began, then paused and shook his head. There was no point pretending. 'Down quite a bit lately. I don't know, maybe I just need more sleep, but little things have been bothering me, and I've been finding it hard to keep a lid on my emotions.'

He glanced up at her, willing her to take the conversation from him. Talking wasn't easy just now.

'I see.' Jean sat back in her chair, notebook balanced on a slender knee. 'Have you had any difficulty sleeping recently?'

'I've had a few rough nights, yes.'

'Difficulty getting to sleep again?'

He glanced up at her and nodded.

Jean wrote something in her book, then inclined her head and gazed silently at him.

'What was keeping you awake?' she asked.

Wasn't it obvious?

'I've been thinking about Alice a lot.' He felt he had to speak carefully, control the rate at which he released the words in case they got away from him, pulled him too close to the edge.

'That's understandable,' Jean said. 'When do you find your-self thinking about her most?'

'Evenings usually,' he shrugged. 'When I get home it's sometimes not too bad, but lately . . .'

. . . it had been getting worse and worse.

'Has she been on your mind more frequently in the last couple of weeks?'

He nodded, eyes downcast, saying nothing.

'All right,' Jean said. She paused for a moment, then asked, 'Can you think of anything that might have triggered this?'

Harland's shoulders sagged a little.

'I fell asleep in our bed.' He hesitated, then sighed. 'In our *old* bed.'

Jean looked up from her notes.

'Are you sleeping in another room?'

'Yes.' No need to elaborate – just keep it simple. For some reason he didn't want to tell her that he camped out on the living-room sofa.

Jean put her book on the table and leaned forward, clasping her hands.

'Why were you in there, in your old bed?'

Harland raised his head a little. He suddenly felt cold, exposed.

'I don't know,' he shrugged. 'I just needed to feel close to her I suppose.'

'Okay,' Jean nodded. 'And what happened?'

'I lay down on the bed, must have fallen asleep . . .' He sighed. 'I had a dream about her.'

'Do you remember the dream?'

Harland nodded.

'Can you tell me about it?' she asked.

'We were together, in a meadow with long grass . . . fooling around.'

'Fooling around?'

He bowed his head, struggling with the memory.

'We were having sex,' he said quietly.

'I see.'

Harland shut his eyes tightly. He hoped she didn't see, hoped she couldn't divine how he'd woken up to that awful moment of confusion, how he'd wondered where Alice was before the sickening realisation had come flooding back. He didn't want her to know how he'd sat there, sobbing uncontrollably as he'd felt the sticky warmth in his shorts, humiliation on top of his loss.

Shame and fear swirled around him – he had to say something, move the conversation on.

'Maybe I just need to drink less coffee,' he said, looking up with a weak smile.

Jean's large blue eyes studied him for a moment.

'Graham, have you been sexually active with anyone since Alice passed away?'

She knew. She knew exactly what had happened. But at least she was allowing him the opportunity to gloss over it.

'No,' he said quietly. There was an uncomfortable thrill in telling her this. Was it the release of opening up, even partially, to someone else? Or was it that he found the discussion of sex with another woman exciting? Jean was certainly attractive. Gazing at her legs, he suddenly felt a guilty flush of arousal.

'No,' he said, more to himself this time. 'I'm not seeing anyone.'

The conflict raged within him but he forced it down, as he forced down other unwelcome emotions. *Bury it deep, starve it of oxygen until he couldn't feel it any more.* He set his jaw and forced himself to meet her steady gaze.

'All right, Graham,' she said after a long moment. 'Have there been any other significant events since we spoke last?'

And just like that, the crisis passed. Her questions moved away to other matters – work, diet, exercise – and he coasted through the rest of their discussion.

But as he sat there, watching the clock above her desk counting down the minutes to the end of the session, he felt an odd sense of resentment building inside him. And unlike lust, that was impossible to subdue.

27

Harland stalked into the meeting room. He'd been in a bad mood anyway, and this part of the morning was unlikely to improve things. Putting his coffee on the table, he walked over to the window and stared out at the traffic for a moment, idly wondering if he had time to slip downstairs for a cigarette. But it wasn't to be. Behind him, the door opened and he turned to see Pope enter, followed by Mendel. He sighed and walked round to his seat.

'What's this little get-together in aid of?' Pope asked, opening his notebook and squinting up at the others through his glasses.

'Progress review on the Severn Beach killing,' Harland said quietly as he sat down. 'And Blake wants to *have a word* with us.'

'Must be serious then,' Pope nodded thoughtfully.

Mendel caught Harland's eye but remained silent. They both knew how this was likely to go, but there was nothing they could do about it now.

Blake arrived exactly on the stroke of ten, breezing into the room and making his way to the head of the table, where he pulled out his chair but remained standing for a moment.

'Good morning,' he said, as though noticing them for the first time. 'All present and correct? Good, good.'

He sat down, leaned forward and clasped his hands on the table in front of him.

'Now then,' he began. 'I've been keeping an eye on this Severn Beach business over the last few weeks and I thought it was high time we had a frank discussion about where we are, and how we see things proceeding.'

Harland listened, his eyes fixed on the coffee cup in front of him. A frank discussion about how *Blake* saw things proceeding would be more accurate.

'Graham's been filling me in on the progress of the investigation, but I thought it might be useful to include everyone in this.' The Superintendent paused, looking at each of them for a moment, then adopted a chilly little smile. 'James, perhaps you'd like to start us off?'

'Sir?' Mendel sat up in his chair.

'I'm interested to hear your perspective,' Blake said. 'How do you feel things are going?'

'Well,' Mendel's eyes flickered to Harland, then back to the Superintendent. 'It's a strange one, really. At first it seemed like a pretty standard sort of job. Boyfriend gone bad, maybe. Or I suppose it might have been an opportunistic hit by some weirdo, but I was never really sure about that, to be honest.'

Pope frowned at this, but Mendel pressed on.

'Anyway, that was how it looked at first, but then everything changed when we got a match on that house key from the Oxford murder.'

'Go on,' Blake nodded, patiently.

'Well,' Mendel shrugged, 'when we connected those two deaths, the theories didn't fit any more. We dug around but there's nothing else to link the two victims, and with the distance between them, it's quite possible our killer comes from outside the area.'

Harland dug his shoes into the carpet as Mendel spoke,

anger welling up inside him. What the hell was Blake playing at, undermining him in such a blatant way? The pompous idiot already knew this, so why ask to hear it all again?

'Then we found out about the body in Brighton and the one in Hampshire,' Mendel continued. 'Again, no apparent connection with the other victims except the single souvenir that linked them.'

'Souvenir,' Blake mused quietly. He didn't look up, but focused on his finger as it traced a series of tiny circles on the table in front of him. 'That word has disturbing connotations.'

'Yes, sir,' Mendel said, risking a barely perceptible shrug towards Harland. 'Anyway, now it looks like we've got hold of something big. This could tie in any number of unsolved deaths, and we're pretty close to the front of things, if the timeline's anything to go by.'

'The front of things?'

'What I mean is, some of these cases go back a good few months. Ours is one of the most recent – there's only the Hampshire one that we know of since.'

'I see.' Blake nodded to himself for a moment. 'Thank you, James.'

Harland glanced at him, suddenly beginning to grasp what was going on. The Superintendent was leading Mendel along, getting him to restate their same unsatisfactory position, before letting Pope muddy the waters.

'Russell?'

'Yes, sir.' Pope looked along the table attentively.

'What's your view on all this?'

'It's been quite a challenging case,' Pope began. He leaned forward in his chair, clearly relishing the audience. 'At first the evidence suggested a failed sexual assault or something of that nature. There have been one or two similar incidences along the Severn Estuary, so it was a natural line of enquiry to follow.'

Harland gritted his teeth as Blake nodded approvingly. This wasn't going anywhere useful.

'The house key we found on Vicky Sutherland did seem to indicate a link between our victim and the man found dead in Oxford,' Pope continued. 'Thames Valley now think there may be some connection to another body found washed up at Brighton, and Mendel did turn up an item belonging to the dead woman on a body recently discovered in Hampshire.'

'And your conclusions are?' Blake asked.

'Well, sir, it *could* all be the work of one man. We might be dealing with a serial murderer of some kind, but I think we have to keep our minds open to all possibilities.'

'What do you mean?'

'Well, just because something from one victim turns up somewhere else, it isn't necessarily proof of a direct link.' He looked around at the others. 'I mean, an item stolen from one victim could well turn up in the possession of another, and that sort of false positive could steer us in the wrong direction. I'm not saying I think this is the case, just that we shouldn't attach too much credibility to any single theory.'

Mendel was shaking his head.

'It's all very well keeping an open mind,' he interrupted, 'but these souvenirs are the only tangible leads we've got. We *have* to figure out what their significance is, and we really need to see if there's another link in the chain, something tied in with the next murder.'

'If there even *is* a next murder . . .' Pope muttered.

From his place at the end of the table, the Superintendent watched the two of them arguing, his face serene. Harland looked away in disgust. Exactly as the scheming old bastard had planned it. And Pope had played his witless part too.

'If I may?' Blake spoke quietly, forcing a sudden silence from the others. 'Thank you, gentlemen. I think it's clear that while there are still a number of avenues for us to explore, this is becoming a more complex matter, and we may need to re-evaluate how we can best serve the ongoing investigation. Certainly, there are local aspects to the case, and we must be seen to be doing everything necessary on these . . .'

He paused, looking briefly at each of them, then sat back in his chair and gazed up at the clock on the far wall.

'However, I do take on board the point about the most recent murder being in Hampshire, so perhaps the ball is now moving more into their court.'

What the hell . . . ?

Harland's head snapped up at this.

'With respect, sir.' The words were coming now, and all he could do was control the volume, stifle the urge to shout. '*We* put this together. We made the link to the Oxford murder and it was Mendel who tied in the Hampshire one. Up until then, these were just three separate unsolved cases.'

As soon as he said it, he knew he'd lost the argument.

So damn stupid.

Blake regarded him calmly for a moment – a figure of patience considering the outburst of a child – then sighed.

'I'm not completely new to this case, Graham,' he said, pointedly. 'I do read your reports, and I understand – and *appreciate* – the considerable effort that the team have put into this.'

He paused until it was clear that there would be no further challenges, then continued.

'Sadly, I don't have unlimited resources, and there are other cases that will need our attention as time goes on.'

'Sir?' Mendel's face was serious, clearly worried that they were about to be shut down.

Blake held up a calming hand.

'All I'm saying is that we may need to consider how we prioritise things over the coming weeks.' His voice was measured now, reasonable. 'A good general fights the battles he knows he can win, but I do feel we may need something more to go on if we're to tip the balance on this one.'

He looked around the table, a firm gaze at each one of them.

'We'll see how things go over the next week or so. I understand there are still some enquiries to be chased down, so let's see if anything new emerges before I speak to the boys in Hampshire. But whatever happens, I want you all to know that you've done some excellent work on this. I'm proud that Avon and Somerset were the ones who first spotted what was going on in these unsolved killings.'

Already talking about the case in the past tense.

Harland bowed his head, numb with anger and frustrated at his own stupidity.

Only Pope looked satisfied as Blake left the room.

★   ★   ★

'Won't be a moment, sir.' Josh looked up from where he was rinsing out the kettle.

'Take your time,' Harland murmured, slowing as he entered the kitchen and turning to lean against the wall. Rubbing his temple, he let his head roll back and stared up at the fluorescent light, listening to the rush of water from the tap and the click of the kettle switch being pressed down. Sighing, he pushed himself away from the wall and moved over to the sink to empty the dregs from his mug.

'Josh?' It was Firth, leaning on the door frame, peering in. 'Still on for tonight?'

Josh turned to her, confused.

'What do you mean?' he replied. 'I thought you said it was tomorrow?'

'No . . .' Firth straightened, an edge of annoyance creeping into her voice. 'It's tonight. I made a point of reminding you.'

Josh frowned, then looked down. 'Damn.'

'So?' She leaned forward, not allowing him to avoid her gaze. 'Are you coming or not?'

'Can't,' Josh shrugged. 'I promised Mary I'd take her to that Thekla place tonight. I could have sworn you said the film was tomorrow.'

Firth sighed and shot him a withering look.

'Heaven help us if you ever make detective, Josh.'

Harland smiled despite himself. He turned round, putting his back to the sink. Firth caught his eye and her expression softened.

'Sorry, sir.'

'Don't be.' He moved over and patted Josh on the shoulder. 'Some people take a while to make detective . . .' a flicker of a grin '. . . others take a while to make tea, right, Josh?'

The young officer looked up at him warily and nodded.

'Yes, sir,' he murmured.

Firth took a step backwards, then hesitated and looked thoughtfully at Harland.

'A few of us are going to the Watershed this evening,' she said. 'They're doing a special showing of *Dirty Harry*, and there's a spare ticket if you're interested?'

Harland leaned back against the countertop.

Thanks, but . . .

He was going to say no, that same automatic response

that insulated him from all the other social situations he could no longer face, but something in her look stopped him.

The simple, friendly offer of an evening out – the sort of thing *normal* people did.

'Sir?' Firth raised a questioning eyebrow.

'Well . . .' His thoughts flitted briefly to the empty house that lay waiting for him. 'If you're sure it's okay.'

'Great!' Her face brightened. 'The film starts at seven forty-five and we'll be meeting around seven at the Pitcher & Piano – you know where it is?'

Ten minutes' walk from where he lived.

'Yeah,' he nodded, 'I know it.'

'Brilliant. See you there then.'

She turned and almost bumped into Mendel, who had appeared behind her.

'After you.' The big man held up his hands, moving aside with a theatrical flourish to let her through.

'Sorry sir, thanks.'

Mendel waited until she had passed before moving calmly over to the sink and lifting the kettle briefly to feel its weight. Satisfied there would be enough for the three of them, he nodded approvingly to Josh, then looked across at Harland and frowned in puzzlement.

'What on earth are you smiling about?' he asked.

* * *

It was cold when they emerged from the small cinema, shuffling out into the darkness to stand on the covered waterfront walkway as the rest of the audience streamed past them. Lights twinkled on the water while Harland fumbled in his pocket for cigarettes.

'So,' Gregg looked at his watch, 'it's quarter to ten. Shall we grab a beer somewhere?'

'Not here.' Jamieson, a stocky young sergeant whom they knew from the Southmead station, cast an unhappy glance at the crowded bar behind them. 'I don't want to be stood around queuing all night.'

'What about The Ostrich?' His girlfriend, Kirstie, was a PCSO with wavy red hair and a strong Bristol accent. 'It's not far and it'll be a lot quieter.'

'Sounds good to me,' Gregg nodded. 'Come on.'

He turned and began to lead the way between the knots of people and the packed bar-front tables.

Harland paused, struggling to light a cigarette in the swirling breeze that blew in off the water, scowling as the flame danced away from the tobacco. While the others started along the quayside, Firth hung back a little, watching with growing amusement as he turned this way and that, pulling his jacket taut like a cloak against the wind.

'Are you okay there?' She looked different out of uniform, with her leather jacket and faded jeans. There was writing on her T-shirt – something French that he couldn't quite make out.

'It isn't easy being a smoker these days,' he sighed. Shielding the cigarette with his hands, he clicked the lighter once, twice, then finally lit up on the third attempt. 'See what I mean?'

She grinned and fell in beside him as they started walking after the others.

'I love that place,' she said, gazing out between the metal pillars and across the rippling gloom of the harbour basin. 'They show all kinds of cool films you wouldn't normally get to see on the big screen.'

'I know,' Harland agreed. 'I used to be a member there. Haven't been for a year or so, but I always enjoyed coming.

It's a more relaxed atmosphere than you get in the big multiplexes.'

They turned left and strolled slowly out onto the sweeping metal lines of Pero's Bridge, the noise of their footsteps echoing out across the dark water below them.

Firth walked with her head inclined to one side, and turned to glance back towards the cinema.

'Do you know what?' she mused. 'I think that's the first time I've watched that film all the way through.'

Harland slowed and peered at her doubtfully.

'You're kidding.'

'Seriously.' She had turned back to him now. 'I recognised a lot of it, but I hadn't seen all that stuff with the ransom bag, or the bit where he tortures the guy in the football stadium.'

Harland chuckled to himself as they came down off the bridge and onto the cobbled pavement, following it around the Arnolfini building.

'So,' he asked her, as they wandered under the glare of the street lights and across the narrow roadway of the Prince Street bridge, 'now that you've seen it right through, what did you think?'

Firth gazed up at the old-harbour cranes lining the quayside ahead of them.

'I love that whole seventies vibe,' she smiled. 'Clint Eastwood was so cool, and didn't he have amazing hair?'

Harland ran an involuntary hand across his scalp and shook his head.

'I think I'd rather have his sunglasses,' he replied.

They crossed the road and walked along the cobbled water-front – luxury apartments and young trees on one side, old boats creaking against their moorings on the other. Ahead of them, the others seemed to have slowed down a little. Gregg, glancing back over his shoulder, noticed them and beckoned them on.

'Keep up,' he called.

Firth raised her hand in polite acknowledgement but made no attempt to hurry.

'Let *them* queue up to get served,' she laughed under her breath.

One last footbridge carried them across a narrow channel to The Ostrich, a grand old three-storey inn that stood alone on an exposed corner of the quayside. Bench tables filled the space between the building and the water, most of them occupied, all lit by the bright warm glow of the pub.

A young couple scampered towards them in a tumble of laughter and echoing footsteps. The girl ran with abandon, long hair swishing from side to side as she dragged her boyfriend along by the hand.

'Sorry guys.' The slender young man smiled apologetically as he jostled past before being pulled away along the shadowed quay.

Firth shook her head, watching them go.

'Funny how differently people treat you when you're not in uniform,' she smiled.

Harland nodded thoughtfully. Firth was wearing make-up. He'd not noticed it before.

'Anyway,' she continued, 'let's get inside before Gregg buys his round.'

Harland began to move, then hesitated, staring up at the illuminated windows.

'Actually,' he said slowly, 'I think maybe I'm going to call it a night.'

Firth turned and gazed at him.

'Oh, I'm sorry; are you on early shift tomorrow?'

Harland met her eyes for a moment, then looked down.

'No . . .' He suddenly felt a cool shiver of guilt.

Enjoying himself, forgetting, letting his guard slip . . .

He forced himself to look up at her. 'I'm just tired.'

She studied him as they stood there under the light of a street lamp.

'Are you sure? More than happy for you to join us . . .'

He looked at her and shook his head.

'It was really good of you to invite me. I enjoyed it.'

'I'm glad you came.' She offered him a brief smile. ''Night . . . sir.'

''Night.'

He watched her push through the doorway into the laughter and murmuring voices of the pub, then turned his back on the glaring lights and walked away, following his long shadow over the cobblestones.

28

It was becoming intolerable. No matter what he did, Harland could feel the sand draining from the hourglass. In the days since the Superintendent's veiled ultimatum, they'd gone over things again and again, but turning up leads wasn't something you could hurry. The momentum was slipping away, and it wouldn't be long before Blake would smoothly pass the buck to Hampshire and quietly reassign everyone.

They needed something tangible, something to keep the investigation alive, but this killer wasn't stupid. He didn't seem to have made any mistakes at all – there was nothing but a single souvenir connecting one victim to the next.

Harland considered this as he walked into the station kitchen, mug in hand. He switched on the kettle, then paused.

Those souvenirs weren't mistakes, they were deliberate. Some killers were compelled to take things from their victims as mementos, or trophies. But this one wasn't keeping his souvenirs. They were subtle markers – the faint initials of the artist on the back of a painting – just enough to prove whose work it was if you knew what you were looking for, nothing more. Their presence spoke of arrogance, a desire for recognition, but tempered by caution and an absolute determination not to be caught.

Pouring water into his mug, Harland shook his head. Real

mistakes, if any ever came, would be few and far between. Unless they were focused – *properly* focused on the case – they wouldn't spot them.

He took a spoon from the cutlery drawer and slammed it shut hard.

So frustrating . . .

The worst part was that it didn't have to be this way. But politics and sheer bloody incompetence would drag them down, no matter how desperately they wanted a result. Blake was certainly a glory hunter, but he was much more interested in avoiding any negative PR. Pope was an idiot who would take the shortest route he could to suck up to the Superintendent, neither of them knowing or caring who he trampled over on the way. Between the two of them, what chance did he have?

Bastards.

He stirred his drink and tossed the spoon, clattering, into the sink.

And it wasn't just Pope who'd acted incompetently. He shook his head as he remembered his own outburst in the meeting, how he'd taken his chance to reason with Blake and thrown it away.

No, it didn't have to be this way . . . but it would be. They were just going through the motions until the whole thing was shut down.

He took a breath, then picked up his coffee and turned back towards his office. He needed a moment to think, time to clear his head. Rounding the corner into the corridor, he moved slowly, as though in a daze.

Laughter. Pope was leaning in the meeting-room doorway, smiling broadly, that irritating laugh echoing along the corridor. The smug little toad was sniggering about something as his head tilted round and their eyes met.

Harland hated him.

That pudgy, leering face and that smug grin. What was so
bloody funny? The clock was ticking and all he could do was
prop up a wall . . .

As they drew level, Pope nodded at him, then turned back
to Josh who was coming out of the meeting room.

'Run out of work, Pope?' The words were out of Harland's
mouth before he could stop them, but it was a reasonable
thing to say, wasn't it? For some reason, Josh had taken one
look at him then anxiously moved away, hurrying down the
corridor.

'Don't worry—' Pope started to drone, raising a placatory
hand.

'Don't *fucking* tell me what to do!' Harland spat. He
suddenly found that he was standing with his face inches
away from Pope's.

Everything seemed to be moving slowly, and even though
he could tell they were very close, it felt as if he was staring
out at Pope from somewhere deep inside his head.

'Now hang on!' Pope was saying something, his face a
blubbery frown. 'You can't speak to me like—'

There was a ringing crack as Harland's mug hit the floor,
splashing coffee along the wall and skirting boards. His hands
were on Pope's lapels, knuckles shining pale as he pushed
the miserable little creep up against the door frame.

'I *said*, don't tell me what to do!' Harland snarled again.
He could feel Pope's rapid breaths on his face, his piggy little
eyes wide. 'Understand?'

The adrenalin taste in his mouth, every muscle taut, ready
to lash out hard . . .

And then Mendel was there, running down the corridor,
his huge arms between them, prying them apart in a moment
of quiet confusion. Pope remained pressed up against the

wall, spluttering and pointing, as everything cleared and Harland found himself being moved back, recoiling from what had just happened.

He was shaking. Mendel was holding him, concerned eyes searching his face, speaking quiet words that he couldn't quite latch on to.

'Are you okay now?'

Harland stared at him for a moment, then nodded mutely.

What the hell had he done?

Pope eased himself away from the wall, drawing himself up and jabbing out an accusing finger.

'What the fuck was that?' he gasped, his cheeks flushing red. 'You're out of order, Harland, bang out of order!'

Mendel's hands released their grip and he sagged a little. He *was* out of order, and he knew it. What had he done? This would mean disciplinary action for sure. Suspension, maybe worse.

'Did you see?' Pope's voice was shrill now. 'You saw what happened, didn't you?'

Mendel spun round and raised a warning finger.

'Nothing happened here,' he hissed.

'But—'

'*Nothing* happened, Pope.' His tone was absolutely serious. There would be no argument.

Pope stared at him, about to say something more, then turned his back and stomped away. A door slammed and suddenly it was just the two of them standing there.

Harland was still shaking.

Mendel looked at him carefully for a moment, then glanced down at the spilt coffee.

'Come on,' he said calmly. 'Let's get this cleaned up.'

29

Harland sat back in his chair, closing his eyes for just a moment, after an hour or so of staring at the screen. An uneasy calm had settled over the station since his outburst the day before, and so far nobody had mentioned it.

At least, not to him.

He swivelled his chair a little, stretching his legs out at the side of his desk. Things had got badly out of hand, and he'd spent every hour since then expecting the call from Blake summoning him to the Superintendent's office for that short, difficult conversation. But the call hadn't come and now he felt rather at a loss. Pope had him on the ropes – what the hell was the little idiot waiting for?

Yawning, he turned back to his screen and tried to concentrate. Charlotte Bensk, the DI from Sussex, had put him onto the files for the Brighton murder a few weeks ago, but nothing had stood out. Khalid Ashfar's body had been in open water, exposed to the elements far longer than the others, and was degrading badly when it was found. Personal effects might have been compromised too, and the length of time that had passed since the body was found made new witness information unlikely.

He allowed himself a wry smile. Even if he managed to hold on to his job, nothing was going to be easy on this one.

There was a brisk knock on the door and he looked up.
'Come in.'

The door swung open and Mendel leaned in, one hand raised in greeting.

'Morning,' he smiled, walking over and nodding towards the screen. 'Anything interesting?'

'Just going over those Brighton case notes.'

'Again?'

'Yeah,' Harland said, without enthusiasm.

'Any better second time around?' Mendel grinned.

'It's not exactly a page-turner, but I just want to make sure we're not missing anything. But what that might be . . .'

'You won't know till you see it.'

'Exactly,' Harland sighed. 'Anyway, what can I do for you?'

Mendel smiled.

'Just stopped in to give you this.' He placed a supermarket carrier bag on the desk between them. 'Want to grab lunch later?'

'Yes, that'd be good.' Harland looked at the bag as Mendel turned back to the door. 'One o'clock?'

'One o'clock.'

He waited until the door closed, then leaned forward and picked up the bag. There was something moderately heavy inside, a small parcel wrapped in tissue paper. Tearing away the layers, he exposed the contents and sat back for a moment, a thoughtful smile on his face.

Mendel had bought him a new mug.

Harland pulled his jacket around him as they walked down the road. It was an overcast day and Portishead was colourless and cold in the wind that blew in from the Severn. They spoke about work as they approached the pub, small talk and minor matters, not yet ready to tackle the events of the previous day. Something like that had to wait until they were indoors and free from interruptions.

'I sometimes wonder what old Blake's playing at,' Mendel was saying. 'First he's banging on about his high-visibility policing, next thing he's up in arms about a couple of over-time requests.'

'It must be the budget review,' Harland mused. 'He always gets like that when they start showing him the numbers.'

'Maybe they shouldn't show him the numbers.'

'Rather him than me.' They paused, waiting for the traffic until they could cross the road. 'Anyway, let him play with his spreadsheets, so long as it gets us our increase.'

'And they say crime doesn't pay,' Mendel chuckled.

They found a table in the corner and sat down with their drinks.

'Cheers,' said Harland, raising his glass. 'And thanks for the mug by the way.'

Mendel nodded slowly.

'Cheers,' he replied, taking a sip of his beer. 'I thought you might need a new one.'

They sat in silence for an uneasy moment. Harland looked down, his fingers nudging a beer mat back and forth across the tabletop.

'And thanks for yesterday . . . I appreciate your stepping in when you did.'

'No problem.'

'It was pretty bad, wasn't it?'

'It wasn't good.'

Harland toyed with his drink, glancing up to find his friend watching him intently.

'Everything okay?' Mendel asked.

'Yes.'

'Sure about that?'

Harland sagged a little, then slowly shook his head.

'It's just been a tough spell recently,' he sighed. 'Sometimes it's difficult to readjust, you know, since . . .'

Mendel looked at him for a moment and nodded.

'Anyway,' Harland slumped back in his chair, 'I've got myself another problem now, haven't I? It's only a matter of time until Pope starts telling tales and I get the bullet.'

'Maybe. But I don't reckon they'll do anything. Not really. You know how it works – there'll be a lot of noise for a week or so then it'll all be back to normal.'

'That bloody Pope,' Harland muttered under his breath. He sat up, shaking his head slowly. 'You're assuming that he'll let it go.'

'And you're assuming he won't,' Mendel replied. 'Come on, even an idiot like Pope knows there's a line you don't cross.'

'I think you underestimate him,' Harland frowned. 'I think there are very few lines that little shit wouldn't cross if it suited him.'

He picked up his drink and sipped it slowly, staring at the table thoughtfully.

'Look at it another way then,' said Mendel. 'There's nothing you can do about it now, so there's no point in worrying about it.'

He was right of course. Harland gave his friend an ironic smile and raised his glass.

'You're a great comfort, Mendel.'

30

Naysmith opened his eyes and blinked, slowly focusing on the unfamiliar ceiling. Soft light glowed through the tall net curtain, revealing the sleeping figure beside him, her auburn hair tangled across the pillow. He gazed at her pale shoulders, her long eyelashes, the inviting pout of her open mouth.

There was no denying that it had been a satisfying evening. He'd often thought of Michaela, speaking to her now and again in the course of his business and gently flirting with her on the phone. But now she was leaving the Merentha Group, and when another appointment took him to Bristol he'd called and invited her for dinner.

'Really?' She'd sounded surprised, slightly hesitant. Perhaps she was seeing someone . . .

'Yes, really.' It didn't matter to him. Even if she was seeing someone, that just made her a little more challenging. 'We can celebrate your new job, and I haven't forgotten your promise about a jazz bar?'

'Wow, you remembered.' She laughed, and he knew then that she was interested.

The meal had been relaxed – there was a definite spark between them and he found himself genuinely enjoying their conversation. Her uncharacteristic shyness betrayed her attraction to him and he carefully guided their discussion so that she could talk about herself and feel good.

'You must be excited about doing something new,' he smiled at her.

'Yes, it's a complete departure for me,' Michaela agreed. 'I am looking forward to it, but working in a different industry will be a bit daunting. Jakob says I must be mad.'

'I think it shows strength.' He held her gaze, enjoying those large, dark eyes. 'The best people always seem to rise to a challenge. Too many are afraid to take risks, afraid to try things, afraid to enjoy themselves. But you're not afraid, are you?'

Michaela stared at him for a long moment.

'No,' she said, with a faint twinkle in her eye, 'I'm not afraid.'

Naysmith smiled, raising a hand to call for the bill.

'Now,' he said. 'What about that jazz place you were telling me about . . . ?'

It was a perfect evening, cold and clear. Naysmith knew where they were going but feigned ignorance and let her lead him. He kept the conversation light, joking with her to make her laugh and teasing her until she gave him a playful punch on the shoulder. By the time they arrived at King Street, she was happily leaning on his arm.

The bar wasn't great, but by this point it didn't matter. The music was loud enough to keep them pressed close together as they talked, and the mood was relaxed.

When he eventually suggested going for a drink at his hotel, she barely hesitated and they were locked in each other's arms as they took the lift up to his room. Over the following hours he'd been quite rough with her, but she'd responded

eagerly, and it had been very late when he finally allowed her
to drift off to sleep.

Now, as she dozed, Naysmith pulled the sheets back and
studied her body. Her skin glowed in the morning light, and
his eyes traced along the gentle curve of her back to her
round bottom. Her breasts were bigger than Kim's though
not as firm . . .

He frowned as he thought of Kim. It was unusual for her
to intrude on his thoughts at a moment like this. He looked
at the bedside clock and wondered if she was awake yet.
But he couldn't call her just now, not with someone else
lying next to him. He sighed. It had never bothered him
before.

He gazed down at Michaela again, taking in her naked
form, letting his growing arousal force out all other thoughts.
She *did* have a great body, and he was eager to fuck her once
more. Rolling over, he gently kissed her neck and slid a hand
under the sheets to wake her.

Afterwards, breakfast was strange. He watched her as she
slowly tore open a warm croissant, her long lashes beautiful
as her eyes looked down at the plate . . . and he tasted the
bitter sadness of disappointment. Women often lost their
appeal after he'd slept with them – there was nothing unusual
about that – but he'd expected more with Michaela. He'd
thought about her often, seeing something compelling and
interesting in her gaze, in the way she spoke, in her attitude.
And yet now, across the hotel breakfast table, he suddenly
knew it wouldn't be enough. It wasn't what he wanted.

She glanced up at him, mischievous eyes sparkling between
strands of long hair. He smiled back at her, but it was an
effort now, when last night it had been so natural. There was
really no point prolonging things.

'Remember I said I had an appointment in town this morning?'

She nodded as she ate.

'Well, believe it or not, that wasn't just a clever excuse to come and see you. I really do have an appointment this morning.'

'Oh,' she shrugged. 'No problem. Who's it with?'

The last of his desire for her evaporated. It was tiresome making up stories for Kim; he *really* didn't want to have to do it for anyone else. But it wasn't her fault, and he had no wish to hurt her feelings if he could avoid it.

'An old friend from university,' he lied. 'He's finance director for a firm of accountants over in Clifton and he wants me to meet his boss, see if there's anything we can do for them.'

'That's great.'

She seemed almost satisfied with this, but he did want to let her down gently if he could.

'I'm not sure what time I'll be done. I could try and meet you somewhere after lunch. Maybe.'

Her mouth was still smiling but her eyes looked at him differently. It was such a pity.

'No, that's okay,' she said. 'You can give me a call later. If you like.'

She raised her coffee cup and held it there, sipping from it thoughtfully. The poor girl understood.

Naysmith wandered aimlessly along the Bristol harbourside, listening to his footsteps, feeling the cobblestones through his shoes. He took out his phone, his finger hovering over the speed dial for Kim, then scowled and put it back in his pocket.

Not now.

Gulls wheeled around the Arnolfini building as he walked over to the edge of the quay, looking out at the grey-painted cranes across the water. The city felt as though it was waiting for him, but he was at a loss. Everything had been arranged so that he could spend the whole day with Michaela – the cover story, the hotel room, everything. With her out of the picture, he suddenly had time on his hands, and he resented it.

A faint breeze touched the tree-lined waterfront, teasing through the branches so that the leaves rustled for a moment, then fell silent once more. Naysmith found an empty bench and sat down. He could make an excuse and go home, but something warned him against seeing Kim while he felt like this.

A couple of women in their sixties strolled by, towed along by an eager West Highland terrier on a long lead. One of them was pointing at something further up the street and he leaned forward to see what it was. There was a white police van there, parked by the main road, and he could just make out a couple of officers talking to a group of kids. He got to his feet and wandered towards them, but as he drew near, the group dispersed and the officers returned to their van. He watched it as it pulled around, noting the insignia as it drove past him.

Avon and Somerset Constabulary.

And suddenly he remembered that haunted face on the TV, the detective on the crime programme with the Severn Beach reconstruction. DI Harland from Avon and Somerset Constabulary. Yes, that was it.

Perhaps fate had brought him to Bristol for a reason after all.

The nearest police station to Severn Beach was at Portishead. Naysmith had looked up the address – it was only ten miles away, and he thought it might be an interesting diversion, or at least give him time to think.

Now he was parked in a quiet residential street, an open
newspaper propped up on the steering wheel in front of him,
but his eyes focused always on the police station a hundred
yards further down at the bottom of the road – two storeys
of uninspiring beige plaster and brick, tucked in behind a
low wall. The entrance porch, decorated with crime preven-
tion posters and overhung by a couple of broad trees, was
clearly visible from his vantage point. Why were so many
small-town civic buildings so ugly?

He'd experienced an odd thrill driving out here. The sight
of the Second Severn Crossing, delicate and pale in the
distance as he'd come over the hill from Bristol, had sent a
shiver of excitement through him, dispelling the angst from
earlier. The last time he'd seen it had been that early morning
on the beach . . .

Portishead was a bleak place on an overcast day like this,
its huddle of Victorian architecture and desolate sixties shops
besieged by a vast sprawl of new developments. Bland industrial units, a generic retail park, a host of waterfront apartment
complexes – everything seemed grey, even the people.

He sat back in his seat and rubbed his eyes for a moment.
It had been a late night, but his mind was alert. DI Harland
could be in there right now, just a stone's throw from where
he was sitting. The idea pleased him.

He checked his watch again. It was 12.50 p.m., which
meant he'd been sitting here for nearly an hour with no
activity except one uniformed officer who'd emerged and
driven off in a panda car. And yet somehow it didn't matter.
The fact that this detective – this man who was hunting him
– might be so close was enough.

Smiling to himself, he leaned forward and switched on the
radio for some music. He would give it another hour.

The street was quiet. One or two cars had turned in from

the main road, disappearing up the hill behind him, and an elderly man shuffled down from a house further up on the opposite side. Naysmith watched his progress in the mirror, fascinated by the agonisingly slow pace, willing him along. Eventually, though, the stooped pensioner passed out of sight at the bottom of the road, and there was nothing to watch but the rhythmic swaying of the trees above the police station porch.

Patience was part of the game, bargaining with yourself to sit still for sixty seconds, then another sixty, and another . . . until you'd burned away five minutes. Same again, and ten minutes were gone, then quarter of an hour. He turned the radio down and focused on the memory of that gaunt man, recalling the troubled expression he'd seen on the screen.

And then, moments later, it was all he could do not to lean forward. The door had opened and two men emerged, both wearing dark grey suits. One of them was broad, tough-looking, with a square jaw and short hair, but it was the other man who held Naysmith's attention.

There was no mistaking that gaunt figure, that pale, drawn face. It was Harland. Naysmith exhaled, watching as the men walked out of the porch and turned away from the car park, out onto the pavement. For a heart-stopping moment he thought they might come this way, but they went down towards the main road. Where were they going?

Naysmith considered starting the engine, then decided against it. Moving quickly, he got out of the car and locked it. Folding the newspaper under his arm, he hurried towards the police station.

When he reached the junction, they had already crossed the main road, but that was fine. He preferred following people from the other side of the street, especially when it was quiet like this. They were talking as they went – the broad one was saying something and Harland was nodding – but it was too far away for him to hear what was said.

Naysmith walked carefully, measuring his pace to stay a little behind them, out of their field of vision. They were approaching a busy junction – they'd need to wait if they wanted to cross there. He took a moment to study the menu in the window of an Italian restaurant, watching the reflection in the glass to see when they'd made it over the road. Resuming his walk, he quickened his pace a little to catch up with them, a thoughtful smile on his face. How strange to be stalking someone who was hunting him.

There was a large, whitewashed pub on the corner. Harland and his companion went inside, still locked in conversation. A lunchtime pint for the boys in blue. Naysmith walked on for a short distance, pausing as if to browse in a travel agent's window.

It was so tempting, and there was really no reason why he shouldn't. They didn't know who he was, didn't know anything about him. And he'd got this close already . . . why shouldn't he go in for a quick drink himself? He turned around and looked at the pub for a moment, then drew himself up with a deep breath.

There was nothing he couldn't do.

Spotting a gap in the traffic, he walked briskly across the road and went inside. It was an old pub, with low ceilings and dark wood everywhere. Light from the small windows cut harsh swathes through the gloom, making it difficult to see. He blinked and walked towards the bar, forcing himself to wait, not to look around, not yet. Just an ordinary guy having a drink.

'Yes, sir?' The barman was in his twenties, with lank hair and an indifferent manner.

'A pint of Stella, please.' He wanted something that would

take a moment or two to pour, something that would give him time to see where they were.

Leaning up against the bar, he glanced around idly. He was careful not to react as he spotted Harland and his friend at a table in the corner, instead picking up a lunch menu to read until the barman returned with his drink.

There was an empty table halfway between them and the door. Walking calmly, he made his way over to it, placing his glass on a beer mat before sitting down and opening his newspaper.

And listening.

'. . . don't reckon they'll do anything. Not really. You know how it works – there'll be a lot of noise for a week or so then it'll all be back to normal.'

The broad man had a rich voice, and a slight London accent. Another officer, no doubt.

'You're assuming that he'll let it go.'

There it was, that same melancholy tone from the TV. Naysmith closed his eyes and focused all his attention on their conversation.

'And you're assuming he won't,' the broad man replied. 'Come on, even an idiot like Pope knows there's a line you don't cross.'

'I think you underestimate him,' Harland replied. 'I think there are very few lines that little shit wouldn't cross if it suited him.'

The conversation ceased for a moment. Naysmith opened his eyes and took a sip of his drink before turning the news-paper to stare blankly at the back page. He was glad he'd brought the paper with him – props like that hid a lot of body language, made it easier not to attract attention.

'Look at it another way then.' That resonant London voice again. 'There's nothing you can do about it now, so there's no point in worrying about it.'

A pause, then a soft chuckle from Harland.

'You're a great comfort, Mendel.'

Mendel. Naysmith noted the name, wondering who was subordinate to whom, or if they were both of equal rank.

A pair of men in grey overalls came over and sat down at the table between them. Their voices were loud and Naysmith was unable to hear anything further that Harland and Mendel said. But it didn't matter. He'd sat just feet from his adversary, close enough to hear him speak. It had been a thrilling and unexpected encounter.

He idly flipped through the pages of his paper, skimming the headlines for a moment before casually glancing across towards the corner as a mobile phone rang. Harland was fumbling in his pocket – someone was calling him. Naysmith smiled and returned his gaze to the paper. No rest for the wicked, not even at lunchtime.

He reached out a hand to take his glass when a raised voice caused him to look round.

'Absolutely not!' It was Harland, but this was a cold snarl that didn't seem to fit with the man. 'I don't care, you just tell him to wait until . . . oh for fuck's sake, I'll do it myself.'

Naysmith watched as he slammed the phone on the table and muttered something to Mendel, who shook his head and put a hand on Harland's shoulder. But the pale detective pulled away, jerking to his feet and knocking the table. A glass tipped over, spilling a puddle of beer that began to trickle onto the floor. Eyes flashing angrily, Harland wrenched himself away, knocking his chair to one side, and stormed out of the door. Mendel got wearily to his feet and went after him.

Naysmith sat for a moment, taken aback. What had just happened? What had made Harland so angry? Clearly there was an aspect to his adversary that he hadn't anticipated.

He considered his drink, but decided to leave it. There was no reason to stay any longer and he was suddenly eager to be away from here, away from the police station, away from Portishead. He stood up, put his paper in his pocket, and walked to the door.

And then, as the door swung open before him and the bright daylight streamed through, he recognised the figure coming back in, and froze.

Shit!

Harland held the door open and stared right at him.

An irrational urge to run, to push past him and run, screamed in Naysmith's head as the hollow eyes bored into him. It had been folly – arrogance and folly – to come here and now he was caught in the glare of the man who hunted him.

But Harland just scowled and tilted his head.

'After you.'

The voice seemed to come from a long way away, and his legs were suddenly numb, but Naysmith forced himself to move, stepping slowly past through the doorway and almost stumbling out into the cold afternoon air.

Harland went inside, and the door closed behind him.

31

Harland barged through the door and out into the cold daylight. He couldn't even have a quick lunchtime drink without someone screwing things up and dragging him back to the damn station. Josh knew better than to get himself caught up in conversations with Blake, letting goodness knows what slip out, but that was exactly what had happened. Why couldn't people just do as they were bloody told?

He paused for a moment, one hand rising to massage his temple, catching his breath.

Slow down and think. It was happening again, and he couldn't afford a repeat of yesterday's performance. His hand went to his jacket pocket, searching for his phone, but it wasn't there. Frowning, he patted his other pockets, then turned to see Mendel emerging from the pub behind him, a concerned expression on his face.

'Don't worry,' Harland said, hands raised in mock surrender, 'I'm not going to do anything silly. I'll wait till I've calmed down before I speak to anyone.'

Mendel gave him a speculative look.

'Good,' he said. 'Because I'm not buying you any more damn mugs if you break that new one.'

Despite himself, Harland smiled, and the anger seemed to lift a little.

'On you go back to the station,' he said. 'I think I left my phone in there.'

He patted Mendel awkwardly on the shoulder, then quickly turned and walked back towards the pub. Where would he have been without the big man's support?

Stepping into the doorway, he reached for the handle and pulled the door open just as someone was coming out.

The stranger hesitated in front of him, tall and slim, well dressed with short, dark hair. Harland glanced at him and paused. Something about the man's expression annoyed him – that same fearful look he'd glimpsed on Josh's face when he'd snapped at Pope yesterday. What did other people see in him that was so disturbing?

He scowled to himself, then moved aside to let the man pass.

'After you,' he murmured.

The man stood still for a second before pushing hurriedly past him, out into the car park. Harland glanced over his shoulder, and went inside.

His phone was there, lying on the table where he'd left it. Walking over, he reached out to pick it up, then stopped.

Mobile phone.

He would need to check, but he felt certain there'd been no mobile phone listed in the personal effects of the Hampshire murder victim. Filled with a new sense of urgency, Harland turned and hurried back to the station.

32

'Come in, Graham. Take a seat.'

Safe behind his desk, Blake pointedly closed the folder he had been studying. There was the customary polite smile but his eyes were alert, watchful.

Harland closed the door and walked over to the chair. Sitting down, he noted an unusual tension in the Superintendent's posture, the hunch of his shoulders, the right hand resting awkwardly on the edge of the desk. Something wasn't right.

Damn. Pope must have dropped him in it after all.

'I believe good communication is key to effective police work,' Blake began. The words sounded uneasy, as though he'd rehearsed this little speech too many times. 'So I wanted to have a one-to-one with you, to explain where we are with the Severn Beach case.'

'Yes, sir,' Harland nodded. He was wrong. It wasn't a disciplinary talk – the first in an inexorable series of meetings that would undoubtedly see him suspended. He exhaled silently. *Thank goodness.* But if it wasn't that, what was it?

'We've invested a lot of time and valuable manpower in this investigation,' Blake said. 'I've put my faith in you and your team from the beginning, and that faith has been rewarded by some significant breakthroughs. It was our hard work that unearthed the connection to the other killings, and I'm proud of that.'

Harland's heart sank as he recognised the empty praise that always seemed to precede bad news. Blake was going to pull the plug.

The Superintendent drew a breath and leaned back in his chair, frowning slightly as though considering where to go next.

'However . . .' he said carefully. 'Just as there are times when it's appropriate for us to lead the investigation, we must recognise that sometimes others are better placed to do so.'

He paused, trying to measure Harland's reaction, but there was none.

'I believe that we've made a significant contribution to this case, Graham . . . but I think the time has come to let Hampshire have a clear run at it. As far as we know, the most recent murder happened on their patch, so they're in the driving seat now.'

'I'm sorry, sir.' Harland knew it was pointless, but somehow he just had to speak. 'How can we give this one up to Hampshire? All the bigger-picture stuff – everything – has come from us.'

Blake gazed across the desk at him.

'Nobody's disputing that,' he said, quietly. 'But we can only take it so far, and things haven't really moved much in the last couple of weeks.'

'That's not true,' Harland protested. 'What about the mobile phone?'

'What mobile phone?'

'Each body seems to have one thing on them, one thing that doesn't belong, that was lifted from the previous victim, yes?'

'Yes . . .'

'Well . . .' Harland forced himself to speak slowly, calmly. He couldn't allow his frustration to get the better of him now. 'We were talking about that, about how we're always two steps behind the killer because it's so hard to spot which murders are linked. About how, if we don't know what we're looking for, then we can't get the other forces to watch for it.'

'So?' Blake shrugged.

'So we've been trying to figure out what was taken from the most recent victim, something that we can watch for, something that's close to the killer *now*.'

He paused, slowing himself down again, taking a breath.

'Our lecturer had no mobile phone on him when he was found,' he said. 'We've gone through the reports, checked with his family . . . nobody knows where that phone is.'

Blake rubbed his hand absently across his mouth, his eyes thoughtful for a moment.

'He definitely had one?'

'Yes, a basic pay-as-you-go phone,' Harland nodded. 'If you'll authorise it, we can get a watch put on the number, see if it's used again.'

Surely, even a self-serving bastard like Blake must see the potential in that. If they could track down the phone it might give them a real edge.

Blake leaned back in his chair, steepling his fingers in front of him.

'Very well,' he said at last. 'We'll put a flag on the phone and see if anything comes of it . . .'

Harland felt a brief surge of exultation, but the Superintendent hadn't finished.

'In the meantime,' he continued, 'I think we need to re-assign people. This isn't our only case, and I have to make the best use of resources.'

And there it was. The neat little manoeuvre that effectively bumped the investigation onto the back burner.

'With respect, sir,' Harland argued, 'things really aren't that busy just now. By all means take Pope, even Mendel if you have to, but you don't need to reassign me just yet.'

Blake drew himself up, his mouth showing a faint smile.

'I agree,' he said in a quiet, level voice. 'Perhaps now might be a good opportunity for you to take some time off.'

'I'm sorry, sir?' Harland was caught off balance by the suggestion.

'You heard me.' Blake stared him down, a flicker of challenge beneath his calm tone. 'Good communication is the key, and I've been listening. Did you really think I was unaware of your little scene with Pope?'

Harland's head dropped. He'd been played.

'Take some time off, Graham,' Blake said calmly. 'That's all.'

part 3
LONDON

33

It was getting dark. He knew he ought to be getting home. His socks were wet and his feet were cold, but it wasn't too uncomfortable as long as he kept moving. He looked down at his school shoes and scuffed them through some long grass to wipe the mud off them. They weren't too bad. His mum would put newspaper in them and leave them on the radiator to dry for the morning.

But it wasn't his shoes that he was worrying about.

He stooped to pick up a broken branch, snapping off a few twigs to make a walking stick. It felt good in his hand as he swished it back and forth, scything it through the grass like a sword. If only he could stay out here for another hour, put it off a little longer. But the street lights were coming on in the village below him, flickering red and faint at first, before settling into a bright orange glow.

It was time.

He sighed and started down the hill.

The dark evening clouds were creeping up over the horizon as he turned into his street, walking with one foot on the pavement and one in the road. He dragged the stick behind him, enjoying the sound as it rattled over the gratings of the gutter drains, then using it to draw a long snaking line in the gravel as he trudged up the driveway. He suddenly felt quite sick.

The back door was open and he went in slowly, trying to scrape the last of the mud from his shoes onto the mat.

'Out with no coat again, I see.' His mother breezed into the kitchen and smiled at him as she went over to the sink. He said nothing as she rinsed her hands, then turned to look at him.

'Are those your school shoes?' she asked, noticing his muddy feet. 'Oh Rob, I asked you to wear your old ones . . .'

She knelt in front of him, her thin fingers fumbling with the sodden laces as she loosened the shoes and helped him out of them.

'How many times have I told you . . .' She looked up at him, her frown melting away as she caught his expression.

'Oh, don't look like that,' she sighed, a weary smile breaking onto her face. 'I can always dry them on the radiator. Come here.'

And then she let the shoes drop and gathered him in her arms, holding him close. It felt different now, but it still felt good. She still loved him and he wouldn't let that change. If he was careful, if he didn't say anything silly, she would keep loving him. It would be like a really difficult game . . .

*   *   *

'We're here, mate.'

Naysmith came to with a start and blinked into uncertain wakefulness. Raising his head from where it had been resting against the rear door, he sat up and nodded to the taxi driver's deep-set eyes watching him impassively in the rear-view mirror.

'I must have dropped off,' he frowned, noting the fare and reaching for his wallet.

'That'll be my beautiful smooth driving,' the cabbie said, without enthusiasm.

Naysmith drew out a couple of notes and passed them through the open hatch in the security glass. Then, stifling a yawn, he gripped his small travel case and opened the cab door. The constant rumble of traffic noise from Park Lane assailed him as soon as he stepped out onto the tarmac, but the early evening air was cool and refreshing after his doze. Straightening his jacket, he glanced up at the soaring tower of the hotel, then extended the handle on his case and trundled it round behind the taxi.

The wide revolving door eased him inside with a whisper and he walked down the three broad steps to the familiar expanse of the foyer, shoes marking out a muted rhythm on the marble flooring. Diffuse lighting bathed the dark, wood-panelled reception desk with a calm aura. Sitting behind it, a raven-haired woman in a smart navy blazer gave him a professional smile as he approached.

'Robert Naysmith,' he said, standing his case up on the floor beside him. 'Three nights. It may have been booked via the CRM conference?'

'I won't keep you a moment.' The receptionist nodded to him, then glanced down at her screen as she tapped in his name. She had a nice voice – soft but confident – and quick, clear eyes that he watched as she studied her computer, enjoying their sparkle as she turned her gaze back to him.

'Mr Naysmith. It's good to have you back with us, sir.'

Always that same line.

He was sure it came up on her screen, a prompt for regular visitors with the right sort of privilege card. Other people might have been disappointed by such realisations, but not him. Seeing the wiring under the board – knowing the world for what it really was – filled him with a deep sense of satisfaction.

'You're very kind,' he said.

She handed over the key card.

'I've given you room 1201. The lift is just over there and it will take you to the twelfth floor. If there's anything we can help you with . . .'

'I appreciate it, thanks.'

He inclined his head to her slightly, then reached for his case and turned towards the lifts.

The room was quiet and cool – clean lines and carefully chosen colours, all of it framing the generously broad windows. They looked out with an unobstructed view across the treetops of Hyde Park, a swathe of dark green across the grey city. Naysmith sat on the window sill, his forehead resting on the glass as he stared down at the street far below, the silent ebb and flow of the traffic, the tiny figures drifting along the pale pavements.

Little people.

He sighed and eased himself to his feet, turning away from the window, eyes adjusting to the comparative dimness of the room.

First things first.

He lifted his case onto the luggage stand and unzipped it. The edge of the small white envelope protruded from a side pocket, and he stared at it for a moment before pushing it firmly back down.

Out of sight, out of mind.

From the case, he drew out three clean shirts, which he held up and inspected for creases, shaking each one so that the sleeves could move freely. Opening the wardrobe, he retrieved a handful of wooden hangers and made sure to smooth the front of each shirt once it was on the rail. Underwear and socks went on the shelf above, as always.

Lastly, his clear plastic ziplock bag of airport-friendly toiletries, which he took through to the large, well-lit bathroom.

Placing his toothbrush in the glass by the sink, he paused to look at himself in the mirror, leaning forward to correct a patch of hair that was sticking up from where his head had been slumped against the inside of the taxi. Restless eyes stared back at him as he studied his own expression, a mask that he alone could see through. Frowning, he walked out of the bathroom and switched off the light.

The sun was sinking below the London skyline now, throwing long shadows across the floor, and he suddenly felt conspicuous, pacing in the stillness, trapped by the silence of the room, which was becoming oppressive. Hesitating for a moment, he checked his watch, then gathered his jacket from where he'd laid it carefully on the bed and opened the door to step out into the quiet, lamplit corridor.

Waiting for the lift, he thought briefly about going to the bar, but it was too early – the unaccompanied women came for their nightcaps and their bar-stool conversations at the end of the evening. There would be time enough for that later if he was so inclined. His hand hovered over the small touch screen, about to tap in 28 – the floor for the restaurant – but he knew that he wasn't really hungry. He paused, then touched 'L' for Lobby. A well-spoken recording murmured 'Going down . . .' as he stepped inside for the descent to ground level. A walk, and some air to clear his head, was what he needed now.

The sky seemed darker as he stepped out from under the entrance canopy and passed between the waiting taxis, the idle rattling of their engines hurrying him forward. On a whim he turned right, following the broad pavement along the tree-lined curve of Park Lane towards Marble Arch, but turned into the Mayfair side streets before he had gone far.

Ugly modern architecture quickly gave way to Regency terraces with grand entrance porticos; iron railings freshly glossed and gilded; basement windows that squinted up at the feet of passers-by. Manicured window boxes reflected in the shine of expensive parked cars, while bursts of loud laughter echoed back off the old stone of blue-plaque build-ings. He stepped around the cigarette-bound throngs that filled the pavements outside the bars, his thoughts drifting ahead of him like the wisps of their smoke.

Veering off Curzon Street, he cut along a narrow alley, forcing his way through the press of people that shuffled between the pavement cafés. There was a casino round the next corner – he'd visited it a few times, and done well there. Was that where his feet had been taking him? He slowed as he approached it, pausing a few yards away from the entrance to think, allowing the bustle of people to flow around him.

Little people.

Gazing up at the casino sign, he frowned, then started to walk on.

It wouldn't do. He wanted a real challenge, something to wake him and set his heart racing. A game where the stakes were more than a few digits on a credit card receipt.

At the end of the street, he could see The Ritz – the distinc-tive arches, the illuminated columns – and the crawl of traffic inching its way along Piccadilly . . .

Of course.

It was perfect. Down to the end of the street and turn right, and there the game could begin. He would follow Piccadilly back down towards Park Lane. The first person to make eye contact would be the target.

A pleasing thrill of adrenalin infused him as started towards

The Ritz, the haze of drowsiness evaporating with each step. Pedestrians stepped out of his way, as though sensing his presence if not his purpose, and he had to concentrate on relaxing his muscles into a neutral expression, so that the terrible eagerness would not show on his face.

One last block to go.

An expensively dressed woman with olive skin and long dark hair met his eye as they passed each other, but she was lucky – had they met a hundred yards further along, it might have been her. Naysmith smiled at her good fortune and walked on, his gaze drawn to a double-decker bus that had drawn up ahead of him, indistinct faces staring out from the upstairs windows. He dropped his gaze to the paving slabs in front of him, not wanting to make eye contact with anyone else until he was in the proper place.

The traffic noise grew louder, and a slight breeze of fumes touched his cheek as he finally stepped out of the side street and, turning right, raised his eyes to look out on Piccadilly.

Game on.

Ahead of him, a young couple were walking arm in arm, threading their way between the oncoming pedestrians. Naysmith kept his distance, staying a little behind them, allowing his gaze to flit across the faces of the people coming in the other direction.

Two suited men in their forties, ties loosened for the evening, passed by without looking up. An Arab woman with a broad, beautiful face and an exotically hooked nose approached with a graceful stride, but her large eyes were turned towards the trees of Green Park, lost in thought. Naysmith slowed as she passed, turning to watch her receding figure with a thoughtful smile, then moved on.

He watched diners, oblivious to his presence, talking to each other across small tables in restaurant windows, and caught glimpses of his own reflection keeping pace with him in the polished dark marble of the Piccadilly facades.

The young couple turned right into Half Moon Street and he walked on alone, the road sloping gently downwards. The traffic still rolled along beside him, but there were fewer people here. A huddled male figure sat with his head down in a darkened doorway and, moments later, a cadaverous-looking tramp stumbled along with unseeing eyes staring straight ahead.

He was approaching Hyde Park Corner now, and still nobody had made eye contact. Surely he would find someone before he got back to his hotel. Perhaps the usual crowd of tourists that milled around outside the Hard Rock Café? He didn't want to end the evening with nothing.

Frowning, he walked on towards the grand old hotels that lined the end of the street. A short, middle-aged man stood between a pair of empty tables in a roped-off section at the front of one of them. The red ember of a small cigar glowed in one hand, and his head was bowed as he studied a phone held in the other. The man smiled to himself and straightened, raising the cigar towards his bearded mouth. Inclining his head slightly, he peered over the top of his glasses, his gaze resting on Naysmith for just a second before looking back to the phone.

He would be the one.

Naysmith allowed his pace to slow very slightly as he focused on the figure, just a few feet away from him now, taking in each detail. Late forties or early fifties. Five foot ten, average build, with wispy brown hair swept back from his face, and a bushy, salt-and-pepper goatee beard. Small eyes peered down through delicate, thin-framed spectacles perched on a pointed nose.

He had on a beautifully tailored jacket and expensive-looking shoes, but wore a dark woollen sweater vest over his shirt. A smart leather shoulder bag lay on the table at his side.

And then Naysmith was past him. Closing his eyes, he committed the man to memory – the shape of his ears, the slight double chin. Picking up his pace again, he walked on, casually glancing at his watch to make certain of the time. Exactly 8.16 p.m. He smiled to himself as he followed the pavement back round towards his own hotel.

34

Naysmith walked across the old entrance lobby and passed through double doors into the beautiful art deco hall of the lounge. Beneath the high, arched ceiling, a central aisle of chequered marble stretched out from the street entrance to the sweeping curve of the bar at the far end of the room, where steps led up to the hotel reception area beyond. Comfortable sofas and padded wicker chairs surrounded the low, linen-shrouded tables, while Japanese murals filled the spaces between the columns on the walls and cream-shaded lamps nestled on tables beneath the large potted palms.

He took a table off to one side of the bar, his seat facing into the room so that he had a good view of the doors. The hushed murmur of conversation wafted across the room as he sank back into what was an extraordinarily comfortable chair. A raised eyebrow summoned the waiter, who approached with a measured step and nodded politely.

'Sir?'

'I'd like a gin and tonic, please.'

'Certainly,' the waiter nodded. 'We have Caorunn, Plymouth, Bombay Sapphire, or London Number One.'

'Excellent,' Naysmith smiled, relishing the choice. 'Caorunn, I think.'

'Very good, sir.'

Naysmith watched him walk over to the bar, then relaxed back into the soft upholstery of his seat, gazing up to admire the beautiful stained-glass ceiling and noting the apparent absence of security cameras. There were worse places to wait for someone.

The bar filled up steadily as the evening progressed, the volume of conversation and laughter rising to overcome the meandering jazz that drifted down from somewhere overhead. At first, Naysmith read a newspaper to pass the time. Later, he amused himself by exchanging glances with an elegant brunette in her forties on the other side of the room. Toying with her drink, she artfully smiled at him while her husband stared at the waitresses, and offered a tiny, apologetic shrug when he finally led her away. Naysmith acknowledged her with a mischievous wink, then returned his attention to the doors.

It was a little after nine thirty when his target appeared.

At the far end of the room, the double doors swung open and two figures walked in, deep in conversation. Naysmith gazed across at them, his expression rigidly neutral but his eyes alert. Small glasses, goatee beard, and that curious sweater vest visible under the jacket. Definitely the same man.

As the pair approached, Naysmith calmly folded away his newspaper and placed a twenty-pound note under his half-empty glass. Easing back his chair, he stood up and yawned, allowing the two men time to make their way across the room. As they drew level with him, he took one last glance at the paper, then abandoned it and turned slowly towards the stairs, falling in just behind the two men as they passed.

'. . . but you know what? Their stock's gonna take a big hit if they don't get out of that market soon.' The target had a West Coast accent.

'And did you tell him that?' The other man was younger,

taller, with short, dark hair. He spoke with a slight Scottish accent, and held the door open for Naysmith as they passed through into the brightly lit reception area and walked over to the lifts.

'I called him like three times but he just wouldn't accept it,' the bearded man shrugged, pressing the button to go up. 'It's actually a shame because they had some stellar growth in the last few years.'

The three men waited as the doors slid open, then stepped into the lift. Naysmith went last, his eyes casually registering the single CCTV camera above his head. The younger man pressed the 5 button for himself before turning to the target.

'It's four, isn't it?' he asked.

'Thanks,' the bearded man nodded.

'Four for me too,' Naysmith murmured, moving to stand slightly behind and to the left of the target.

The young man pressed the polished metal 4 button and stood back as the doors slid together.

'Still, I thought tonight was very positive,' he observed as the lift started to move.

'It sure was,' the target chuckled. He was wearing the bag over his left shoulder. It was clearly expensive – soft black leather with reinforced gunmetal edges. A small plastic tag swung on a miniature leather loop, and Naysmith leaned back against the mirrored rear wall of the lift, his head inclined as he watched it.

An American Airlines executive-flyer logo, with what looked like a membership number embossed on it, along with a name: MR D. LENNOX.

'Anyways,' Lennox was saying, 'it was useful to meet their people, and I think there may well be something we can do together.'

Naysmith straightened, studying the man's clothes, his bag

. . . and above all his bearing. Mr D. Lennox was clearly a wealthy man. The wristwatch, the executive-flyer tag – innocuous details that all spoke quietly of money. Naysmith recognised them but wasn't impressed. Money was power, but only of a sort. What *he* did was more powerful, more absolute. And when the time came, and he stood face to face with this wealthy man, all the money in the world wouldn't be enough to save him.

'Well, I guess this is me.' Lennox watched the lift doors slide open and turned to nod at his colleague. 'I'll see you in the morning.'

'See you in the morning,' the younger man replied.

Naysmith brushed past him, following Lennox out of the lift, his feet sinking noiselessly into the deep blue carpet as the doors slid shut behind them. The corridor curved away to the left and right, broad deco uplighters creating pools of soft illumination on the ceiling.

No cameras here. Good.

Naysmith slowed in the shadows between two of the lights, pretending to tap something into his phone. His head was inclined forward, but his eyes peered out beneath the brows, looking along the corridor. He had to let the target get ahead of him, so that he could see which room he was staying in. And he had to do it without appearing suspicious himself.

Lennox walked a little further, then paused, fumbling in his pocket for his key card. Naysmith began to move again, calmly sliding the phone back into his jacket and picking up his pace as he heard the click of the lock. They were only a few yards apart as the door opened and Lennox passed inside.

For a second, Naysmith felt the urge to run forward, to burst in through the slowly closing door and overpower his victim in a sudden explosion of violence. But he mastered the compulsion, maintaining his relaxed pace, his disinterested expression.

He drew level with the door just as it clicked shut, continuing past it with nothing more than a sidelong glance to confirm the room number.

408.

Walking on, he went to a door at the end of the corridor, feigned searching for a lost room key, then retraced his steps back towards the lift.

It wasn't going to be easy.

The fact that his target was a business traveller meant he would need to act quickly. Lennox was probably visiting from the US, and would have to be eliminated before he could return home. But how long would that be?

And then there was the problem of access.

The lift was much too risky – a confined space with CCTV coverage, but also the unpredictable delay in waiting for it to arrive if he needed to leave in a hurry. He glanced over his shoulder, then nudged a side door open with his elbow and slipped into the stairwell. Moving slowly, calmly, his eyes swept the space above him, but there were no cameras to be seen. He trotted down the broad, shallow steps, the carpet deadening his footfalls. This was much better – a discrete way to and from the fourth floor.

He counted the flights down, emerging to one side of the reception area, close to the hotel's rear entrance. Adopting the confident air of a paying guest, he walked over to the glass doors and slipped out into the cold night air. A claustrophobic little back street sloped down between the tall buildings, but he could see a four-way junction, just a few yards up to the left, that presented several different ways to leave the area.

Naysmith smiled. It was important to have options. He took one last look up at the hotel behind him, then turned, walked to the corner and disappeared.

35

Naysmith moved quietly, preserving the hushed tone of the room as he stepped around the bed, laying out the things he would need. A strange peace descended on him as he prepared – the calm before the storm. Everything was ready, but he checked each item once more to be sure. There would be no margin for error, no time for a second attempt.

Surveying the items laid out on the bed, he nodded with satisfaction. It had been quite a challenge, getting everything together so quickly, but he had done it.

Clothing had been the biggest issue – usually he had the luxury of time, with plenty of opportunities to source anony-mous, untraceable garments from different supermarkets – but time was tight on this one. He'd briefly considered wearing his own clothes, or perhaps even stealing a bag from one of the other hotel guests, but that would have been a dangerous compromise; he had to act quickly without being careless. In the end, he'd remembered the big sporting retailer near Piccadilly Circus and reached it before it closed for the night. Under the glaring strip lights, hunting quickly through the crowded racks of discounted football shirts, he picked up a nondescript tracksuit, T-shirt and trainers – all suitably generic items, all paid for with cash.

As he'd approached the sleepy cashier, his gaze had rested

briefly on some cellophane-wrapped baseball bats and a rack of substantial-looking golf clubs. He'd hesitated, weighing up the possibilities, but they were memorable items to travel with, and difficult to conceal. After some thought, and needing to find something that could serve, he'd picked up a long black umbrella with a steel-tipped spike.

Better.

Rubber gloves, a packet of wet wipes and a selection of plastic bags had come from a Metro supermarket on the way back through Mayfair, and everything would be stowed in a small fabric bag with 'I ♥ London' printed on it, purchased from a street vendor. Backpacks and holdalls attracted the wrong sort of attention on the capital's streets these days, but obvious tourists were virtually invisible.

Walking thoughtfully back towards the hotel, he'd gone over his plan, testing and refining it, working out every eventuality. His hand gripped the umbrella, dragging the steel tip along the pavement beside him, scraping it, sharpening it. Everything was ready.

Now, he walked out onto the pavement and looked up at the steel grey sky of an overcast London morning, savouring the swell of pent-up anticipation. His thoughts flitted momentarily to Lennox, and he pictured the man lying in bed, resting as his final minutes bled quietly away, blissfully unaware of the abrupt end that was closing in on him.

A powerful man made powerless.

Naysmith smiled to himself and set off, melting into the early-morning pedestrians. Men and women cradling their coffee cups, insulated by their iPods, eyes downcast as they hurried along. Nobody would notice him; nobody would remember him, a single face in the crowd.

He took a roundabout route through Mayfair, winding his

way around several back alleys so that he could approach
the target's hotel from the opposite direction. A black taxi
rattled past him as he turned the corner onto the narrow
tarmac of Brick Street. Ahead of him, he could see the rear
entrance of the hotel and he slowed his pace, watching the
single uniformed figure emerge to place a pedestal sign beside
the carpeted steps before returning inside. The glass doors
glinted as they swung shut.

Time to go.

Naysmith quickly covered the distance and walked briskly
up the carpeted steps. Pushing it open with his forearm, he
passed through the glass side door and crossed the lobby
with his head slightly forward and away from the reception
area he knew lay just to his left. He measured his steps carefully, deliberately. He absolutely must not hurry. Pace and
body language were the secret to going unnoticed.

Casually, he made his way round the corner, moving as
though towards the lift, but turned quickly, nudging through
the door to the stairwell with his elbow.

And now he paused, allowing the door to swing shut behind
him, allowing his racing pulse to slow a little, holding his
breath as he listened. But there was nothing. No sound.
Nobody was following him.

He was in.

Leaning on the central banister, he gazed up through the
sharp angles of the flights of stairs above him, then began to
climb, slowly and silently. Occasional bumps, muffled voices
and the regular hum of the nearby lifts echoed through the
stairwell, but he reached the fourth floor without encountering
anyone.

Almost there.

He opened the bag and drew out the gloves first. He hadn't
worn them before, to avoid attracting attention to himself, but

now he pulled them on carefully, forcing himself to take the extra seconds, making sure they were on straight, fitting snugly to his fingers. Only once they were on did he unwrap the clear plastic bag that had protected the handle of the umbrella from fingerprints, screwing it up tightly and jamming it into his pocket. Lastly, he drew out two more bags and slipped them over his shoes. The fit was inexact but it would do – he knew that he couldn't afford to track blood through the hotel corridors and the bags could be discarded if required, leaving his soles clean. Stepping to one side, he studied the floor to ensure he hadn't dropped anything, then folded the top of the fabric bag over on itself. Testing the feel of the umbrella in his now gloved hand, he took a deep breath and listened once more.

Ready.

Shouldering the door open, Naysmith stepped out onto the fourth-floor corridor and turned left. He walked quickly but calmly, counting the numbers on the doors, adrenalin building steadily until he stood outside room 408.

Bowing his head, he took a last breath, a heartbeat, forcing his shoulders to be loose, ready. He looked up at the door. Was there a chain? Maybe, but the chances were good that it wouldn't be latched in place, and as long as Lennox didn't suspect anything was wrong there was no reason for him to chain the door.

He took a step forward, measuring his position, then raised a gloved hand and knocked.

'Housekeeping.'

His voice sounded very loud in the carpeted stillness of the hotel, but it was necessary to explain the knock. Leaning forward, he exhaled slowly onto the tiny spyhole in the door, misting the glass, then bowed his head in readiness.

He pictured Lennox, just a few feet away, hearing the knock, turning and moving towards the door. The rubber gloves squeaked as his fingers tightened their grip, holding the umbrella in a low, two-handed stance like a spear. His feet were planted in a well-braced position, ready to thrust forward, to burst open the door and knock his victim back into the room.

Any second now . . .

But there was no sound from inside, only the beat of his pulse.

Frowning, he knocked again, louder this time.

'Housekeeping.'

And waited. Again, nothing.

A cold knot of doubt began to grow in his stomach.

He knocked once more, leaning forward to remist the spyhole, the gleaming metal tip of the umbrella hovering just below the handle of the door.

At last, he heard a sound – movement, indistinct – but it was coming from another doorway, further along the corridor.

Shit.

Stifling a snarl, Naysmith spun on his heel and strode quickly back towards the lift. Pushing through the door to the stairwell, he paused for a moment, leaning against the wall as he tore the bags from his shoes and peeled the rubber gloves from his hands. Dropping everything into the fabric bag, he jogged quickly down the broad steps, his movements hastened by frustration.

Where was Lennox?

On the ground floor, he walked swiftly out of the rear entrance and onto the street . . .

. . . but it didn't matter if anyone saw him now. Nobody cared. As he stood in the morning light, he felt the crash of anticlimax, as though the whole world had been holding its breath, but had now lost interest in him. He had done nothing. Accomplished nothing.

Knuckles whitening around the handle of the umbrella, he strode angrily along the back street, turning the corner. Ahead

of him stood a red telephone box, one of the traditional ones
that tourists liked to photograph themselves beside, despite
the windows being plastered with cards advertising call girls.
Gripping the handle, Naysmith hauled open the door and
stepped inside, insulating himself from the noise of the city.

Where the fuck was Lennox?

He rammed a pound coin into the slot and dialled the
number for the hotel, breathing deeply, forcing his voice to
be calm as he heard the receptionist answer.

'Hotel Park Lane. How may I help you?'

'Ah yes,' he smiled. People could hear when you were
smiling on the phone. 'I need to speak to one of your guests,
please. Mr Lennox in room 408?'

'I'm sorry, sir, but Mr Lennox left earlier this morning.'

Damn.

'I see.' Naysmith thought quickly, formulating an appropriate lie. 'Will he be returning? I just realised I have his
laptop charger and I wanted to get it back to him.'

'Oh dear.' The voice sounded genuinely dismayed. 'I'm
afraid not. I was on the desk when he asked for a taxi back
to the airport.'

Shit.

'Thank you,' he sighed. 'You've been most helpful.'

Replacing the handset carefully, Naysmith paused for a
moment, then lifted the receiver and smashed it hard against
the metal wall of the booth, beating it again and again until
the plastic cracked and shattered.

The target had escaped him.

★   ★   ★

There was something soothing about looking out across
London late at night. Lights scattered like twinkling jewels

across the silhouette of the city, blurring into an orange glow on the horizon. The ebb and flow of tiny cars, the warm yellow of illuminated old buildings, and the cool white glare from office-block windows.

Naysmith sat on a cream leather sofa beside the full-length windows, gazing down on Hyde Park Corner, condensation pooling around the untouched drink on the low glass table in front of him. The twenty-eighth-floor bar was winding down now, with slow jazz filling the gaps in quiet conversations. Stretching his legs out in front of him, he checked his watch. It was five to midnight – 'almost tomorrow', as Kim would say. He rubbed his eyes and yawned.

The day had been a blur of dreary speakers and awkward conference delegates, and he'd stumbled through his appointments like a sleepwalker. This evening there had been an industry social event at Bar Dokidogo – the sort of networking opportunity he usually worked so well – but tonight his mood had been too unsettled and he'd found himself leaving early, staring out of a taxi as it drove him back to the hotel.

He sighed and leaned closer to the glass, propping his chin in his hand as his eyes followed a tiny figure hurrying across the road below to disappear behind a building.

He'd lost targets before – it was an inevitable part of the game – but for some reason this one gnawed at him. Turning to the table, he reached out to take his glass, tracing a clear line through the mist of condensation with his finger.

Where was Lennox right now?

He sipped his drink, wondering what the man was doing, wondering how his life would unfold from here, a life that should have ended this morning. Would he ever have any inclination, some subconscious sense, that he'd been given a second chance?

Turning back to the window, he caught sight of the rueful

smile on his reflection, but his eye was drawn to an indistinct female form passing just behind him. He watched her slow, then move to sit down on a seat nearby. He could see her better now – a businesswoman in her forties, maybe five foot seven, though two inches of that must have been in her heels. She wore a charcoal blazer suit that suggested a pleasing figure, rectangular glasses and blonde hair in a bob that framed a patient face.

He subtly turned his body, angling himself more towards her while watching her reflection. Then, as she glanced in his direction, he casually leaned forward to put his glass down, accidentally catching her eye and allowing an instinctive smile to flicker across his face.

She smiled back.

'It's a beautiful view.' Her tone was relaxed and she spoke with a soft, low voice.

Naysmith let his eyes dwell on hers for a moment.

'It is.' He turned his gaze out to the city lights. 'You get a different perspective on things up here.'

'We're looking west?' she asked, leaning forward to peer down through the glass.

'Yes,' Naysmith nodded. 'That's Knightsbridge over there.'

He glanced at her as she stared out across the glittering vista. No wedding ring. On another person, he might have equated that with less challenge, but there was something about her – an air of sadness perhaps, or insecurity – that he found interesting.

'London looks so peaceful from up here,' she murmured, settling back into her chair.

'It's an illusion,' he said softly, 'but a pleasant one.'

She studied him for a moment, then nodded to herself and looked down.

'I suppose you're right,' she sighed.

Loneliness.

It was the loneliness in her voice that fired his senses. Blood in the water, to the seasoned sexual predator.

'Tough day?' An open question, to let her talk.

'Does it show?' she asked.

He smiled and shrugged slightly.

'Let's just say it makes two of us.'

She gazed at him over her drink.

'You too, huh?'

He sat back in his seat, choosing his words carefully.

'Sometimes, no matter how hard you try . . .' He hesitated, pressing his palms together, tapping his fingertips against his chin as he pictured Lennox standing inches away from him in the lift. '. . . things don't go the way you want them to.'

'I'm sorry to hear that.' She seemed so genuine in that moment that Naysmith was suddenly struck by her concern, however misplaced it might be. He looked down and shook his head.

'Don't be,' he told her quietly. 'Really.'

He knew how it was meant to unfold from here; the gentle fencing, the coy responses, another drink.

But he suddenly knew that his heart just wasn't in it.

'Actually, *I'm* sorry.' He straightened and got slowly to his feet. 'You'll have to excuse me.'

She looked up at him, the light glinting on her glasses, her expression confused. She really was quite attractive, and he didn't want her to misunderstand.

'I wish we'd met on a different evening,' he whispered truthfully. 'But tonight . . . I'm just not good company.'

He gave her a last smile, then turned away and walked down the steps to the lift.

36

Thursday, 30 August

He was awake, the last tendrils of sleep still curling around him as he felt the comfort of the pillow against his face. Sighing softly, Harland lay for a moment, eyes closed, enjoying that blissful uncertainty on the edge of wakefulness, relaxing as though about to drift back into nothing.

Somehow, this was different. Through his eyelids, he became vaguely aware of something that bothered him. It seemed bright, much brighter than usual . . .

His eyes flickered open, and just as suddenly snapped shut, his mind recoiling from the sunlight that glared in at him. Mind rushing, he fumbled blindly for his watch, then screwed up his eyes as he tried to make out the figures.

Ten past eight! Shit!

He had slept in, badly! Jerking up into a sitting position, he swung his legs over the edge of the sofa bed, his heels thudding down onto the carpet. Bracing himself, standing up, swaying unsteadily. How could he have slept so late? Everything was wrong . . .

And then he remembered, understood, and crumpled down to sit, hunched over, his eyes closed against the morning light as he waited for his pulse to slow down again.

There would be no work for him this morning. Blake's suggestion that he take some time off had been non-negotiable, and with nothing to get out of bed for in the past few days, he'd found himself staying up later and later into the night, hiding from the painful descent into sleep. It was those transitions that he feared the most, when he felt most vulnerable: that point in the darkness when he had to surrender all distraction and wait for oblivion to find him, and the other evil moment, when the peace of sleep was torn away and bad memories were rubbed in the wound.

Swearing softly, he cupped his face in his hands for a moment, then slowly sat up straight. He daren't lie down again now. Eyes red, he shakily got to his feet and stumbled through to the kitchen in search of coffee. Pausing at the doorway, listening to the overpowering silence of the house, he knew that he had to get out today – no more excuses.

He drove without purpose, just letting the flow of traffic take him where it would. Passing through Bedminster, he gazed out at the colourless buildings, everything dull despite the sunlight. People with bleak expressions stared at him from the pavements, and nobody cared.

He hadn't been suspended – not yet anyway – but things were going badly. The Superintendent had wanted him to deliver a quick win, but the Severn Beach case had unravelled into a serial murder investigation that would taint everyone associated with it. And then, on top of it all, there was his encounter with Pope. It was difficult to say just how bad things were, but they would certainly get worse. Blake disliked a fuss, so he wouldn't be obvious or hasty. But he would remember, and sooner or later he would respond with vengeful subtlety. And when it came, Harland would know that he had brought it all on himself.

Pope. If only he hadn't lost it with fucking Pope.

He sighed.

The city slid away behind him but the road stretched on, winding between the reservoirs and out into the undulating countryside beyond. The white sun glared off the tarmac as he coasted up another hill, the gentle rise and fall of the road strangely hypnotic.

He found himself skirting the edge of Bristol Airport, the endless perimeter fence following the road as it swept round in a long arc. A plane passed low overhead, very close against the bright blue sky, seeming to move slowly despite the roar of its engines. He leaned forward, staring up at it through the windscreen, wishing that he could be up there, flying somewhere far away . . . anywhere but here.

And then, suddenly, he knew where he was going.

As he followed the road down through Redhill, he could feel the cold knot in his stomach, that sense of grim inevitability chilling him despite the warmth of the sunlight through the windows. It had looked very different, that night all those months ago. He hadn't passed this way since.

The houses gave way to open countryside as the road levelled out and he drove on, forcing himself to concentrate on the landmarks – the hotel, the bend at the bottom of the hill, the little bridge, the lone dead tree – familiar images that he'd buried deep but could never forget. It wasn't far now, along here somewhere . . . The road was climbing again, cutting across the fields towards the crest of a long hill. There was a little lane on the right . . .

. . . and then the blind summit, where the road swept round to the right, with a junction on the left. This was the place, the turning signposted to Burrington. The very name chilled him, though he'd never been there, had no idea what it was like.

He pulled off the main road and drove a short distance

down the lane, slowing to a stop beside a narrow grass verge. What the hell was he doing here? He sat for a moment, rocking gently back and forth in his seat, wrestling with the urge to drive away, but he knew that he couldn't. Taking a deep breath, he switched off the engine and felt the dreadful silence flood in around him. A reluctant figure, he got out of the car and began to walk slowly back towards the junction.

It had been very different that night. The cold glow of blue lights, normally so familiar to him as a police officer, suddenly took on an ominous aspect. Was that how they looked to normal people?

He wasn't sure where he'd parked – probably up on the main road somewhere – and he hadn't been walking, he'd been running.

But he'd been too late.

Another officer had seen him running through the glare of the headlights, had rushed forward to intercept him, strong arms folding round him in a dreadful embrace from which he couldn't break free. Together with a paramedic, they'd managed to keep him back from the tangle of metal, illuminated under the harsh glare of the fire-engine lights. Their restraint had eased when he'd identified himself as a fellow police officer, then tightened as he told them why he was here. He couldn't make out the words they said to him then – too many voices speaking at the same time – but he remembered their faces, the first time he saw that painful sympathy that would become so familiar in the days to follow.

He struggled, but there were too many of them, and he was suddenly so very tired.

'That's my wife's car,' he'd howled, arms outstretched as they pulled him backwards into the gloom. 'Alice!'

37

Naysmith woke and slowly opened his eyes. The sheets felt stiff as he turned over and focused on the bright blue digits of the hotel alarm clock glowing in the darkness beside him: 6.07 a.m. He let his head sink back into the pillow, but he knew that he wouldn't be able to sleep again now. Rolling onto his back, he yawned and gazed up at the ceiling. What had woken him so early?

The bed wasn't particularly comfortable, but he savoured the warmth for a moment more before propping himself up and slipping a foot out from under the covers. Hotel carpets all felt the same. He yawned again as he sat on the edge of the mattress and wearily stood up, shivering a little as the cool air touched his naked skin. Wandering over to the window, he pulled the heavy curtains aside and reached out to put his hand on the cold glass. The foredawn sky was still quite dark, tinged with a faint glow on the horizon. Before him, the long, thin basin of Heron Quays stretched away towards the distant Millennium Dome and its illuminated pylons. To his left, the towering skyscrapers of Canary Wharf stood like a line of sheer glass cliffs, looming high above him, the reflection of their lights glittering in the water below. An expanse of buildings divided by narrow waterways, like some futuristic Venetian landscape overtaken by steel and mirrored windows. It was strangely beautiful and he stood for some time, watching the still-quiet city as it slowly began to stir and the glow on the horizon grew almost imperceptibly brighter.

The lobby was still quiet when he came downstairs, and the vacant-eyed staff didn't acknowledge his presence. He'd tasted the hotel coffee last night and wasn't about to repeat the mistake, but he remembered there was a Starbucks in the mall under Canary Wharf – it wasn't too far and the walk would clear his head. As he went down the broad carpeted steps and out onto the street, the air felt cold, but a few minutes later he was warming up as he turned off the road and took a short cut through a private car park. A train rumbled slowly overhead as he passed under the elevated track and on to the footpath that ran along the edge of the water. It was peaceful here, with nobody around save for a lone fisherman perched on one of the old steel moorings beside a 'Fishing Prohibited' sign. Naysmith smiled, but his eyes were drawn by habit to the CCTV camera overlooking the path. It was the third one he'd seen since leaving the hotel. That familiar restlessness was growing inside him once again, but he didn't want to think about it yet.

Not now, not so soon.

His shoes echoed with a soft metallic ring as he made his way over the suspended steel footbridge that arced across to the far side of the quay, where the first commuters were making their way to work, dwarfed by the towering office blocks. Little people, inconsequential people, hurrying along unaware of who was walking beside them. He smiled for a moment, despite himself, then shook his head.

Coffee. He was just going for some coffee.

Walking into Canada Square, he gazed up at the skyscraper

before him, its pinnacle nearly scratching the cloud cover, red lights on each corner blinking against the dull grey sky. A steady stream of people poured out of the tube station entrance on his right – so many tailored suits and big watches, so much macho posturing . . . and yet he could almost smell the fear on some of them. This was no place for the weak.

There was already a queue in Starbucks when he arrived. Waiting in line behind a middle-aged woman with a sour face and an expensive coat he gazed out at the concourse, watching people pass by. So many powerless lives, drifting blindly until chance brought them into his path. It could be any one of them . . .

'Let me have a large hazelnut latte.' The woman in front of him had a scornful tone, and lacked the courtesy to say 'please'. He stared at the back of her head, at her dry, bleached hair, with slight regret. It was tempting, but he knew he couldn't choose his targets – to do so would be to break the rules of the game.

When it was his turn, he thanked the attractive Asian girl who served him and was rewarded with a friendly smile. Taking his drink, he made his way through into the brightly lit mall and wandered along between the still-closed shops.

Sometimes he resented the thoughts that rose, unbidden, in his mind. So compelling, so dominant that they drove out everything else. Sometimes he almost wished things had been different, all those long years ago, and that his life might have followed a less turbulent path, an easier path. So many victims, their lives suddenly able to play out, uninterrupted. Altered fates and different histories, all because of him. And he might have been one of them, one of the little people, free to drift through their insignificant little lives.

But that wouldn't have been *his* life. He wouldn't be the

person he was now, without those experiences. This life, this extraordinary existence, was his and he could not – *would* not – hide from it.

He took the escalator up to the DLR station platform, emerging into thin daylight under the high glass-canopied roof. The conference he was attending ran for the whole week at the ExCeL Centre, but there were no direct trains from here – he would have to change at Poplar.

As he stood there, gazing out along the tracks, he could feel the anticipation growing, but he pushed the thought away once more.

Not yet . . .

He watched the train as it crept into the station, got on board and found a seat by the window, then stared out through his own reflection as they emerged from the forest of skyscrapers to trundle out above the water and building sites beyond. Canary Wharf was surrounded by an expanding swathe of redevelopment, like a smouldering fire slowly consuming everything around it.

And as he gazed across the changing cityscape, the idea began to take shape. A new challenge, something to make his week in London more meaningful, more exciting.

This time, he wouldn't find the target – he would let the target find *him*. He wasn't exactly in a rush, and there was plenty of time before his first appointment at the conference. Yes, this could work very well. The next station was Poplar, where he had to change trains anyway. He would get off there and wait on the station platform. The first person to make eye contact would be the one. It would be perfectly random, and acquiring a target there could lead to an extremely intriguing game.

The train bumped slowly round a turn in the elevated track before sweeping down into the little station. As it slowed,

Naysmith got calmly to his feet and moved towards the doors. He stepped out of the carriage into the cool morning air of the exposed platform, allowing his gaze to be drawn up to the impressive view of Canary Wharf in front of him. Tiny aircraft warning lights blinked on the tops of the buildings, and a ribbon of steam trailed out from the pinnacle of the tallest tower, fading gently into the overcast sky.

Behind him the carriage doors hissed shut, and the train slipped away with a resonant electric hum.

Slowly, he lowered his eyes from the office blocks and turned his head to look along the platform. Several people stood waiting under the long glass roof, morning commuters staring into space while they waited for their trains. One or two had got off here as he had – a red-headed woman in her twenties with a short denim jacket and a leopard-print bag, a black businessman in a nicely cut suit listening to his iPod – others were coming down the steps from the footbridge at the other end of the station.

An older man was walking towards him – a security guard by the look of him, with the standard-issue shirt and tie, a badge stitched onto his jacket and a battered rucksack slung over one shoulder. Would he be the one?

Naysmith watched him intently as he approached but the man passed behind him without ever looking up.

A girl with a tight woollen jumper and skinny jeans made her way hesitantly down the steps, paused to study a poster on the inside of the shelter, then meandered on along the platform. She carried a heavy bag and slowed as she approached – just a few yards between them now. Her long dark hair was gathered up in a large clip, and she wore a lot of costume jewellery. If she would just look up . . .

. . . but she didn't.

He waited there as another train arrived, passengers got

on, new arrivals got off. His searching eyes moved from face to face, but nobody looked up, nobody met his gaze. Taking a sip from his half-empty coffee cup, he found that it was getting cold.

Another train, another set of people, but still nothing.

He frowned as he stood there, rocking from one foot to the other, jamming his hands down into his pockets as a chill breeze gusted along the exposed platform. This was East London. People didn't make eye contact lightly around here.

He sighed and looked out along the tracks at the distant grey cityscape and the thin morning sun, ghostly behind the clouds. Perhaps this wasn't going to work out as well as he'd thought. The lights of another city-bound train approached and he turned expectantly, but it swayed and rattled across the points to slide in along the opposite platform. He bowed his head in frustration. How long was he going to have to wait on this miserable strip of concrete?

The passengers were disembarking, but they were stepping out through the doors on the far side of the train. He sighed.

And then, just as he began to think that this whole thing might have been a bad idea, his gaze flitted across one of the carriage windows.

A man was looking at him. From a seat inside the waiting train, a clean-shaven man in his early thirties stared out at him with an expression of boredom. Naysmith peered at him intently. He was slight, with a weak chin and a complexion that looked pasty under the artificial lights of the train. Lank, sandy hair was swept back across his scalp, and his eyes were small and dark. He wore a blue anorak over his shirt and tie, and sat with a brown leather case clutched to his chest. After a moment, the man seemed to become self-conscious and looked away, but the contact had been made.

He would be the one.

There was a change to the noise of the motor, and the pitch of the hum rose as the train began to move. Naysmith felt a strange exhilaration as the man looked up and stared at him again, their eyes locked until the train disappeared under the footbridge and out of the station. Would the man remember him if they saw each other again? He'd certainly been aware that he was being studied . . .

. . . which meant this hunt would have to be undertaken with considerably more care than usual. Good!

Naysmith glanced up at the time on the electronic information board above him: 8.27 a.m. A twenty-four-hour head start, and a week-long conference before he had to go back home to Wiltshire. In every sense, the clock was ticking.

38

'Can I get you anything else?' The waitress was a tall woman with long blonde hair that shimmered as she moved. She wore a high-collared white shirt and a satin waistcoat with black trousers.

Naysmith looked up at her.

'Just the bill, please.'

He watched her as she walked away across the polished wooden floor, admiring the lithe tone of her body that her outfit was unable to conceal, then turned back to the balding man who sat opposite him.

'You would, though, wouldn't you?' said the man, in a light Welsh accent. He adjusted his steel-rimmed glasses and inclined his head towards the receding waitress with an eager grin.

Naysmith smiled. 'Somehow I don't think you're her type, Ken.'

It had been ages since he'd seen Ken. Slightly thinner on top, slightly heavier around the middle, but still good company. They'd worked together for three years at TTC – just long enough to secure their stock options and get out. Naysmith had moved to Winterhill and Ken, after some enforced gardening leave, had joined one of TTC's largest competitors. Today, they'd met by chance at the conference and spent an enjoyable evening talking shop, and running up a tab on Ken's corporate credit card.

'Anyway,' Naysmith continued, 'you're a married man.'

'Not *that* married,' Ken murmured, still gazing after the waitress. 'Nobody's *that* married.'

They laughed, and Ken poured out the last of the wine, then leaned across to hand a glass to Naysmith.

'And what about you, Rob?' he asked. 'Still happily unencumbered?'

'I'm sort of living with someone now.'

'Really?' Ken raised an eyebrow. 'Who'd put up with a rascal like you?'

'I don't know if you ever met her. Her name's Kim.'

'Not that little dark-haired one you brought along to the last Christmas party at TTC?'

'Yes, that's her.'

'Bloody hell,' Ken said slowly, leaning back in his chair. 'You've fallen on your feet there, boy.'

'Yes,' Naysmith nodded thoughtfully. 'I suppose I have.'

The waitress reappeared and placed a small leather bill folder on the table.

'My treat,' Ken beamed, sweeping up the folder and handing it with his card to the waitress.

'If you insist,' Naysmith shrugged, putting his wallet away. 'I'll get the next one.'

Ken nodded as he took the credit-card machine, squinted at it through his glasses, then entered his details.

'You're still down in Hampshire or wherever it was?'

'Wiltshire. A couple of miles from Salisbury.'

'That's right, I remember now. Charming place, Salisbury. Stonehenge, druids, that sort of thing . . .'

He handed the machine back to the waitress and grinned at her.

'Thank you,' she said with a slight nod, then handed him his card and receipt. 'Have a good evening, gentlemen.'

Ken folded the receipt as he watched her walk away.

'Did you see that?' he sighed. 'A twenty-quid tip and not so much as a smile from her.'

'You've still got it,' Naysmith laughed, getting to his feet.

'I should've let you pay,' Ken muttered.

A squall of wind caught them as they walked down the steps from the restaurant, but an evening of drinking had numbed them to the chill night air.

'Where are you staying?' Naysmith asked as he raised his hand to hail a taxi.

'Nice little boutique place on Threadneedle Street, just round the corner from the Gherkin.'

'Any good?'

'A bit quiet,' Ken shrugged. 'First-class breakfast, mind you.'

Across the street, a black cab with its light on had slowed. As a gap in the traffic opened, it executed a tight U-turn and pulled in at the kerb beside them. Naysmith reached out and held the door open.

'Come on,' he said, 'I can drop you on my way – I'm out by Canary Wharf.'

They told the cabbie where they were going, then settled back into the broad rear seat and gazed out at the bright shopfronts as the taxi set off. Crackling snatches of conversation and static drifted through the hatch from the driver's radio.

'So are you happy at Winterhill?' It was an abrupt question, but Ken had always been the master of the surprise attack.

'Yes.' Naysmith shot him a quizzical look. 'Why do you ask?'

'Don't get me wrong, but it doesn't sound like it's stretching you,' the Welshman explained. 'You were always one for a challenge, that's all.'

'There're plenty of challenges . . . if you know where to look.'

Ken nodded, studying him.

'So you're enjoying it there?'

Naysmith thought for a moment.

'It gives me freedom, and that suits me just now.' He relaxed into his seat, tilting his head back, then grinned over at his former colleague. 'Why, are you going to make me an offer I can't refuse?'

'Well, what could be better than working with me?' Ken winked at him. 'Just like old times, eh? Dream ticket and all that . . .'

Naysmith laughed.

'I'm flattered,' he said, 'but I'm not sure this is the right time for me to move. Ask me again in a few months.'

'The offer might not be there.' Ken shook his head in mock seriousness. 'Hell hath no fury, and so forth . . .'

They drove on into the financial district, where the cars were less frequent but more expensive. A white Ferrari pulled up beside them at a junction, then sped away with a roar when the lights turned green.

'Tell me that wasn't what tonight was all about . . .' Naysmith left the question hanging.

'Not at all, not at all.' Ken smiled, then leaned over conspiratorially, making the vinyl seat cover creak. 'I was really hoping to get some decent client leads off you, but you've been a cagey so-and-so even after three bottles of vino collapso.'

They laughed as the taxi pulled up outside the small hotel.

'You never change, Ken.'

'Neither do you.' Hunching over, he struggled out onto

the pavement, then straightened up and adjusted his spectacles with a grin. 'You *need* a challenge, you do.'

Naysmith smiled back.

'I'll try and keep busy,' he said, softly.

The city slid by, bathed in the lonely orange glow of street lights and illuminated signs. Knots of people drifted like eddies in the current, silhouettes against the glaring shop windows as the taxi paused then sped on again.

Naysmith held up his watch so that it was lit by the headlights of the car behind them: 11.07 p.m. Just over nine hours until he could begin what promised to be an interesting game. The conference meant he'd be in London until the end of the week and he wondered how far he might progress things in that time . . . Crucially, would he be able to find his target again by Friday?

The taxi rattled along a sweeping curve, then finally slowed as it turned in to stop just outside his hotel, the engine idling.

'Here you are,' the cabbie called over his shoulder, stopping the meter. Naysmith sat forward in his seat and was just reaching for his wallet when he felt the vibration of his phone in his jacket pocket. Frowning, he took it out, saw Kim's name on the screen and busied the call. He always felt it rude to answer the phone when you were dealing with someone else.

Once he'd fished out his wallet, he paid the fare, folded the receipt into his pocket and clambered out. The taxi drove noisily away, leaving Naysmith at the foot of the carpeted steps, bathed in light that spilled from the glass doors.

Yawning, he made his way into the foyer, his phone pressed to his ear. Kim sounded odd when she answered.

'Hello?'

'Hi. Sorry about that, I was just getting out of a cab.'

There was a pause.

'Where are you now?' she asked, quietly.

'Back at the hotel. Just heading up to the room now,' he replied.

What was the matter with her? Was she tired? It wasn't really that late.

'Okay.'

Another pause.

'Are you alone?' she asked.

Naysmith stopped at the foot of the stairs and leaned back wearily against the wall. Demons of suspicion took his place when he left her by herself.

'Of course I'm alone,' he sighed. 'And what's that supposed to mean anyway?'

'Nothing.'

'Don't start this, Kim,' he warned her. 'I've been at the conference all bloody day and catching up with Ken from TTC this evening. Just him and me, in a restaurant, talking about work. Okay?'

'Okay.'

She sounded as though she was beginning to believe him. And this time, it was actually the truth, for heaven's sake.

'And I busied the phone because I was paying the taxi driver. Really, you're being paranoid.'

She began babbling out an awkward apology. Once they started apologising, you knew that going on the offensive had worked, that you had them where you wanted them.

'It's okay,' he hushed her. This was really the time to press his advantage, to make her feel so foolish that she wouldn't dare question him again. And yet he found that he didn't want to do that. Not to her. He imagined her huddled in the corner of the living-room sofa, her feet tucked under her as she cradled the phone, strands of hair falling across her anxious face. No, not to her.

Changing the subject now would let her off the hook completely.

'Anyway,' he said, 'while we were out Ken offered me a job.'

'Really?'

'Really. We worked well together before, so it makes sense for him.'

'What did you say to him?'

'I told him I'd think about it,' he lied, patiently.

'Oh Rob,' she said softly. 'I'm sorry about everything. Sometimes I just get worried about things, you know?'

'All you have to do is trust me,' he told her. 'Everything else will work itself out.'

★   ★   ★

There was a steady drizzle the next morning. Naysmith sat on a cold metal bench and gazed along the station platform, his mood as bleak as the grey sky overhead. It had seemed quite simple in theory, but the reality was different – it was almost impossible to spot someone if you didn't know which train they were going to be on.

He'd only been at Poplar for twenty minutes or so, but already it was enough to convince him that he wouldn't find the sandy-haired man today. Naturally, he'd not started looking until 8.27 a.m. – the twenty-four-hour grace period was sacrosanct – and if the target had travelled by an earlier train they would have missed each other.

Nevertheless, it seemed unlikely that he'd locate him this way. The DLR trains were short and reasonably well lit, but it was still difficult to see exactly who was inside each carriage.

He'd tried standing towards the end of the platform, so that the length of the train had to move past him as it entered the station, but it was no good. The windows whipped by too quickly, people were moving around inside and, worst of all, he could only really see the passengers sitting on his side of the train. It simply wouldn't work.

He sat back and rubbed the sleep from his eyes – too much wine with Ken last night. Stifling a yawn, he stretched and gazed out at the overcast city. If he was going to find the target, his best chance would be to spot him while he was on a platform, either before he got on his train, or after he got off.

He stood up and wandered over to study a large route map on the wall behind the seats. His finger traced along the blue-green DLR line until he found Poplar, where they'd first made eye contact. The train had been heading into the city, so the target would have got on somewhere before that. But where? There were two different routes leading in from East London, and an awful lot of stations to cover . . .

Frowning, he looked across to see where the train went *after* Poplar. There were just five possible stations, and two of them were main terminus points – significantly better odds.

There was really nothing more he could do until tomorrow morning – he might as well head over to the conference and get some breakfast. Yawning, he turned and made his way across to the opposite platform to await his train.

39

Naysmith paid the taxi fare and added a good tip – the driver hadn't attempted to make conversation on their thirty-minute journey and that was always a relief. Standing there on the pavement, surrounded by the steady roar of early evening traffic, he turned to gaze up at the imposing building behind him – four storeys of pale Georgian permanence, right on Hyde Park Corner.

It was an expensive place, and if his clients were staying here then they certainly had money. Considering this, he allowed himself a slight smile and made his way towards the entrance portico.

A sombre-faced doorman in a grey coat and bowler hat moved smoothly to intercept him, quietly opening the tall wooden door before him.

'Thank you,' Naysmith nodded as he strode up the stone steps and passed into the small entrance lobby.

Behind him, the rumble of the city was gently snuffed out as the great door slid shut, and the only sounds that remained were his footsteps on the polished marble floor. The space smelled of old wood and furniture wax, and it was accented with some lovely nineteenth-century pieces. Ornate lamp fittings hung by long chains from the tall ceiling, occasional tables carried vases filled with beautiful sprays of flowers, and carved mahogany chairs sat in every corner. He walked through to the long reception desk where an immaculately dressed man acknowledged him with a deferential nod.

'Good evening, sir. May I help you?' he enquired.

'My name's Robert Naysmith. I'm meeting one of your guests – a Mr Vernon Kapphan – but I'm a little early.'

The receptionist glanced down at his screen for a moment, then smiled politely.

'Very good, Mr Naysmith. Perhaps you'd care to wait in the room across the corridor and I'll let Mr Kapphan know you're here.'

'Thanks.'

He walked through the doorway the man had indicated and stepped into a long, bright room decorated in Regency style. Crimson and gold drapes framed the windows, matching the velvet upholstery on the low sofas, and small pedestal tables gleamed with polish. He selected a beautiful wood-framed chair that had its back to the doorway, but which commanded a good view of the foyer in the reflection of a glass-fronted cabinet.

There was a heavy stillness in the room that seemed to swell and grow as he waited. Through the window, he could see the tops of trucks and red buses as the incessant traffic slid by outside, but no sound reached him here behind the thick cream walls and spotless glazing. The oppressive silence was briefly disturbed by muted voices drifting through from reception before it returned to smother the room.

He checked his watch again, his face registering a slight flicker of annoyance as he noticed that he was no longer early – *they* were now late. Leaning back into the chair, he wondered how long they would be. Wealthy clients were often late, but in a way that was understandable. Time-wasters might be apologetically punctual but people who were serious – people who actually had the money to place an order – they naturally thought of themselves as customers, and felt no need to rush around after a salesman.

In any case, there were worse places to pass the time, and it was certainly better than being at that bloody conference. He'd endured another tiresome afternoon, sitting there listening to lectures given by people with limited public-speaking skills, and a particularly awful keynote speech from an enthusiastic halfwit who would probably be out of business within a year.

Naysmith sighed and leaned back, stretching out his legs and feeling the deep carpet springing against his heels. It had been another long day, another early start. Once again, he found his thoughts drawn to that sandy-haired man looking back at him from the train – an ordinary person with an ordinary life, unaware that he might be staring death in the face. Had he felt anything as he made eye contact? Did he sense that something profound had happened, even though he couldn't know what it was? Naysmith hoped so. A moment like that must surely resonate in even the most mundane of people. He wondered where the man worked, where he lived . . . and where he might die.

Of course, he had to find him first. It had dawned on him that the man's journey might well take him further into London than the DLR ran, that he might need to change trains. This greatly increased the odds that he would find the target at one of the two main terminal stations where the DLR connected with the Underground. He'd felt a real buzz of anticipation as he lay in wait at Tower Gateway, the ambush predator standing at the foot of the escalator, watching as passengers streamed out onto the pavement, but it had been a washout. The man had not appeared. Tomorrow morning he would try Bank station instead . . .

His eyes flickered across to the two figures that had appeared, reflected on the glass in front of him. Smiling quietly to himself, he leaned forward and got to his feet without looking round.

'Gentlemen,' he said, finally turning to face them and extending his hand. 'It's good of you to see me . . .'

40

Mercifully, the waiting room was empty again. He'd sat there
before, angry and self-conscious, while a middle-aged woman
had sat opposite him. He'd felt her eyes on him as he'd leafed
through an ancient magazine, staring at him, judging him.
Just sitting here meant you were tainted, damaged.

But today, there were no covert glances, no quiet coughs
to disturb the breathless silence. Harland leaned forward,
sifting through the magazines as noisily as possible, suddenly
eager to dispel the dreadful stillness.

When Jean appeared in the doorway, beckoning him through,
it was almost a relief. She was wearing jeans and boots, with
the snug-fitting sweater he always seemed to picture her in
when he thought of her. It highlighted her figure in a way that
distracted him, and he forced himself to think of other things
as he followed her into the small room and sat down.

Jean put her notebook on the table, then opened her spec-
tacle case and pulled out a different pair of glasses to the ones
she usually wore. Harland watched her put them on.

'They're new, aren't they?' he asked.

'What?' She glanced up at him.

'Your glasses,' he explained. 'They suit you.'

Her expression softened and she smiled with a warmth
he'd not seen from her before.

'Thank you,' she said as she retrieved her notebook. She read for a moment, then looked up at him. 'So, how have you been?'

He returned her gaze and sighed before answering.

'I'm still on leave,' he said, half shaking his head. 'A break from work, whether I want it or not.'

'Okay.' Jean paused for a moment, then asked, 'And do you want it? A break from work?'

'No.' He found that he had answered her too quickly, too urgently. She nodded and wrote something down.

'Why do you think that is, Graham?' she said, sitting back in her chair and looking at him.

'I'm not sure.'

'Is there something that you're missing at work perhaps? Or are you just not in the mood for time off just now?'

Harland leaned forward in his chair, elbows on his knees, gazing at the carpet.

'A bit of both,' he shrugged. 'I certainly don't like to walk out on a case halfway through. Something might come up that I need to take care of.'

'Can't one of your colleagues deal with things while you're away?'

'That all depends on which colleague it is,' he said grimly. 'But yes, I suppose so.'

Jean looked at him for a long moment.

'And do you feel as though you're walking out on something when you take time off?' she asked.

He struggled with this for a moment, then sighed again.

'Not really,' he said eventually. 'It's just that I want to see things through . . .'

'I know you do, Graham,' she said gently.

They sat for a moment, the room quiet except for the sound of the pen scribbling in her notebook. He picked at the neutral blue fabric on the seat of his chair, then looked up to find Jean staring at him.

'You said that you might not be in the mood just now,' she said. 'Do you usually enjoy your time off or are you maybe happier when you're at work?'

Harland frowned.

'Happier at *work*?'

He dealt with murder and other violent crimes. Misery and loss. That wasn't something that should make anyone happy. And yet part of him was desperate to be back on duty.

Jean leaned forward a little.

'Some people find the regular routine helps them to structure their lives,' she said. 'It's not uncommon.'

No. That wasn't him. Or at least, it didn't used to be . . .

'I think maybe I just like to keep myself busy.'

He used to say that he didn't have enough time to get everything done. Now, he didn't have enough to fill his time.

Jean nodded thoughtfully.

'Perhaps you could tell me what you usually do when you're not working. How do you spend your regular days off?'

Harland considered this.

'Depends what the rotas are like, but usually I catch up with chores, try and keep the house tidy, that sort of thing.'

He paused, aware that it wasn't much of an answer, that there must be more.

'I also read a lot. Sometimes I go for a walk . . .' *Damn it, what did he do?* 'Oh, and there's the swimming of course.'

Jean noted something, then smiled encouragingly at him.

'And what about this week?' she asked. 'What have you been doing with your time while you're on leave?'

He sat back, trying to think, but only one thing came to his mind. There seemed no point in trying to hide it.

'I drove out to the place near Redhill,' he said slowly.

She waited, sensing how hard he suddenly found it to speak.

'Oh, I see. Is that where . . .' her eyes flickered down to her notebook '. . . Alice had the accident?'

You had to check her name there, didn't you?

A shiver of anger brushed over him, but it somehow lightened the burden, made it easier for him to talk.

'Yes.' He sat up, forced himself to breathe. 'I drove out there a few days ago.'

Jean waited.

'It was strange,' Harland mused, half to himself. 'I wasn't planning to go there. I was just driving around and I somehow ended up on that road. I haven't been there since . . .'

Jean nodded.

'How did you feel going back there?'

'Empty,' he shrugged. 'At first there was a sort of dread – so many memories stirred up there – but after a while I just felt numb. Empty.'

'That must have been difficult for you.'

Harland looked up at her.

'I thought it would be,' he nodded, 'but I didn't really feel it properly until afterwards.'

'Afterwards?'

'When I got home.'

'Well, as you said, an experience like that can stir up a lot of memories. Coming to terms with bereavement takes time . . .'

She made it sound like a legal disagreement, something to be negotiated with, settled with. As if he could ever *come to terms* with it. As if he could ever change the way he felt about Alice. He shook his head.

'. . . she was your wife and—'

'Alice *is* my wife,' Harland spoke abruptly. And in that instant the room seemed different, suddenly less intimidating to him. 'You weren't even sure of her name a moment ago. Why am I listening to you on a subject you don't really understand?'

His voice was raised now, and he could sense her drawing back from him, concern in her eyes. Why did people always look so worried when he got upset recently? What did they see in his face that hadn't been there before?

She began to speak, but he held up a hand for her to wait, turning his head away from her as he spoke, hiding whatever it was that lay behind his eyes.

'Please,' he scowled, his voice careful now, 'I don't mean any offence, but you don't understand. You *can't* understand.'

They sat there in silence for a long time, until he slowly lowered his hand. Jean waited for a moment, then spoke in a soothing voice.

'I understand that it isn't easy to rebuild your life when someone important is taken from you.'

Harland laughed, a desperate, almost sobbing sound.

'How can I rebuild my life?' he snapped. 'She *was* my life. I don't want to move on, I don't want to get over her . . . I want her back. I want all of this to just *stop*, and I want things to go back to the way they were before . . .'

He looked at her, her expression still guarded, but tinged with a curious sympathy.

'Don't worry,' he sighed, getting to his feet. 'I'm not losing it. I know that I can't go back. But I also know that everything *isn't* going to be all right.'

'Graham,' she began, but he just smiled sadly and shook his head.

'I think our time's up for now,' he said, opening the door. 'Thanks for everything, Jean.'

41

Thursday, 6 September

Naysmith bowed his head as the train swept down into the tunnel and the grey morning light of East London was extinguished. Swaying in his seat as the carriage rattled from side to side, he closed his eyes, quietly preparing himself for another rush-hour vigil, recalling the face of his target and fixing it in his mind.

Early thirties, clean-shaven, with sandy hair and a pale complexion. Slight build, weak chin and small, dark eyes. Impossible to be sure of his height – the man had been seated when he'd seen him – but the blue anorak and brown leather case might be worth watching out for.

He opened his eyes and looked around, calmly taking in the dull expressions on the faces of his fellow passengers, already drained from the morning commute before they'd even made it to work. Scrubbed skin, combed hair and newly ironed clothes, but all withdrawn, dead eyes staring away into nothingness. Adopting that same tired expression, Naysmith sat back in his seat. Everything now depended on his ability to blend in, to avoid attention. An underground station wasn't somewhere he could stay for long without arousing suspicion. He'd mentally allowed himself thirty minutes, but that would be a very long time to stand there in the glare of so many CCTV cameras.

This train was some fifteen minutes ahead of the one he'd seen his target on at Poplar. As it slowed, and the darkness of the tunnel was replaced by the bright walls of the DLR station sliding into view, he got to his feet, ready to disembark with the other passengers. His face was bored, expressionless, but as the doors opened and he stepped out onto the platform, his eyes swept back along the other carriages, flickering from face to face. A long line of glaring strip lights hung from the curved white ceiling, illuminating the head of each person who got off. There was no sign of that short, sandy hair he was looking for, but he *was* early . . .

As the passengers made their way towards the exit, he allowed himself to drift along with them, slowing as they mingled with other groups of commuters who were making for the train. He paused for a moment, making a pretence of checking his phone, then started walking again. Except now he was walking back *towards* the platform, just another ordinary person on his way to work. He had already identified the best places to stand, not far from the platform exit, where the target would have to pass by as he made his way out.

The clock was ticking – twenty-three minutes left. Leaning against the glossy white wall, Naysmith unfolded his newspaper and gazed idly at the back page, noting a couple of London Transport staff in their orange vests standing at the far end of the platform. He had already decided that he was waiting for a colleague, if anyone should ask. It was important to get your story straight in advance – any hesitation could give you away if you were challenged. But having that story in mind – almost believing it – infused your actions with a certain credibility, masking your body language and making you less likely to attract attention. In the wake of the bombings, London stations were watchful places, and he knew he was very exposed here.

There was a change in the air, and a faint vibration before he heard the next train. It emerged from the dark opening at the far end of the platform and swept into the station, its motor dropping in pitch as it slowed and stopped. The doors slid open and Naysmith looked up from his newspaper

He caught a few tantalising glimpses of people with the right hair colour, tracking each one as they approached him.

Too heavy . . . female . . . hair too long . . . one with a beard . . . damn, he wasn't on this train . . .

As the last of the passengers made their way towards the exit, Naysmith slipped in among them for a short distance, then casually steered himself back to a slightly different point on the platform. As long as he was moving with the crowd, he was virtually invisible – the less time he stood still the better. And changing position would avoid the obvious giveaway of a loitering figure occupying the same spot on a CCTV screen . . .

He turned to study the London Transport map on the wall beside him, willing the next train to arrive. This one should be the one he'd seen his target on at the start of the week, but was he such a creature of habit that he caught the same time train every day? When they'd made eye contact, the man could have been running late, or going to work earlier than usual. Perhaps his trip wasn't a regular journey at all – just a one-off visit to a client in another part of the city . . .

He felt the muscles in his jaw tighten, grinding his teeth together.

Would this target elude him as well? Would it be two failures in a row?

No!

Angry at himself, he shoved those thoughts out of his mind. This was no time for pessimism.

The thirty minutes were almost up when he spotted him. A fleeting glimpse, between the other figures milling around the carriage doors, but Naysmith was immediately alert. A heartbeat later, he recognised the pale skin and dark eyes as the sandy-haired man walked towards the exit, wearing that same blue anorak.

He felt a surge of excitement, that dreadful thrill coursing through his veins like a stimulant, quickening his pulse and urging his chest to breathe faster. The sudden, howling lust for that ultimate power of life and death was almost insatiable, but he fought it down, got himself under control. He had to stay focused.

As the target passed, Naysmith calmly folded his newspaper and melted into the crowd behind him. They shuffled through the exit and turned right into a long, brightly lit corridor signposted to the Central Line. Was he changing trains?

An escalator rose at the far end of the corridor, creating a bottleneck for the crowd of commuters as they funnelled onto it. Naysmith pushed through the throng, judging his pace carefully and stepping onto the escalator just three people behind the sandy-haired man.

As they ascended, he gazed around at the faces on the escalators. Solemn pinstriped bankers, eager interns, power-dressed women . . . so many irrelevant people, little more than a fog that obscured him as he tracked his prey. He glanced ahead, noting how the back of that sandy-haired head was moving towards the ticket barriers. Good. The man worked somewhere close by.

Climbing the last few steps into the blinding daylight and

traffic noise, Naysmith paused and looked left and right along the pavement. The target was a short distance ahead of him, walking east alongside the old stone buildings of Threadneedle Street. It was almost nine o'clock – wherever he was heading, it wouldn't be far now.

A double-decker bus crawled along, keeping pace with Naysmith and bathing him in warm fumes. He glanced up at a girl staring vacantly out from her seat inside. He smiled as their eyes met and she grinned back before nudging a friend sitting next to her. *If only she knew.*

Ahead of him, the blue anorak disappeared from view as the target turned down a side street. Naysmith quickened his stride and hurried to the corner, not wanting to lose track of the man. They made their way down a quiet road, then turned right into a narrow cutting, gleaming new tower blocks on one side dropping vast shadows across the grand old office buildings on the other.

The man was only twenty yards in front of him when he veered over towards a modest, stone-arched doorway. Padding lightly up the steps he pushed through the tall glass doors and disappeared inside.

Naysmith glanced up at the building, noting the name of it as he walked past, then strolled on towards the end of the street with a satisfied smile on his face. It had been a most productive morning.

42

Harland trudged across the grass, his hands in his pockets. He moved slowly, like a reluctant child called home at bedtime, head hanging and eyes downcast. The sun was bright just now, bleaching the colour from the morning, but it was still cold. Or was that just him? He wondered about that as he walked up the slope, following the worn path, taking the same route he always did. Perhaps it was all in his head, a natural reaction to a place with such strong emotional associations.

Blooms of dark lichen gnawed at the older headstones and heartbroken angels gazed down on him as he came to the paved track. Even the wind seemed hushed here, sighing softly through the trees. Pressing on into the newer sections of the cemetery, he left the tarmac and walked up the slope, picking his way between the plots, careful not to step on any of the graves. Flowers were more frequent here, and the odd mourner could be seen, kneeling in quiet grief.

Should have brought flowers.

He passed a tragic little plot, lovingly adorned with children's toys and hand-drawn cards sealed in cling film, but even that couldn't move him. Not here, not now, so completely insulated by his own loss.

He hesitated near the top of the slope, then took the last few steps towards a small, simple headstone, the polished marble pale against the grass. He stood for an awkward moment using his sleeve to gently clean the top of the stone before sitting down beside it.

How long was it since he'd come here last? Weeks? Months? His visits had become shorter and less frequent as he'd found less comfort in them. The turf had knitted together now, a soft green covering that marked the passage of time as the world moved on without him. His hand reached out, caressing the grass, just as he used to caress the duvet when she lay beside him, asleep.

The tears came suddenly, and he slumped down, overcome with anguish, weeping uncontrollably. Deeper and deeper he sank until he had nothing left to give, and the darkness passed, leaving him weary, disoriented.

He opened his eyes, taking in his surroundings, feeling the cool blades of grass pressed into his hand, the cold marble against his face.

'I miss you,' he whispered.

He knew she was there, knew she could hear him. The presence was so strong that he was almost overcome. Suddenly aware of his own appearance, he wiped his eyes, struggling to adopt the brave grin that he used to wear when he was trying to reassure her.

But he knew that she could see through him, just as she always had.

He pictured her, standing there beside him, a small hand on his shoulder, her beautiful eyes full of compassionate sadness. Sitting, propped up on the grass, he put his free hand on his shoulder, gently touching where hers would have been.

'I'm sorry, baby . . .' He choked on the words he wanted to say, sitting in trembling silence as he struggled to compose himself.

'I don't mean to be like this, but it hurts. It hurts so much.'

A wry little smile, flashed through the tears, the best he could manage.

'You made quite an impression on me, you know?'

He sat for a while in silence, just as they used to, not needing words, satisfied and complete in each other's company.

Sniffing, he closed his eyes, shutting out the emptiness around him, imagining her kneeling down on the grass beside him.

'I suppose you know I'm not doing that well without you.'

Instinctively, he knew how she would have reacted to that, her perfect little brows furrowing into a frown.

'Okay.' He smiled sadly. 'I know you'll always be with me. Maybe that's what makes it so difficult.'

He slowly opened his eyes and squinted out across the rows of gravestones and the gently rustling trees beyond. Hurting him was the last thing she would have wanted.

'It's impossible, isn't it?' he grinned. 'Can't live with you, can't live without you . . .'

She would have laughed at that, a brave little smile on her worried face as she gazed up at him.

'The worst part is, I actually feel guilty for not thinking about you. I *know* you wouldn't want that, but I'm just being honest. If I'm feeling good about something, laughing, whatever, and then I suddenly remember what happened?' He shook his head. 'Enormous feelings of guilt. Stupid, isn't it?'

He ran his fingers through the grass again.

'But I could never leave you,' he said. 'How can I just abandon you here, in this . . .'

He gestured with his hand, taking in the lines of grey stones that lay all around.

'Maybe that's why I don't visit you here that often, because I keep you with me at home . . .' He bowed his head, hoping it wouldn't sound like an excuse. 'You understand, don't you?'

And she would have understood him, only too well. She was always more practical than him, always had more common sense. He pictured her, regret on her serious little face, moving apart from him and sitting down silently by her own headstone.

She would want him to live. She'd insist on it, but it was asking an awful lot.

'Oh my beautiful girl,' he sighed. 'Why did it have to be you? I wish it had been me . . .'

But he knew how stubborn she could be. Sitting on the grass, feeling the warmth of the sun as it climbed in the sky, he stayed with her until a strange peace came over him. Eventually, he got to his feet and took a few steps forward, looking out across the cemetery. In the distance, the rattle of a passing train rose above the background rumble of the city. He turned his head, speaking over his shoulder.

'I love you, Alice,' he said softly.

I love you.

That familiar smile, those wonderful bright eyes that always seemed to sparkle when she heard those words. She would be here, waiting, whenever he needed her.

Sighing to himself, he trudged down the hill without looking back.

43

Naysmith had left the conference early. The late afternoon seminars were frequently space-fillers and networking opportunities would be limited – he really wasn't missing much. In any case, he'd already had several very productive meetings, so he'd earned a few hours off.

It hadn't taken him long to travel back to Bank and retrace his steps to that narrow cutting between the office buildings. Now he sat in a claustrophobic little pub, looking out through the grubby window onto Throgmorton Street. From here he couldn't quite see the glass doors of the office where the target worked, but it was the best vantage point available – anyone heading towards the station from here would have to pass him.

He checked the time again – it was just after 5 p.m. Hopefully, the sandy-haired man wouldn't be working too late. Fortunately today was Thursday – if it had been Friday there would be more chance of the man going out for a drink, but with luck he'd be heading straight home tonight.

Gently turning a beer mat with his finger, Naysmith wondered where he lived, what his home would be like. He clearly came from somewhere to the east of the city, but what sort of place? Would it be a good neighbourhood or bad? Did he live alone, or was there someone waiting for him? He found himself hoping that there wouldn't be children, but quickly pushed that train of thought away, unwilling to go where it led.

Frowning, he closed his fist around the beer mat, crumpling it into a jagged ball, and went back to his patient study of the street.

The target didn't appear until 6:15 p.m., a slightly weary figure in that same blue anorak, trudging past the window in the direction of the station. Naysmith swallowed the last mouthful of drink that he'd been nursing and slipped out after him. The street was busier now as the offices released their staff into the evening rush hour. It was easy to hide in the swirling flow of commuters, hurrying along the pavements then disappearing down the steps to the underground station, like water down a storm drain.

Naysmith shadowed his target through the crush of the ticket barriers, along the passageways and down to the busy DLR platforms. He stood a few yards away from him, not near enough to be noticed, but close enough to keep him in sight.

When the train arrived, he felt the crowd surge towards the doors. The sandy-haired man was caught up in a tight knot of passengers and swept forward to the edge of the platform. Naysmith kept him in view until he was on board, then shouldered his way through the slow commuters to secure his own place in an adjacent carriage. There was no need to get too close just yet – he knew the target was travelling at least as far as Poplar.

As the doors hissed shut, and the passengers jostled around him to maintain their personal space, he closed his eyes in disgust. Brash fragrances, body odour and bad breath, all sealed in the heat of a busy train. How did these people do it every day? Why would anyone settle for this sort of existence? He sighed. Life was too short for this kind of misery – he knew more than most how quickly it could be snuffed out.

The train rattled through the noise and darkness of the tunnel and out into the evening gloom. Rising steadily, the rails climbed to an elevated track that swept along, carrying them eastwards between the grim-looking neighbourhoods that sprawled out below. Grey tarmac streets and endless parked cars slid by, all bathed in the tainted glow of street lamps and garish shop signs.

Stations came and went – islands of harsh white light in the darkening evening – and gradually the passengers around him began to thin out. He found a seat where he could see the target in the next carriage, head bowed, reading a book.

Outside, the towering heights of Canary Wharf obscured the horizon. There was a lonely beauty about this part of Docklands as the glittering buildings bloomed with lights, and shadows hid the wasteland around them. Naysmith smiled to himself and turned away from the window. They had just passed through Poplar – from here on, he would need to be ready. The train was bound for Woolwich Arsenal, so at least he now knew which line the target travelled on, but that wasn't enough. He had to find out where the man lived.

Outside, everything was growing darker as they sped onwards, leaving the vast glow of Canary Wharf behind. After a while, a faint sense of unease began to gnaw at him. The Dome lay a long way behind them now, and several stations had slipped by – how far out of the city were they going? The train rattled across a junction and sloped off to the right. An unfriendly landscape of high fences and dark industrial buildings finally gave way as the track curved up beside a long expanse of water. Apartments looked out between the old dockyard cranes and there, in the distance, he could make out the ExCeL Centre where the conference was being held.

And now, finally, the man was putting his book away. Naysmith watched until he was sure, then quietly got to his feet and moved to the doors at the opposite end of the carriage as the train began to slow down.

There was a delicious coolness to the air as he stepped out onto the bare concrete platform. After the smothering humidity at the start of his journey, the slight chill was very welcome. They had alighted at West Silverton, an elevated station with two short platforms that hugged the tracks, each side enclosed by a curved metal roof.

Naysmith walked slowly, letting the man get slightly ahead of him as they moved to the exit – only two other passengers had got off here and he didn't want to spook his prey.

As he descended the flights of steps that led down to street level, the train rumbled away somewhere above, the noise fading as it crept off into the darkness. Suddenly, this station seemed a very lonely place, and he felt a shuddering thrill of anticipation. The man had no idea what was behind him, following him out onto the pavement that ran beneath the elevated tracks. His irrelevant life, ebbing away with each step as he led his killer home.

Naysmith measured his pace, but his muscles were taut and eager from the adrenalin. He suppressed an urge to howl with excitement as they crossed the road and headed north into a warren of newly developed apartment blocks. It couldn't be far now.

He slowed down, allowing the distance between them to stretch out a little as the sandy-haired man turned to cut across a grassy open space surrounded by houses. A forlorn figure, brightly lit, then silhouetted, then brightly lit again as he walked between the street lamps that lit the curving path. Naysmith glanced around – a lot of windows overlooked this

little area. When the time came, he would have to find somewhere more secluded than this.

Ahead of him, the target had reached a line of houses.
Naysmith strolled slowly out onto the grass, shunning the
well-lit path. There was no need to rush in – he could see
everything from here.

The man had turned and was walking along the pavement,
bag under one arm, reaching for his keys . . .

Which house would it be?

His eyes followed the target as he slowed and turned onto
a brick-paved driveway. There were lights on in the house
– the man clearly didn't live alone. A moment to fumble with
the lock, then light spilled out across the drive as the door
opened and he disappeared inside.

Naysmith smiled and made his way calmly across the grass
and onto the pavement. He gazed across at the street sign
– Evelyn Road – then strolled slowly past the house, noting
the number, and walking on.

He had everything he needed.

44

Harland opened the cupboard and pulled out a handful of DVDs, all still sealed in their cellophane wrappers. These days he seemed to buy more films than he watched. Idly shuffling through them, he tried to judge which would suit his mood, or which might best improve it. Eventually he chose one and settled down in front of the TV to escape.

When his phone rang, he couldn't quite remember where he'd left it. Pausing the movie, he followed the sound through into the kitchen. The ringtone grew louder as he drew the phone from the pocket of his jacket, still draped over a chair, and quickly answered it.

'Hello?'

'Graham?' It was Mendel's voice.

'Evening,' Harland smiled. 'How's life in the police force?'

Mendel chuckled.

'Consistent,' he replied. 'Are you at home?'

'Yes.'

'Okay if I swing by?'

'Sure, if you want.' Harland was puzzled. This was unlike his colleague. 'You remember the address?'

'I'm parked outside,' Mendel replied. 'Stick the kettle on.'

They sat down in the living room. Mendel leaned forward, placing his mug on the coffee table and picking up a DVD case.

'I really enjoyed this one,' he nodded. 'Great twist at the end when you find out that the crippled guy is actually the villain.'

'Thanks for that,' Harland sighed. 'Saves me the trouble of enjoying it myself.'

'You're welcome.' His colleague smiled. He eased himself back into the armchair and looked around the room, automatically cataloguing, noting things – a bad police officer's habit that they both shared.

'So what brings you to this part of town?' Harland asked. 'Consorting with a known troublemaker like me could be bad for your career.'

'Don't be daft,' Mendel rebuked him. 'Things have pretty well calmed down now. In fact, a little bird told me you'll be back in scenic Portishead next week.'

'Are you sure?'

The big man spread his palms wide.

'It makes sense,' he said. 'Leighton's being transferred, so Pope and Jackson are picking up his work on that Shirehampton thing. And that leaves us short-staffed . . .' He paused, then added, 'Not that Pope's a great loss, mind you.'

Harland leaned back, his fingers steepled in front of his face.

'So they just need me back to make up the numbers,' he mused.

Mendel shot him a disapproving look.

'If I'd known you were going to get all enthusiastic about it, I'd have come round sooner,' he said pointedly.

'Sorry, you're right.' Harland held up a hand. 'It'll be good to get back to work. That's all that matters.'

Mendel nodded.

'You'll probably get the call tomorrow,' he said. 'Try and sound surprised, okay?'

'Okay.' Harland laughed. He reached out for the remote control and switched the TV off, then looked across at his colleague. 'You came round just to tell me that?'

'Well, I'm not here for your tea.' Mendel made a face and put down the mug. 'No wonder you drink coffee.'

Harland looked at his friend and nodded slowly.

'I appreciate it,' he said. 'You've not been round here for ages . . .'

There was an awkward silence, as they both recalled that last time, shortly after Alice had died. Mendel finally spoke.

'So, what've you been up to?'

Harland started to say something, to answer without thinking, but the words wouldn't come. He floundered for a moment, then looked away.

'You all right, Graham?' Mendel leaned forward in sudden concern.

'Yeah.' He had been caught off guard, thinking about her, but he gathered himself now, speaking tentatively, testing each sentence before trusting his weight to it. 'I'm just not used to so much free time . . . so much time at home. This is the first proper leave I've taken since . . . Alice.'

Managed to say her name. Good.

Mendel nodded at him.

'It must be tough,' he said. 'But you're keeping yourself busy?'

'Yeah, just catching up on a few things, you know . . .'

Harland trailed off, bowing his head. 'Went to the cemetery – first time in a long time. Did some thinking . . .'

Again, words failed him, but once again Mendel didn't.

'I still don't know how you scored someone like Alice,' he said, lifting his mug and studying it.

Harland, jolted out of silence, looked up at him.

'What?'

'Well,' Mendel reflected, 'she was way too good for the likes of you. Thought that the first time I met her.'

A wry smile spread across Harland's face.

'Thanks for that,' he said.

Mendel glanced up from his mug.

'Be honest, though,' he said. 'You were lucky there.'

Harland nodded for a moment but his smile had become hollow.

'Not so lucky now though,' he said, looking down.

Mendel frowned at him.

'How can you say that?' he asked. 'How can you *possibly* say something like that?'

Harland's head snapped up sharply. Wasn't it obvious how much he was suffering? How much her loss hurt him?

'Would you rather you'd never met?' Mendel pressed him. 'Would that have been better?'

Harland stared at him for a moment, then gently shook his head.

'No,' he said softly.

'I should think not,' Mendel sighed. 'Tell you what, Graham – for a clever bloke, you do say some stupid things.'

They ordered a pizza and watched the rest of the movie. Afterwards, Mendel agreed to one more cup of tea before he left, but insisted on making it himself.

'You need to give it a chance to infuse properly,' he

explained, mashing the tea bag against the side of the mug with a spoon. 'Otherwise there's no flavour.'

Leaning against the kitchen counter, Harland watched him doubtfully.

'I'll stick to coffee,' he said. 'Anything that strong would probably keep me awake.'

'Your loss,' Mendel shrugged.

Opening the back door, Harland moved outside and stood on the step while he lit a final cigarette.

'So what about the Severn Beach thing?' he asked. 'I guess by the fact you haven't mentioned it that there's not been much progress.'

Mendel came over to stand beside him, his large silhouette framed in the light of the doorway.

'No,' he said. 'Shame about that one.'

'Shame?'

'Well . . .' Mendel lifted his mug, inhaling the steam. 'It's all over, isn't it?'

Harland looked at him, then nodded slowly.

'I suppose so,' he said. There was nothing more they could do unless they got a hit on that mobile phone. 'At least until he kills another one.'

45

Painting the little soldiers was difficult. He dipped the thin brush – just a few fine hairs in a tight point – into the small pot of black gloss, then carefully applied the glistening paint to the infantryman's tiny rifle. He held his breath as he worked, not blinking, not moving, except for his brush hand. When it was done, he exhaled, and held up the soldier to survey the finished figure.

Perfect.

He set the soldier down on the window sill, beside the others, then crouched in close to see them at eye level. A whole box of them, twenty-four German infantrymen, all painted. He wished they didn't take quite so long to dry, but his father said it was good for him – that it would teach him patience.

Reaching down, he retrieved a jam jar filled with paint thinner and placed it on the old newspaper that protected the top of his bedside cabinet. Carefully, he lowered the tip of the brush into it, watching as little swirls of black bloomed out like upside-down smoke in the clear liquid. Then, checking his hands to make sure they were free from paint, he lay back on his bed and stared up at the patterned plaster ceiling, inhaling the delicious smell of the gloss and the thinners.

It was his room now. There were still two beds, but he didn't have to share any more. He could do whatever he wanted, wherever he wanted, which was brilliant. Nobody moaned about the fumes from his paints, nobody told him to move his things back to his own side of the floor. In fact, he could even use Gary's things, as long as he was careful with them and put them back before his mother noticed.

He sat up and glanced across at the empty bed opposite him, frowning for a moment. Sometimes, when he was pretending to be asleep, she would come in and sit there, just running her hand across the cold bedspread or gently stroking the unused pillow in the dark. He reached out, his fingertips brushing across his own pillow. She wouldn't pack away any of his brother's stuff, even after all this time. He wished she wasn't so sad. If only he could tell her . . .

But it really wasn't so bad. And he had discovered another, even greater advantage. He didn't have to share *her* any more either. She held him for longer now; she loved him more than she had before. He smiled and got to his feet. Things were better now, he was sure of it.

★   ★   ★

Naysmith woke with a start. Glancing around the bedroom, it took him a few seconds to get his bearings before he sank back into the soft pillows and exhaled slowly. He stretched out his arm, caressing the bulging duvet, but it crumpled under his hand. Kim must be downstairs. Fumbling on the bedside table for his watch, he focused on the time – 9.37 a.m. He frowned for a moment then remembered it was Saturday.

Yawning, he stretched and kicked off the duvet, letting his feet drop to the floor and sitting for a weary moment. The light coming from between the curtains was dull and without warmth. He shook his head – another overcast Saturday. Rubbing his eyes, he got slowly to his feet and padded through to the bathroom.

The kitchen smelled of coffee and toast when he came down. Kim was sitting at the large wooden table reading a book.

'Morning, sleepyhead.' She smiled up at him as he wandered over to the fridge. 'I did make you some toast . . . but then I ate it.'

'It's the thought that counts,' Naysmith murmured, pouring himself an orange juice. 'Why didn't you wake me?'

'You looked so peaceful, it seemed a shame to disturb you,' Kim said. 'Plus, when I tried shaking you, you didn't respond.'

'I'm still asleep now.'

'Sit down and I'll make you some coffee.'

'Thanks.'

She got up and tousled his hair as she went over to the counter.

'Do you remember Javier? From Sam and Dave's barbecue?'

Naysmith lifted his head and shot her a bleary frown.

'Wasn't he a photographer or something?'

'That's right.' Kim glanced over her shoulder. 'He's got an exhibition in Bristol. Sam asked me if we wanted to go with them.'

'Sure.' Naysmith rested his head on his hands. 'When is it?'

'Next Sunday evening.'

Her voice continued but Naysmith barely heard her, his mind suddenly racing.

'I thought you were going out next Sunday?' he asked casually.

Not next weekend – any time but then. He'd spent too much time planning the climax of the current game, checking things, arranging things, all for a weekend when she was supposed to be busy . . .

'No. Jane had to cancel. And this might be more interesting anyway.'

Shit. He sleepily rubbed his eyes to avoid looking at her.

'Not sure if I can do Sunday night,' he said carefully. 'I've got a breakfast meeting on Monday and I told Ken I'd go up to town for a few drinks, then stay over.'

Kim said nothing. He glanced across at her but her face was unreadable.

'You said you were out that night,' he shrugged.

'It doesn't matter.'

Naysmith watched her as she took her book from the table and left the room. Changing his plans now would certainly be tiresome and might introduce unnecessary complications. He really didn't want to risk it. Kim might be a little sulky for an hour or so, but she'd be okay. And he'd make it up to her, maybe take her somewhere nice for dinner . . .

He downed the last of his orange juice and sat for a moment before pushing back the chair and standing up.

'I'm going to go and get the papers,' he called as he moved through to the hallway. 'Do you want anything?'

No answer. She must still be cross with him. He shook his head and reached for his jacket.

Outside, the village was dull and shadowless beneath an ugly grey sky. Pulling the front door shut behind him, Naysmith jammed his hands into his jacket pockets and walked briskly down the lane.

He stopped off at the bakery on the way back to buy a crusty loaf, then made his way home, tearing off little pieces of warm bread and eating them as he walked. The clouds were darker now, and he was glad to get back before it started to rain.

Entering the kitchen, he placed the loaf in the bread bin and dropped the papers on the table. Kim was probably still annoyed about her weekend plans and he thought it might be better to give her some space. He knew he had some emails to check so he went upstairs to the study and settled into his chair. Most of the mail was unimportant – follow-ups to meetings and a couple of conference calls to add to his calendar – but there was also a draft contract that he'd been waiting for and he decided to go through it now while he had the time. There were a couple of minor errors, but those were quickly fixed and, once satisfied, he hit the print button.

Nothing happened.

On the screen, a message flashed up: *Out of paper.*

'Kim?' he called, as his eyes searched the room. 'Have we got any more printer paper?'

'Is it on the shelf?' Her voice came from the bedroom.

'There's none there.'

'Then we must be out.'

He sighed and saved the file for later – it could wait if it had to. As he shut down the email program, he caught a movement at the edge of his vision. Turning his head, he saw Kim standing in the doorway, watching him.

'What is it?' he asked.

She shook her head. 'Nothing.'

He held out his hand to her but she turned away and started down the stairs. Naysmith rubbed his eyes for a long moment, then reluctantly got to his feet and slowly followed her down to the kitchen. All this fuss over an exhibition for someone they barely knew – it was just getting silly now.

She had her back to him, standing at the sink and filling the kettle as he walked into the room.

'Kim?'

She turned round, her eyes on him as she returned the kettle to its base and switched it on.

'Yes?'

'What's bothering you?' He realised that he had instinctively positioned himself directly between her and the doorway. He hadn't meant to . . .

'Who says anything's bothering me?' Her voice was measured, but she folded her arms as she spoke.

'I do,' he said softly. 'Now what is it?'

The kettle began to steam and bubble on the counter. Naysmith waited patiently, his eyes locked on Kim until she finally raised her head and met his gaze.

'Are you seeing someone else?' she asked, quietly.

He had misread her. It wasn't missing the exhibition that bothered her, it was the thought that he might be deceiving her. And he wasn't, at least not in the way she thought . . .

'No,' he said, gently.

There was a long pause and Kim eventually lowered her head to stare at the floor. *Didn't she believe him?*

'Really no,' he told her, more firmly.

Kim bit her lip and peered out at him between strands of hair that had tumbled down across her face.

'Do you believe me?' he asked.

She said nothing, absently toying with her hair as she stood with her back to the counter. Naysmith moved across the room and took her hand.

'Do you believe me, Kim?'

She hesitated for a moment, then nodded slightly. 'Yes.'

He moved closer, putting his arms around her shoulders. She remained still, passive, as he leaned forward, gently kissing her cheek, nuzzling her neck, loving the smell of her hair.

'Rob?' Her voice was soft, almost a whisper. 'Are you keeping something from me?'

He paused, just for a heartbeat, and kissed her neck. Straightening up, he gazed down into her large eyes. So beautiful, so vulnerable.

'Does it matter?' He reached up and began slowly to unbutton her blouse, gradually revealing her smooth, pale skin. Her breathing was quicker now, her exposed chest rising and falling beneath his hands.

'Please, Rob. Is there something?'

So perfect, her dark eyes shining, his brave little Kim.

'Yes,' he told her simply. At this moment, any other answer would have been unworthy of her, and unworthy of him.

Still gazing up at him, Kim blinked and sighed. It sounded almost like relief.

'Thank you,' she whispered. Her arms crept up to encircle his neck and she buried her face in his shoulder. It was a curious reaction, and he was surprised how much this glimmer of honesty had meant to her.

She yielded to his kiss, her body arching in response as his hands caressed her back, then stood pensively as he hitched up her skirt and calmly slid her underwear down to her feet.

'Rob?'

'What is it?' he asked as he undid his belt buckle.

'Will you tell me?'

Naysmith put his hands on her hips and lifted her up to sit on the edge of the kitchen counter, then gazed thoughtfully into her eyes.

'Not yet,' he said softly.

Kim nodded hesitantly, reaching out to touch his arm.

'But one day you will?'

'Shhh.' He gently put a finger to her lips and smiled kindly. She studied him for a moment and shyly smiled back.

He caressed her smooth legs, spreading them apart and moving between them. When had she become so important to him? The door was open now – only slightly, but it would be almost impossible to close. He moved forward, kissing her slender neck, closing his eyes as he nuzzled her hair. Her body felt warm against his, and suddenly he didn't care – the desire for her swept aside the growing turmoil of emotions.

For now.

46

Harland pulled the front door closed behind him and dropped his keys in the bowl. The house was silent but somehow that didn't matter just now. He rubbed his eyes as he walked through to the kitchen. It had been a quiet day but he felt strangely weary as he shrugged off his jacket and draped it over a chair. Opening the fridge, he took out a bottle of sparkling water and held it against the side of his face, relishing the invigorating cold on his skin.

Work had settled down again, back to a dull routine that was almost welcome after the recent upsets and problems.

Almost welcome.

He'd spent an unrewarding afternoon behind a parade of shops on the Lawrence Weston Estate. There, between the commercial wheelie bins and the torn black refuse sacks, someone had noticed a pair of feet sticking out from under a piece of old cardboard. They'd called it in, and somehow it had fallen to Harland – perhaps as a punishment, perhaps because he didn't have anything more important to do.

The worst of it was done by the time he got there, and it was outside, so the only real smell was the reek of the rubbish, but it wasn't pleasant. There was nothing special about the body – a white male vagrant in his late forties – and he knew as soon as he arrived that it was just another miserable old soak, someone who'd finally lost his tenuous grip on life and slid into the dark. Tragic but meaningless. He knew that the investigation – and everything he was doing – wouldn't really matter. When a person's life had so little worth, his death didn't seem to count.

He pierced the plastic covering on a pasta meal and put it in the microwave, setting the timer for three minutes.

At least these dregs jobs were keeping him away from Blake. He hadn't seen the Superintendent since he'd returned to work, which was probably the way both of them wanted it. The less they said to each other the better. And Pope had been conspicuously absent too, first with the Shirehampton case, and then recently working on something 'rather important' over in Fishponds. Doubtless the little brown-noser was chasing the high-profile stuff, anything to get himself noticed, promoted. And good luck to the little bastard, just so long as it took him somewhere far away from here.

The microwave was beeping impatiently. Harland opened the door, removed the plastic tray carefully and sat down at the table to eat.

Later, when the washing-up was done, he clicked through the channels for a while, but there was nothing on TV. Switching the set off, he stood up and moved across to the bookcase. Head tilted, his eyes scanned the spines, looking for inspiration. So many books, each with its own associations and memories. Here was one he'd read by the pool in Italy a couple of years ago, and there was another that had been his companion when he'd been laid up in bed with the flu. They were both good, but he wanted something else, something he hadn't read, something where he didn't know the ending. Tracing a finger along the uneven books, he mouthed the titles silently to himself, until his hand paused.

It was a novel that he'd started reading once but never finished.

It had been at his bedside when he came home to the empty house that first night, one more thing overtaken by his loss. He pulled it from its place on the shelf and looked at it. There was still a till receipt acting as bookmark, only a few chapters in.

By nine thirty, he was yawning. He put the book down on the kitchen table, and opened the back door. Standing in the garden, he lit a final cigarette and exhaled smoke that drifted up into the evening sky, his eyes following the wisps as they spiralled and faded.

He thought back to the dead vagrant, a man not much older than himself, skin leathered by the sun and years of drinking. The matted black hair, shot through with grey, eye sockets deep and dark, Salvation Army clothing stained and wrinkled. He wondered if anyone else was thinking of the man, if anyone wanted to know about him, if anyone cared. He wondered if the man himself even cared – had he lost his grip on life, or had he deliberately let go?

He stubbed out his cigarette against the brick wall, tiny orange sparks cascading to the ground, then went inside. Bolting the kitchen door behind him, he yawned and made his way through to the living room. Out of habit, he moved towards the sofa bed, then paused, remembering. Straightening up, he turned and walked back to the doorway, where he stood for a while, thinking. Then, head bowed, he switched off the light and closed the door.

In the kitchen, he retrieved the book from the table and took it to the foot of the stairs. Everything down here was in darkness now – the only illumination came from the upper landing, yellow light spilling down from above to pool around his feet. He placed his free hand on the banister and sighed. Then, yawning and weary, he went upstairs to bed.

47

Sunday, 16 September

It wasn't the sort of hotel he usually stayed in. Places like this catered for the basic business traveller – tables for one in the nondescript restaurant, a cheerless bar with intermittent Wi-Fi, and a discreetly billed porn channel in the room if you were lucky. Bland and sterile accommodation for bland and sterile people; an experience that was utterly impersonal . . .

. . . and that was what made it so suitable. The few staff that were there took no interest in him – he was just another lonely figure walking along the featureless, carpeted corridors, and tomorrow he'd be forgotten. Just as he wanted to be.

At least the room would be clean. Naysmith put his shoulder against the door to keep it open as he lifted the holdall in from the hallway, then found the light switch. He turned to fasten the security chain behind him, pausing as he went to slide it home, staring thoughtfully at the shiny metal chain in his hand. He stooped to the holdall, unzipping it and drawing out a pair of black gloves, which he pulled on. Opening the door slightly, he carefully rubbed clean the outer and inner handles with the edge of his sleeve, then repeated the process on the light switch. Replacing the chain, he turned to look at the room, with its many smooth and polished surfaces. He would keep his gloves on.

A vague sense of unease had followed him all day – perhaps

just frustration that his previous game had ended in failure – but he'd been cautious from the moment he checked in. The reservation had been made using a real name and address, but neither was his. Feigning an embarrassing but unspecified problem with his credit card, he'd managed to pay for the room in cash, and even had the presence of mind to use his own pen when signing the registration form. The hardest part was avoiding the CCTV cameras, but he'd noted their positions on a previous visit and moved carefully to avoid his face being recorded. The weary-looking youth at the reception desk had barely looked up at him throughout the exchange.

He lugged the holdall onto the bed, then walked over to the window and pulled the long net curtain aside to peer into the evening gloom. The room looked out across the mile-long rectangle of water that was once the tidal basin for the Royal Victoria Dock. Heavy iron cranes, embalmed in weatherproof grey paint, lined the quayside – giant pieces of engineering, now little more than period decor for the waterfront apartment blocks. Leaning forward, he could see the angular suspension bridge, slung between two box-like elevator towers, that took pedestrians from one side of the water to the other.

Over there somewhere, beyond those waterfront apartments, was the quiet little street where his victim lived. He was probably no more than a mile away right now. Naysmith idly wondered what he was doing, then dismissed the thought.

The victim was not important. His preparation was.

He turned and surveyed the small room. A narrow double bed, a long desk with a TV at one end and a kettle at the other, and a single armchair. It was unlikely that he would sleep and he resolved not to use the bed. With so many different people passing through them, hotels were littered with DNA, making it easier for him to avoid discovery. He wasn't about to let his guard down, though. One bit of carelessness – one mistake – might be all it took to finish things.

Unzipping the holdall, he began checking through the contents. As usual, everything was new and unremarkable. He was already wearing anonymous, supermarket clothing, and had a second spare set in the bag. Underneath it, nestled on top of the black refuse sacks, was a white envelope that rattled as he moved it. He frowned and drew it out of the bag. Opening the flap, he tipped the mobile phone and its disconnected battery out into his hand. Absently, he snapped the battery into place so that it would make no noise, then put it down on the bed with the envelope. Lastly, beneath a packet of clean-up wipes, his gloved fingers touched a thin, towel-wrapped bundle. He slipped the towel aside to reveal the gleaming tip of a long kitchen knife.

It wasn't his first choice – he knew from experience that knives could be messy to use – but this challenge was being played out in a big city, where stabbings were commonplace.

When in Rome . . .

Smiling, he covered the blade with the towel. Everything was ready.

He glanced at his disposable watch. It was just after 7 p.m. Tomorrow morning the target would leave home just before eight in order to catch the 8.19 train from West Silverton. Naysmith had initially considered going to the man's house, but the fact that he clearly lived with someone made that approach problematic. In the end, he'd decided to wait for his victim near the station. It was a better location than Evelyn Road – somewhat isolated, without shops or houses in the immediate vicinity, and there were plenty of ways out of the area when he was done. It wasn't that far away, but he would set off before 7 a.m. to ensure he was positioned in good time. He picked up the mobile phone, toying with it, turning it in his gloved fingers. Absently, he pushed the power button, but the screen did not light up.

A bang from just outside the room jerked him to his feet. He stuffed the phone back inside the envelope and dropped both into the holdall as he moved silently round the bed and over towards the door. Drunken laughter echoed along the corridor as he peered out through the spyhole, his shoulders relaxing a little when he saw the distorted shape of a balding, middle-aged man fumbling with the door opposite.

Nothing to worry about.

He waited until the man disappeared, then turned away from the door and sighed. It would all be worth it in that instant when he held the target's life in his hands. When he burned away the failure of the last game.

He looked at his watch again – just under twelve hours to kill. Yawning, he eased himself down into the chair and reached out a gloved hand for the TV remote control.

48

Something was wrong. Harland stirred and buried his face in the pillow, sinking into the welcoming softness of the bed. But something was wrong. Slowly the sound filtered through to him, a smouldering ember in his consciousness that suddenly took flame.

His phone was ringing.

Groggily, he rolled over, his hand fumbling for the lamp switch, and he groaned as the sudden light jarred him awake. Blinking, he reached for the phone and answered it.

'Hello?'

'It's me.' Mendel's voice sounded serious.

'What time is it?'

'Just gone midnight. You weren't asleep, were you?'

'I had an early night,' Harland yawned.

'Sorry if I woke you,' Mendel said. 'I thought you'd want to know about this, though.'

Harland struggled to sit up, pushing away the duvet and rubbing a hand through his hair.

'No problem,' he said, letting his eyes close as he leaned back against the headboard. 'What is it?'

'Remember that mobile phone? The one from the Hampshire murder?'

'Yes.' Harland's eyes opened and he leaned forward.

'Well, we just got a hit on it. Somebody switched it on a couple of hours ago.'

Harland frowned, shaking off the sleep, forcing himself to concentrate.

'Any calls on it?' he asked.

'None, so far as we know. It just popped up on the network.'

'Okay. Where was this?'

'London somewhere. Hang on, let me see what they gave us . . .'

Harland swung his legs over and sat on the edge of the bed, rubbing his eyes. It could be nothing, but on the other hand . . .

'East London . . .' Mendel's voice was distant as he sifted through the information he'd received. 'Yeah, here we are. It's over in Docklands somewhere. I've got a grid reference, but it's only approximate.'

'Get a map and take a look.' Harland rose wearily to his feet and padded out onto the landing, the phone pressed to his ear. 'I'm just going to the computer downstairs.'

He hurried down, bare feet sensitive on the carpeted steps, and shielded his eyes as he switched on the light in the study. Then, dropping into his chair, he opened his laptop and powered it up.

'Okay,' he said after a moment. 'Give me the reference and let's see what's there.'

Mendel read the details back to him and he entered them in quickly, then clicked on the Search button. On the screen, a large map expanded. There was the Thames, snaking up and around the Dome, with London City Airport on the right. The reference marker was in the middle of the screen, by a long stretch of blue marked 'Royal Victoria Dock'. He zoomed in closer.

'Has the phone changed location at all?' he asked. 'Since it was switched on, I mean?'

'I don't think so,' Mendel replied. 'Position was constant. It's still there as far as I'm concerned.'

Harland nodded as his eyes scanned the more detailed view of the area.

'Most of this is water,' he said, half to himself. 'Lots of open areas, a car park, building developments, nothing residential . . .'

He paused, looking at the small lettering that had just popped up near the centre of the grid.

'What is it?' Mendel asked.

'Get onto the Met,' Harland said quickly. 'We need to get some bodies on the ground there. Maybe the phone's just been dumped, or sold on to someone, but . . .'

He hesitated, staring at the word 'Hotel' close to the reference marker at the centre of his screen. There seemed to be little else close by.

'I'll call you when I'm in the car,' he said. 'Oh, one more thing?'

'Yes?'

'The number of that phone – it's in the file somewhere. Look it up for me.'

49

It was past 4 a.m. now. Naysmith shivered, fighting off the temptation to sleep, and yawned deeply. He looked away from the screen and wearily rubbed his eyes . . .

And stopped.

For a moment, he wasn't sure where the noise was coming from. Leaning forward, he took the remote control from its place on the desk and aimed it at the TV, tapping the volume down to zero.

There it was. A thin, muffled tone, accompanied by a dull buzzing. He lifted his head, trying to identify what it was, and where it was coming from. Slowly, he got to his feet, moving towards the bed, where the sound seemed to be louder. His hand stretched out to the holdall, carefully sliding open the zip. The ringtone was clear now and he tentatively reached into the bag, feeling the vibration of the white envelope through his gloves.

The phone was ringing.

Turning back the flap of the envelope, he took the handset out and stared at the word on the brightly illuminated screen.

Unknown.

He stood for a moment, frozen. The ringtone filled the room as his mind cried out for him to do something. His thumb, unbidden by him, hovered over the green Answer key, then gently squeezed it.

Silence.

On the screen, a timer began to count up the seconds. Someone was on the other end of the line, and he thought he could hear a faint voice. Holding the phone as though it might burn him, he raised it to his ear.

'Hello?' said a man's voice.

Naysmith stood absolutely still, making no sound.

'I'm going to assume that you can hear me.'

A long pause.

'I understand your reluctance to speak,' the voice continued in quiet, measured tones, 'but I think it would be good if we could communicate somehow.'

There was something familiar about that voice, but Naysmith was too off balance to place it.

'Tell you what,' the voice said, 'if you can hear me, press the 1 key. Just so I know I'm not talking to myself.'

He lowered the phone a little, unsure of what to do, then lifted it again to listen.

'Whenever you're ready,' the voice was saying. 'Just press 1, or any of the number keys, so I know you can hear me.'

Naysmith lowered the phone and stared at it, unsure what to do. He had planned for everything, but nothing had prepared him for this. His thumb hesitated over the 1 key for a moment, then pressed it, making a quiet tone.

'Thanks,' said the voice. 'It's good to know that somebody's there.'

Naysmith closed his eyes, forcing himself to breathe normally, willing himself to calm down as he listened.

'I appreciate,' the voice said slowly, 'that you're a very careful person . . .'

This wasn't a random wrong number – somebody knew something.

And just as suddenly, he thought he knew where he'd heard a voice like that before. That quiet, impassive speech . . . but it couldn't be.

'. . . so I understand you might not want to answer any questions . . .'

With the phone pressed to his ear, Naysmith walked softly over to the window and carefully pulled back the net curtain. Was that the reflection of a flashing blue light on one of the tall cranes, or was he letting his imagination run away with him? It looked quiet down at street level, but he couldn't see much from here.

'. . . I was just wondering if you'd ever been to Severn Beach.'

Shit.

Naysmith stepped back from the window. He was sure now.

'Maybe you could press 1 if you have?'

Slowly, he leaned in close to the door and put his eye to the spyhole. The distorted corridor appeared to be empty. He had to get out.

'Or perhaps I'm moving a little fast,' the voice continued. 'It's a failing of mine. But it would be good if we were able to communicate. In fact, I rather think you'd like it if we could . . .'

Naysmith closed up the holdall, working quickly, quietly. His mind was racing. Were they about to burst into the room? Surely they would have done so already if they knew where he was. How much did they know?

'Still there?'

Putting the holdall under one arm, he pressed the 1 key on the phone and listened again.

'That's good,' the voice said. 'I know that the circumstances are difficult, but I really would like to understand more about what you do . . .'

Appreciate. Know. Understand. Suddenly, the spell was broken. Naysmith shook his head in disgust as he recognised the language – he wasn't going to fall for a thinly veiled empathy play, allow some halfwit to try and build a rapport with him.

Scowling, he took one last look around the room – not rushing, forcing himself to take the time and double-check everything.

'Do you think we could do that?'

Enough. Naysmith pressed the 1 key and listened. He waited until the voice started to speak again, then immediately hung up.

'Fuck you,' he muttered, switching off the handset and slipping it into his bag. Moving to the door, he reached for the handle, but hesitated. There was no point making it easy for them. He put down the holdall and stalked into the bathroom. Crouching, he pushed the plugs into the bath and the basin, blocked the overflows with toilet tissue and turned both sets of taps fully on. A flooded room would make the forensics job that much tougher.

Retrieving the bag, he checked the spyhole once more, then took a deep breath and opened the door. Outside, the corridor was empty. Pulling his door so it shut quietly behind him, Naysmith turned away from the lifts and made his way quickly towards the illuminated fire exit sign at the opposite end of the corridor. Pushing through the double set of doors, he emerged into a windowless stairwell and paused, listening for any movement below.

Nothing.

He took the stairs several steps at a time, dropping swiftly

down the short flights. Four floors to go . . . now three . . .
two . . . his movements fluid as he twisted on each landing
to leap down the next set of stairs.

He bent his knees to deaden the sound as his feet hit the
ground floor, then straightened up slowly, straining to hear
if anyone was nearby. In front of him was a wooden door
with a small window set into it. Tensing himself in readiness,
he slid up against the wall and slowly leaned over to peer
through the glass.

The foyer was partially visible – a collection of brightly
upholstered easy chairs and leaflet-strewn coffee tables – but
he couldn't see anyone through there.

Taking a deep breath, he placed his hands carefully on the
door and gently pushed, ready to stop if it made any sound.
As it opened, he leaned across, eyes alert, and eased himself
partly round it.

There was nobody at the front desk, and his eyes swept
urgently across the space.

There!

The receptionist was standing with his back to him, over
by the full-height windows at the front, watching something
happening in the street outside.

A rhythmic flicker of blue light touched the building across
the road.

Shit! They were here!

His breathing quickened. He had to find another way out,
right now.

Eyes fixed on the receptionist, he edged round the door,
easing it quietly closed behind him. Then, moving silently,
he slipped along the wall and round the corner into the
restaurant. The room was dimly lit, rows of tables and chairs
arranged ready for breakfast. He moved swiftly, weaving
between them as he made for the opposite end of the room,

the thicker carpet muffling his careful footsteps. Tall smoked-glass windows looked out onto a paved walkway that ran along the side of the building and there, at the far end, a green fire exit sign shone out brightly.

He reached the door and paused. It would be alarmed, but his chances would be better outside, and at least he'd be away from the front of the building. There was no other way.

Breathing quickly, he put his gloves on the release bar and pushed the door open. Somewhere in the building behind him a distant buzzer sound went off, but he ignored it and stepped out into the night. Cold air enveloped him as he paused for a moment, alone in the alley, listening for any sound of pursuit. Then, lugging the holdall, he walked along the pavement towards the back of the hotel.

Don't rush, just walk, nice and easy.

He was between two tall buildings, with the street behind him and the water in front. As he approached the corner, a glow of red flared in the shadows. Someone was standing there, smoking.

He couldn't turn around now – it would look odd, guilty. Besides, the front of the hotel could be crawling with police by now. He had to keep calm, keep walking.

The distance between them closed and he could see the silhouette of a man in a long coat, pale smoke drifting out into the light of the street lamps.

Don't make eye contact. Just look straight ahead, look at the lights across the water . . .

There was nowhere to go but forward. He just had to hold his nerve – walk straight past and he'd be out of there, free. Just the briefest glance across as he drew level with the figure . . .

A lean man, features wreathed in shadow, but the head had turned, following his steps.

It didn't mean anything.

All he had to do was keep on walking. The corner was only a few yards away.

As he passed by, he sensed movement behind him and a voice spoke out.

'Excuse me . . .'

It was like a physical blow. That voice – that same voice – from the phone moments earlier. Everything inside him cried out, but he fought it down, mastered it. He *wouldn't* run. Just ignore the howling storm of adrenalin and keep walking, calmly, slowly. He *mustn't* run. Almost at the corner now . . .

'Hey, you!' It was a shout this time.

Naysmith ran.

50

It had seemed like such a promising lead. He'd not been able to round up much manpower – he would never have got it authorised anyway – but he'd subconsciously built up his hopes on the long drive down. They were going to find something, he *knew* it. A solid lead now could bump the case back onto the radar again, give them a fighting chance.

And then, when he'd arrived on the scene, it had all started to come apart. He saw straight away that the online map was wrong, or at least out of date. There were *two* hotels on the site, not one. With only a few uniformed officers, no clear indication on where to begin searching and no suspect, he suddenly found himself wondering if he'd made a fatal mistake. Unless he turned up something good, like the missing mobile phone, he was just making it easy for Blake to get rid of him. He thought of the Superintendent's humourless smile – *'So sorry, Graham, but you've left me no other option . . .'* – and imagined Pope's smug satisfaction when the word got out . . . it was infuriating. But there was nothing he could do about it – things had taken on a momentum of their own now and, win or lose, there was no option but to play it through to the end.

And so, standing there in the cold glow of the street lights, he'd decided to try one last, desperate gamble.

There had been no voice at the other end of the line, but he wasn't really expecting the killer to talk back to him. Someone so clever, and so careful, wasn't likely to reveal himself that easily. And yet, as Harland heard that first numeric tone in response to his own words, he felt sure that he was speaking to the murderer. If it was just someone who'd picked up a stolen mobile, they'd probably try to bluff their way through the conversation, or hang up immediately. But there was a dreadful curiosity in the silence at the other end – and surely that could only come from the killer.

Straining to hear better, he pressed the phone hard against his ear as he walked into a narrow alleyway at the side of the buildings, away from the distracting chatter of the other officers.

Don't rush things . . . try to empathise with the subject . . .

All the things they'd told him about speaking to unstable people came back to him now, and he tried to infuse his voice with a steady, reasonable tone as he undertook his one-sided conversation.

Whatever happens, just don't let him hang up . . .

'Still there?'

Another numeric tone. Harland breathed a sigh of relief.

'That's good,' he said, trying to keep his voice calm. 'I know that the circumstances are difficult, but I really would like to understand more about what you do . . .'

I really would like to know where the hell you are . . .

'Do you think we could do that?'

He listened intently, then clenched his fist in triumph as he heard the answering tone. The bastard *wanted* to communicate with him.

'All right then,' he began. 'Let's try to—'

There was a click and the line went dead.

No!

Harland stared at the handset in horror. What had just happened? Had he hung up or was there a problem on the line? He looked around, panicked, but there was nobody else near him. Trembling, he redialled the number and pressed the phone to his ear once more.

Come on, come on, ring . . .

But all he got was a number-unobtainable tone. He tried again, then once more, but it was no use. Something had happened – perhaps the killer had simply run out of battery, or perhaps he'd switched off the phone.

Shit!

As he stood there, alone in the shadows, he was struck by the appalling realisation of what he'd done. He'd ignored procedure and tried to contact the suspect directly. This might have been their best chance to find the killer and he'd rushed it like a bloody amateur. They'd hang him out to dry for this. He was screwed.

Reeling, he stepped back to lean against the wall. It was over, and this time it really was all his own stupid fault. Trembling, his free hand searched his pockets, fingers closing around a box of cigarettes. Fumbling, he jammed one between his lips and sparked his lighter. In the darkness, the flame blinded him, but the tobacco caught and he drew in a desperate wave of smoke. Eyes closed, he held it for a moment before exhaling slowly.

He was still shaking, but it wasn't as bad now.

Bowing his head, he gripped the cigarette tightly as he wondered what the hell he was going to do.

The distant rumble of the city came to him from far away, mixed with the hum of air-conditioning units on the walls high above him. He wasn't sure how long he'd been standing there, but he'd lit a second cigarette and was rolling it between his fingers when he heard the click. Further back along the alleyway, a door swung open. In the darkness it was hard to see, but he could just make out a figure emerging from the building to his right, carrying a holdall. Soft footsteps reached his ears, echoing off the walls. There was nothing furtive about the figure's movement, in fact the man was coming towards him – just another weary worker heading for home at the end of a late shift. Harland relaxed, and raised the cigarette to his mouth. The figure walked calmly along the side of the hotel, a silhouette, backlit by the orange glow that filtered in from the street.

He drew on the cigarette, blowing out the smoke as he tried to clear his head, tried to think what he would do now. He closed his eyes for a moment, listening to the rhythm of the footsteps passing by . . .

. . . *and hearing them quicken.*

His eyes flickered open. The figure was just beyond him now. Harland watched with a frown, wondering for the first time where this person had come from, where he was going. And his movements seemed somehow different, not so weary now.

He felt the hairs rise on the back of his neck as he stepped out from the wall and peered after the man. He had to be sure.

'Excuse me . . .'

The dark shape didn't stop or show any sign that he'd heard as he walked on up the alley. Harland stepped forward, cold adrenalin rising in him.

'Hey, you!' he shouted angrily, and the retreating figure suddenly broke into a run.

A profound sense of fury exploded through Harland as he sprinted after the man. Racing to the end of the alley and around the corner, they emerged onto the broad paved walkway that led along the edge of the dock basin at the back of the two hotels. Lights from the apartment blocks on the opposite side glittered on the dark water below as his feet pounded along the pavement, his quarry no more than fifteen or twenty yards in front of him.

As he ran, Harland glanced around but there were no other officers within shouting distance, and the hotels were soon behind him. He couldn't stop, couldn't risk losing the man – he had to stay with him no matter what.

They raced onwards, the figure ahead of him struggling with his bag, which swung around wildly as he powered forward. They ran between the legs of the enormous black cranes that loomed along the quayside, their erect iron arms lost in the darkness above. On the left, a broad plaza stretched away, with uniform rows of ornamental trees slipping by, their thin branches eerily lit by cold blue fairy lights. The man was moving fast, but Harland was holding the distance between them. And still, he saw no one, nobody he could call out to for assistance – it was just the two of them now.

Ahead of them, flights of broad steps led up to the illumin-ated glass entrance of the exhibition centre, but the man kept right, following the pavement along the water's edge.

He was making for the bridge.

It dominated the skyline before them – two boxy towers clad in metal, with a slender footbridge slung between them, high above the water. Triangular suspension struts gave the appear-ance of sails, and a series of red lights glowed in silent warning at the top of each mast. It was the only way across the dock.

Ahead of him, the man turned right, the bag flying out wide from his left hand as he sprinted onto the wooden-floored gangway that led to the nearest of the towers. The rhythmic impact of his footsteps seemed very loud as Harland rounded the corner and pounded onto the gangway after him, the whole structure bouncing under his feet. He was breathing hard now, legs feeling heavy, but a righteous fury carried him on. He wouldn't let go, not this time.

At the far end of the gangway, his target ducked into the metal-clad tower and disappeared from view. Harland hurried after him, determined not to lose ground.

As he reached the open doorway, he could hear the sound of urgent footsteps echoing down through the tower from the metal steps above him. His breath was failing now, legs burning as he forced himself on, into the cramped stairwell and up the first flight of steps. Head tilted back, he looked up as he climbed, straining for a sight of the hurrying figure above him, but all he could see was a confusing maze of steel stretching up to the deck of the bridge.

At the first landing, he turned and drove himself up another flight, then another. His breathing had become ragged, the metallic echo of his feet reverberating around the enclosed space, drowning out everything else.

Yet another flight of identical steps. Surely this was near the top now. How much further could it go on?

Exhausted, he rounded what must have been the final landing, gasping for air, urging himself to go on. As his eyes flickered up, he saw the movement but by then it was too late.

Dark against the reflected fluorescent lamps, the waiting figure launched himself down from the top of the stairs, blotting out the light behind him. Harland stumbled, desperately trying to dodge to one side, but an outstretched foot caught him in the chest, smashing the last breath out of his lungs. The full weight of his attacker crashed into him, sending him tumbling backwards until his head smacked against a handrail and there was nothing more.

51

'Ha ha, you got your shoes wet.' Gary was looking down at him from the riverbank, and laughing. 'You'll be in trouble with Mum when we get home.'

'Shut up.'

'Shut up yourself, *Robbie.*' Gary always called him Robbie, emphasising the second syllable. He hated it.

Scowling, he scrambled up from the slippery stepping stones, drained his shoes as best he could and followed his big brother along the grassy bank. They picked their way slowly along the meandering course of the river, swollen with dark water from several days of rain, before turning aside onto a faint path that led up into a stand of trees. A breath of wind sighed through the leaves overhead, making them shimmer.

'Where are we going?' he asked.

'To the waterfall, stupid.'

'All right, I was only asking.' Why did his brother have to be so mean all the time? It was no fun with him around; he spoiled everything.

They emerged from the woods and walked down a long, grassy slope. It was quiet here – the village was far behind, and the only sound was the occasional bleating of the sheep on the side of the valley above them.

'We can cut across here,' Gary said, pointing towards the broad expanse of reeds and grassy hummocks that stretched out to their left.

Rob hesitated. The ground looked marshy, and he didn't want to get muddy.

'Can't we go round by the path?' he suggested.

'What's the matter?' Gary sneered at him. '*Scared*? Your shoes are already messed up, and this way's quicker.'

'I'm *not* scared!'

'Prove it then.'

Gary turned his back and walked down into the reeds. Frowning, Rob followed him. The ground felt soft at the foot of the slope but he hurried on, determined to keep up. He wasn't scared of *anything*. Following Gary, he kept his eyes on where he was treading, trying to avoid getting any wetter than he already was. The long tangled grasses were thicker now, hiding the muddy ground completely, and dark water bubbled up between the mounds as his shoes pressed them down.

They were almost halfway across when Gary stumbled and swore. Rob looked up to see his brother, some twenty yards ahead of him, shaking his head in annoyance.

'Aw, sod it!' He turned to glance back at Rob. 'I've stepped in a hole or something. The water's gone right up over my knee.'

'Ha!' Rob called over to him. 'Who's got wet shoes now?'

'Shut your face.'

Rob carefully picked his way forward, moving round the side of a large hummock. The ground suddenly felt very strange beneath his feet and as he paused he could feel it moving under him, as though he was walking on a giant trampoline.

'Rob, come here.'

'In a minute.' The moving ground didn't feel right at all.

'Come here right now and help pull me out.'

Slowly, he crept forward, placing his feet carefully on the

squelching reed bed. He could see Gary clearly now, just a few yards in front of him, bent as though in a crouching position, one leg buried to the thigh in the grass. There was water all around him.

'Blimey, you're soaked!' Rob said, steadying himself on a mossy tuft of reeds.

'Of course I'm soaked,' Gary said. 'You're such an idiot, Robbie. Now get over here and help me.'

Rob paused.

'What are you waiting for?' his brother snapped. 'Get over here now!'

He looked funny, bent over like that, water swirling up around his leg. He ought to be polite if he wanted help. Maybe even say sorry for being so horrible . . .

'*Rob!*'

He looked different now, sort of worried and angry at the same time. And he'd said Rob not Robbie . . .

'You're nasty to me, Gary.' He watched his brother staring up at him uncertainly. 'Maybe you should say sorry to me . . . if you want me to help you.'

There. He'd said it. His brother might rub his face in the mud later on, but at least he'd said it.

'Say sorry? To you?!' Gary's face went red and he started to say something, then tried to lunge at Rob. There was a loud bubbling as his trapped leg dragged him down and he fell sideways with a dull splash. Water sluiced around him as the ground sagged and he began to struggle, trying to get to his feet.

'Shit! Oh shit!' His arms slid into the water as he tried to push himself up and the floating grass gave way under his hands. 'Help me, Rob, help me!'

And suddenly it wasn't funny any more. Rob looked around desperately, but there was nothing to hold on to except for the reeds. Grasping a clump tightly, he leaned forward and stretched out his hand towards his floundering brother.

There was a strange sensation in his tummy, like an icy knot of excitement, as he reached out. It was an amazing feeling, to suddenly be so important. Gary was totally dependent on him at this moment, totally in his power. It felt so good . . .

And then, as he stared at his brother, he withdrew his hand a little.

'Say sorry, Gary.'

'What?!'

'Say sorry.'

'Okay, I'm sorry, whatever you bloody want,' Gary yelled, arching his body to keep his face out of the water. 'Now give me your fucking hand.'

He didn't mean it.

Rob looked down on his tormentor thrashing around in the water, both legs now snared below the tangle of reeds.

He would never mean it.

Rob leaned back to the safety of the large clump of reeds and closed his eyes.

'Please! I can't get my legs out!' Gary was begging now, but he'd be nasty again soon enough. 'You've got to help me, Rob!'

He could get himself out.

Turning away, Rob pulled himself up and edged his way back towards the firmer ground. Behind him, he could hear Gary swearing and yelling, but with every carefully placed footstep, the noise grew a little less. He bit his lip, concentrated on where he was walking, trying to push everything else out of his mind.

He wasn't doing anything wrong. He wasn't doing anything at all.

And then the noise behind him changed to a strange half-screaming, half-sobbing sound. It pierced him, making him pause and look over his shoulder, but the reeds hid Gary from view.

And then it stopped.

An eerie peace fell across the valley, and the only sound was the mournful sigh of the wind. For several long minutes he stood alone, listening, until a cold trembling gripped his body, forcing him to move. Turning away from the marsh, he started back towards the village.

52

Stephen Jennings looked up from his monitor and watched the clock hands as they traced the last long minutes to lunch-time. It had been a dull morning, but even from his cubicle – tucked away at the very back of the office – he could see that the weather had changed and the sun had come out. Yawning, he pushed a hand through his short, sandy hair and got slowly to his feet. Reaching for the blue anorak draped over the back of his chair, he hesitated, then changed his mind. He wouldn't need it today.

Downstairs, the reassuring rumble of the city greeted him as he pushed aside the heavy glass door and wandered down the steps onto Throgmorton Street. It was already getting busy with other office workers breaking for an early lunch, and he quickened his pace. He saw so little sunlight at his desk that he was determined to get a place by the window today.

Casa Mia was quite full, but in the end he was lucky. Finding a table where he could sit in the sun, he reserved it by folding his jacket over the chair and went to the counter to order his usual sandwich and drink.

When he returned to the table, there was a padded brown envelope sitting on it.

Frowning, he looked around, trying to identify who might have left it there, but he couldn't see anyone. Taking his seat, he felt a flush of annoyance – this was *his* table, and he didn't want to share it with anyone else.

Several minutes passed and people bustled all around, but still nobody came, nobody joined him. Curious now, he took another bite of his sandwich and casually lifted the envelope, feeling its weight in his hand. There was something inside – not too heavy, but he suddenly thought about all the terrorism warnings – what if it was a bomb?

Growing alarmed, he scraped his chair backwards, ready to stand up and move away from the sinister package, when he noticed the photograph.

It had been under the envelope, lying on the table, and when his eyes fell on it his worried expression turned to one of puzzlement.

The photograph was of him.

It was small and blurry, like one of those Polaroid snaps that developed instantly inside the camera, but it was definitely him. There he was, walking along the road, wearing his blue anorak and his new grey trousers . . .

. . . exactly what he was wearing today. Had it been taken on his way into work this morning?

He looked around, half expecting to find one of his colleagues playing a joke, or to see someone filming him for something, but there was nothing. Nobody was paying him any attention. He looked down at the photograph again, wondering who might have taken it, and why?

As he turned it over in his hands, he saw a single word, handwritten in block capitals on the reverse.

REPRIEVED

Reprieved? Reprieved from what? What was this all about?
He turned his attention back to the brown padded envelope.

Glancing around once more, he slid a cautious finger under the sealed flap and opened it. Inside he found a second envelope with a neatly printed label:

FOR DETECTIVE HARLAND
AVON AND SOMERSET CONSTABULARY
WITH COMPLIMENTS

Standing up slowly from his table, Stephen gathered up the two envelopes and the photograph, hesitated, then took them over to the man at the counter.

'Excuse me,' he asked, 'but can you tell me where the nearest police station is?'

53

Harland was late but it didn't matter. He'd been on compulsory leave ever since he got out of hospital. Now, they'd finally decided to call him in – an eleven o'clock appointment with Superintendent Blake – but he was in so much trouble that there seemed little point in hurrying. The bollocking would keep.

He walked calmly up the steps and into the station, smiling at Firth as he made his way through to the back offices.

'Good to see you, sir,' she said, her face bright, interested. 'Feeling better?'

'Fine thanks,' he nodded, lifting a hand to the tender spot at the back of his head. 'Just a concussion and some bruised ribs.'

'Well, it's good to see you back.'

Back, yes. But maybe not for long.

He went upstairs and made his way along the corridor. Should he go and make himself a coffee first? No, might as well get it over with. It was already ten past – he'd kept Blake waiting long enough.

Walking along to the meeting room, he opened the door and went in. The Superintendent was there, but he was surprised to see Mendel and Pope sitting on opposite sides of the table. Had he got the time wrong?

Pope's expression was aloof, but Blake looked up pleasantly.

'Ah, there you are, Graham,' he said, removing his glasses and cleaning them with a handkerchief. 'Fully recovered, I trust?'

'Yes, thank you, sir,' Harland replied.

'Good.' The Superintendent beckoned him into the room. 'We may as well begin then.'

Harland pulled out a chair next to Mendel, catching the big man's eye as he sat down, but it was clear that his friend was in the dark too. What was going on?

'There have been some . . . developments,' Blake began, 'and I thought it would be appropriate to share them with you all.'

He put his glasses back on and, opening the folder in front of him, drew out several large photographs.

'Last week, a man called Stephen Jennings walked into a police station in London with an envelope.' He slid the first photograph across the table. Pope had to rise from his seat to see the picture of a plain brown envelope. 'It was left on the table of a café near Bank, at lunchtime last Wednesday. Inside, there was a second envelope . . .' He paused, then glanced up at Harland. 'And that one was addressed to you.'

'Sir?' Harland frowned.

Blake slid a second photograph across the table. This one showed the front of an envelope, with a printed label. They leaned forward, reading the words on it.

'I don't understand.' Harland shook his head as he stared at his own name. 'What's this all about, sir?'

'What indeed?' The Superintendent gazed at him for a moment, sharp eyes peering over the top of his glasses, studying, evaluating. 'You weren't here at the time, so we took a look at the contents in your absence . . .'

No, I wasn't here, was I? I was on 'leave' again, pending your bloody review.

'. . . and we found something rather interesting.'

Blake pushed another photograph towards them, showing a black mobile phone.

'This phone was inside. It used to belong to a certain Morris Eddings.'

'Eddings?' Pope looked up. 'Isn't that the name of the guy in Hampshire?'

'The victim in the West Meon killing,' Blake nodded. 'This is the phone we put a watch on, if you remember.'

'So the envelope came from our killer.' Mendel whistled. He turned to Harland, then frowned. 'But it's addressed to you.'

Harland sat back heavily in his chair.

'Was there anything else in the envelope?' he asked, quietly.

A faint smile passed over Blake's face.

'As a matter of fact there was,' he said, sliding another photograph across the table. 'This short note was with the phone, presumably intended for you.'

Harland stared at the image – a small square of white paper with two lines of text printed in the centre:

THE GAME IS OVER
WE'LL CALL THIS ONE A DRAW

Pope read the message, then looked over at the Superintendent.

'What does it mean?' he asked. 'He thinks of all this as some kind of game?'

'Perhaps,' Blake mused. He paused for a moment, his hand resting inside the folder, before pulling out a fifth photograph, toying with it as he looked at them. 'Stephen Jennings brought us something else that was quite significant.'

He pushed the photograph into the middle of the table, waiting for them all to crowd in and look. It was a photo of a photo – a small Polaroid snapshot by the look of it. It showed a sandy haired man in a blue anorak – unposed, as though the man didn't realise that his picture was being taken.

'That is a snapshot of Mr Jennings,' Blake said. 'He found it with the envelope on the café table.'

They sat for a moment, taking this in.

'That'd give you the creeps,' Pope muttered to himself.

'I think it probably got his attention,' Blake shrugged. 'Perhaps that was the idea. However, there is one thing further . . .'

He slid a final photograph over. It showed the back of the snapshot, with one word written in large capital letters.

'"Reprieved",' Mendel read aloud. 'So perhaps this Jennings bloke was lined up as the next victim?'

Blake looked at him, his face impassive.

'It's possible,' he said. 'Jennings lives in Silvertown, close to the Royal Victoria Dock.'

Harland sat forward.

'Where the hotel was,' he said. 'That's why he was there.'

The Superintendent gave a slight nod as he ran a finger along the edge of the folder.

'The Met are running with this now,' he explained. 'They've been over the hotel, and they're working through CCTV footage from Docklands, London Transport, and the area around the café.'

'What about Jennings?' Pope asked.

'He seems to be genuine,' Blake replied. 'They've done some digging and there's nothing untoward. Naturally, they'll keep an eye on him, just in case. That word "Reprieved" is encouraging, but I don't think they'll want to take any chances.'

'If he knew how close he'd come . . .' Mendel said, looking at the snapshot and shaking his head.

The Superintendent sat back in his chair, looking at each one of them in turn.

'So there we are,' he said. 'While there are things that might have been done differently, it does seem that we may have interrupted the killer . . .'

Harland noted his slight emphasis on the 'we'.

'. . . for now at least. Although there were a number of decisions taken that I cannot condone, I think it's best that we draw a line under the whole thing and move on. The case is now with the Met – we've done our part and there is no need for *any* further involvement, from any of you, without my express direction.'

He wasn't looking at Harland as he finished, but it was a clear, absolute warning.

'Are the Met close to making an arrest?' Pope asked.

'The investigation is ongoing,' Blake replied. 'But they know what they're doing, don't you worry.'

Harland stared down at the table in silence, keeping his doubts to himself.

'Pity the DI didn't get a better look at the suspect,' Pope murmured. Mendel shot him a withering look.

Seeing there were no further questions, Blake reached across and gathered up the photos, returning them to the folder.

'Anyway, I thought you should know how things stand. Good communication is the cornerstone of effective policing.'

He closed the folder, then looked up at them.

'That will be all.'

'Thank you, sir,' Pope nodded, as they all pushed back their chairs, getting to their feet.

Blake watched them stand, then added, 'Stay for a moment, Graham.'

Harland stood to one side, letting the others by. Brushing past, his back to the seated Superintendent, Mendel held up two crossed fingers in front of his chest and gave a subtle nod of encouragement.

'Close the door, would you?'

Harland pushed the door shut and turned back to the table. Blake got to his feet, considered him for a moment, then turned and walked over to the window.

'A most unusual business, Graham,' he said as he looked down on the street below. 'There's been some highly irregular behaviour, to say the least. I'm still not entirely clear about the chain of events that brought our suspect out into the open, but I feel certain that it wouldn't do either of us any good if I were to dig any deeper into it.'

He turned round and stared meaningfully at Harland, then moved to the table and put his hand on the folder.

'My opposite number in Thames Valley rang to congratulate me,' he smiled to himself. 'Did you know that?'

'No, sir.' Harland frowned.

'Said we'd "got a result". Under the circumstances, I think we've acquitted ourselves rather well, and we've certainly given the Met a tough act to follow.'

The idea seemed to amuse him for a moment. He shook his head and made his way around the table and paused by the door.

'I want to bring you in from the cold, Graham,' he said quietly. 'You're a good officer; you were lucky this time.'

Harland stared at him, unsure what to say.

'Just make sure you stay lucky,' Blake mused.

Then, without turning round, he opened the door and strode out.

Harland stood for several minutes before walking along the corridor to his office. Pushing the door shut behind him, he moved around the desk, dropped into his chair and slowly massaged his temples with his fingertips.

Mendel had called him lucky too.

He looked at the picture of Alice, light catching on the little gold frame, but his thoughts drifted back to the note, the snapshot.

The game was over. Reprieved.

He wondered where Stephen Jennings was right now. A name in a report, a man he'd never met. But whoever he was, he was alive.

Harland smiled. Alice would have been proud.

EPILOGUE

Naysmith propped himself up on one elbow and watched Kim as she slept. The first night in a new bed always made him eager and he'd taken her twice since they'd arrived that afternoon. Now sated, he gazed down at her slender form, his mind clear, able to think without distraction.

The cottage was ideal – and the perfect place for a romantic getaway. Perched in a remote location on a windswept stretch of coastal cliffs, with no neighbours for miles, and nothing to do except go for long walks or fool around in bed. But he must have known when he booked it. At least on some subconscious level, he *must* have.

Kim had been so pleased when he'd mentioned it. A whole week without work, or email, or mobile phones. Perhaps even a whole week without clothes, she'd suggested naughtily. And of course, that was what he wanted. A whole week with her, just the two of them together, enjoying each other, growing closer as the waves crashed on the rocks far below.

But they *had* been growing closer. Somehow, her life and his had become more entwined than he'd ever anticipated. Or allowed for.

Yes, she was very attractive, but there were plenty of other women out there for him . . . at least there *had* been until he'd found himself comparing them to her.

He pulled the duvet aside to reveal her naked back, smooth skin lit by the warm glow of the bedside lamp. She was just a person, fragile and beautiful and interesting, but still just a person. Why then did his thoughts return to dwell on her so much? He bit his lip. He'd never intended for things to go this far.

For so long, the game had sustained him, driven him forward. In many ways it had defined him, given him both purpose and pleasure. He couldn't ignore it, or pretend it hadn't happened. But he also knew the gnawing pain of hiding it, the hollowness that grew inside until it consumed everything else. He remembered how bitterly he'd wanted to tell his mother, and how much it had cost him not to.

And he knew that stifling his desires just made them hungrier.

He looked down at Kim, listening to the gentle sigh of her breathing as she dozed peacefully beside him.

What if it was all just too much for her to take? He dreaded the thought of what he would have to do if she couldn't accept it. But the time might come when he had no choice – when he could no longer risk telling her because he could no longer bring himself to deal with her if she ran.

He shut his eyes.

Of course he'd known when he booked the cottage. He'd known for some time that this was coming, however much he'd wished otherwise.

He opened his eyes again, studying Kim, fixing the image of her in his mind. So very beautiful, so utterly submissive to his will. She had accepted everything he'd done to her, even seeming to gain pleasure from her surrender. But some things were more difficult to accept than others . . .

And that's why he'd booked this place. A remote cottage, with lonely clifftop walks, where lovers might stand on the edge of the precipice, gazing down at the breakers below.

Lovers.

He sighed, forcing the hope from his mind. Hope would only cloud his judgement and he couldn't allow that. Not just now.

Sliding quietly out of bed, he padded through to the living room and found Kim's bag. Her mobile phone was switched off as he'd requested, but he took it along with the car keys and hid them in the bottom of his case, where she wouldn't be able to find them in a hurry, though he prayed it wouldn't come to that.

She stirred slightly as he got back into bed, and he kissed the top of her head, inhaling the soothing smell of her hair. Then, turning off the lamp, he lay back and closed his eyes.

He would tell her in the morning.

ACKNOWLEDGEMENTS

I'm deeply grateful to the following people:

Brendan McCusker, whose creative writing class started it all, and Chris Wild for the conversation that ignited the idea;

Andrew Oates for his valuable procedural insight, and Sarah Prince for introducing me to him;

Sally Spedding, Linda Regan and Lesley Horton for their guidance and encouragement, and Barbara Large for the excellent Winchester Writers' Conference where I met them all;

Julia Painter, Kate Ranger, Martyn Heasman, Helen Lynch, Angie Moysak, and Eveart Boniface for their feedback on early drafts;

Nick Day, my literary wingman, for reading and commenting every step of the way;

Caroline Johnson, my copy editor, who hid a multitude of my literary sins;

Eve White, my agent, for finding me a wonderful home at Hodder & Stoughton;

and my editor Francesca Best, who's more observant than the finest TV detective, and who helped make the story so much better.